Praise for *USA TODAY* bestselling author Delores Fossen

"Fossen cer[...] [...]owboy, and when s[...] [...]nger... crank up th[...]

—[...] *[...]k Reviews*

"Overall, this romance is a little sweet and a little salty—and a lot sexy!"

—*RT Book Reviews* on *Texas-Sized Trouble*

"With a great combination of drama and romance, plus a huge twist, this might be the best one in the [Blue River Ranch] series. *Roughshod Justice* has it all."

—*RT Book Reviews*

"*Always a Lawman*...includes plenty of thrills, romance, suspense and a hot cowboy/lawman hero."

—*RT Book Reviews*

"This is much more than a romance."

—*RT Book Reviews* on *Branded as Trouble*

"Nicky and Garrett have sizzling chemistry!"

—*RT Book Reviews* on *No Getting Over a Cowboy*

"Clear off space on your keeper shelf, Fossen has arrived."

—*New York Times* bestselling author Lori Wilde

"Delores Fossen takes you on a wild Texas ride with a hot cowboy."

—*New York Times* bestselling author B.J. Daniels

Also available from Delores Fossen and HQN Books

To see the complete list of titles available from Delores Fossen, please visit www.deloresfossen.com.

DELORES FOSSEN

LONE STAR
Christmas

HQN™

ISBN-13: 978-1-335-04104-3

Lone Star Christmas

Copyright © 2018 by Delores Fossen

Recycling programs for this product may not exist in your area.

To my wonderful editor, Allison Lyons.
Thank you for everything.

LONE STAR
Christmas

CHAPTER ONE

DEAD STUFFED THINGS just didn't scream Christmas wedding invitation for Callen Laramie. Even when the dead stuffed thing—an armadillo named Billy—was draped with gold tinsel, a bridal veil and was holding a bouquet of what appeared to be tiny poinsettias in his little armadillo hands.

Then again, when the bride-to-be, Rosy Muldoon, was a taxidermist, Callen supposed a photo like that hit the more normal range of possibilities for invitation choices.

Well, normal-ish, anyway.

No one had ever accused Rosy of being conventional, and even though he hadn't seen her in close to fourteen years, Billy's bridal picture was proof that her nonnormalcy hadn't changed during that time.

Dragging in a long breath that Callen figured he might need, he opened the invitation. What was printed inside wasn't completely unexpected, not really, but he was glad he'd taken that breath. Like most invitations, it meant he'd have to do something, and doing something like this often meant trudging through the past.

Y'all are invited to the wedding of Buck McCall and Rosy Muldoon. Christmas Eve at Noon in the Lightning Bug Inn on Main Street, Coldwater, Texas. Reception to follow.

So, Buck had finally popped the question, and Rosy had accepted. Again, no surprise. Not on the surface, anyway, since Buck had started "courting" Rosy several years after both of them had lost their spouses about a decade and a half ago.

But Callen still got a bad feeling about this.

The bad feeling went up a notch when he saw that the printed RSVP at the bottom had been lined through and the words handwritten there. "Please come. Buck needs to see you. Rosy."

Yes, this would require him to do something.

She'd underlined the *please* and the *needs*, and it was just as effective as a heavyweight's punch to Callen's gut. One that knocked him into a time machine and took him back eighteen years. To that time when he'd first laid eyes on Buck and then on Rosy shortly thereafter.

Oh man.

Callen had just turned fourteen, and the raw anger and bad memories had been eating holes in him. Sometimes, they still did. Buck had helped with that. Heck, maybe Rosy had, too, but the four mostly good years he'd spent with Buck couldn't erase the fourteen shitty ones that came before them.

He dropped the invitation back on his desk and

steeled himself up when he heard the woodpecker taps of the high heels coming toward his office. Several taps later, his assistant, Havana Mayfield, stuck her head in the open doorway.

Today, her hair was pumpkin orange with streaks of golden brown, the color of a roasted turkey. Probably to coordinate with Thanksgiving since it'd been just the day before.

Callen wasn't sure what coordination goal Havana had been going for with the lime-green pants and top or the lipstick-red stilettos, but as he had done with Rosy and just about everyone else from his past, he'd long since given up trying to figure out his assistant's life choices. Havana was an efficient workaholic, like him, which meant he overlooked her wardrobe, her biting sarcasm and the occasional judgmental observations about him—even if they weren't any of her business.

"Your two o'clock is here," Havana said, setting some contracts and more mail in his in-box. Then she promptly took the stack from his out-box. "George Niedermeyer," she added, and bobbled her eyebrows. "He brought his mother with him. She wants to tell you about her granddaughter, the lawyer."

Great.

Callen silently groaned. George was in his sixties and was looking for a good deal on some Angus. Which Callen could and would give him. George's mother, Myrtle, was nearing ninety, and despite her advanced age, she was someone Callen would classify as a woman with too much time on her hands. Myrtle would try to do some matchmaking with her lawyer granddaughter, gossip about things that Callen didn't want to hear and prolong what should be a half-hour meeting into an hour or more.

"Myrtle said you're better looking than a litter of fat spotted pups," Havana added, clearly enjoying this. "That's what you get for being a hotshot cattle broker with a pretty face." She poked her tongue against her cheek. "Women just can't resist you and want to spend time with you. The older ones want to fix you up with their offspring."

"You've had no trouble resisting," he pointed out—though he'd never made a play for her. And wouldn't. Havana and anyone else who worked for him was genderless as far as Callen was concerned.

"Because I know the depths of your cold, cold heart. Plus, you pay me too much to screw this up for sex with a hotshot cattle broker with a pretty face."

Callen didn't even waste a glare on that. The *pretty face* was questionable, but he was indeed a hotshot cattle broker. That wasn't ego. He had the bank account, the inventory and the willing buyers to prove it.

Head 'em up, move 'em out.

Callen had built Laramie Cattle on that motto. That and plenty of ninety-hour workweeks. And since his business wasn't broke, it didn't require fixing. Even if it would mean having to listen to Myrtle for the next hour.

"What the heck is that?" Havana asked, tipping her head to his desk.

Callen followed her gaze to the invitation. "Billy the Armadillo. Years ago, he was roadkill."

Every part of Havana's face went aghast. "Ewww."

He agreed, even though he would have gone for something more manly sounding, like maybe a grunt. "The bride's a taxidermist," he added. Along with being Buck's housekeeper and cook.

Still in the aghast mode, Havana shifted the files to her left arm so she could pick up the invitation and open it. He pushed away another greasy smear of those old memories while she read it.

"Buck McCall," Havana muttered when she'd finished.

She didn't ask who he was. No need. Havana had sent Buck Christmas gifts during the six years that she'd worked for Callen. Considering those were the only personal gifts he'd ever asked her to buy and send to anyone, she knew who Buck was. Or rather she knew that he was important to Callen.

Of course, that "important" label needed to be judged on a curve because Callen hadn't actually visited Buck or gone back to Coldwater since he'd hightailed it out of there on his eighteenth birthday. Now he was here in Dallas, nearly three hundred miles away, and sometimes it still didn't feel nearly far enough. There were times when the moon would have been too close.

Havana just kept on staring at him, maybe waiting

for him to bare his soul or something. He wouldn't. No reason for it, either. Because she was smart and efficient, she had almost certainly done internet searches on Buck. There were plenty of articles about him being a foster father.

Correction: the hotshot of foster fathers.

It wouldn't have taken much for Havana to piece together that Buck had fostered not only Callen but his three brothers, as well. Hell, for that matter Havana could have pieced together the rest, too. The shit that'd happened before Callen and his brothers had got to Buck's. Too much shit for him to stay, though his brothers had had no trouble putting down those proverbial roots in Coldwater.

"Christmas Eve, huh?" Havana questioned. "You've already got plans to go to that ski lodge in Aspen with a couple of your clients. Heck, you scheduled a business meeting for Christmas morning, one that you insisted I attend. Say, is Bah Humbug your middle name?"

"The meeting will finish in plenty of time for you to get in some skiing and spend your Christmas bonus," he grumbled. Then he rethought that. "Do you ski?"

She lifted her shoulder. "No, but there are worse things than sitting around a lodge during the holidays while the interest on my bonus accumulates in my investment account."

Yes, there were worse things. And Callen had some firsthand experience with that.

"Are you actually thinking about going back to Coldwater for this wedding?" Havana pressed.

"No." But he was sure thinking about the wedding itself and that note Rosy had added to the invitation.

Please.

That wasn't a good word to have repeating in his head.

Havana shrugged and dropped the invitation back on his desk. "Want me to send them a wedding gift? Maybe they've registered on the Taxidermists-R-Us site." Her tongue went in her cheek again.

Callen wasted another glare on her and shook his head. "I'll take care of it. I'll send them something."

She staggered back, pressed her folder-filled hand to her chest. "I think the earth just tilted on its axis. Or maybe that was hell freezing over." Havana paused, looked at him. "Is something wrong?" she came out and asked, her tone no longer drenched with sarcasm.

Callen dismissed it by motioning toward the door. "Tell the Niedermeyers that I need a few minutes. I have to do something first."

As expected, that caused Havana to raise an eyebrow again, and before she left, Callen didn't bother to tell her that her concern wasn't warranted. He could clear this up with a phone call and get back to work.

But who should he call?

Buck was out because if there was actually something wrong, then his former foster father would be at the center of it. That *Please come. Buck needs to see you.* clued him into that.

He scrolled through his contacts, one by one. He no longer had close friends in Coldwater, but every now and then he ran into someone in his business circles who passed along some of that gossip he didn't want to hear. So the most obvious contacts were his brothers.

Kace, the oldest, was the town's sheriff. Callen dismissed talking to him because the last time they'd spoken—four or five years ago—Kace had tried to lecture Callen about cutting himself off from the family. Damn right, he'd cut himself off, and since he would continue to do that and hated lectures from big brothers, he went to the next one.

Judd. Another big brother who was only a year older than Callen. Judd had been a cop in Austin. Or maybe San Antonio. He was a deputy now in Coldwater, but not once had he ever bitched about Callen leaving the "fold." He kept Judd as a possibility for the call he needed to make and continued down the very short list to consider the rest of his choices.

Nico. The youngest brother, who Callen almost immediately discounted. He was on the rodeo circuit—a bull rider, of all things—and was gone a lot. He might not have a clue if something was wrong.

Callen got to Rosy's name next. The only reason she was in his contacts was because Buck had wanted him to have her number in case there was an emergency. A *please* on a wedding invitation probably didn't qualify as one, but since he hated eating up time by waffling, Callen pressed her number. After a couple of rings, he got her voice mail.

"Knock knock," Rosy's perky voice greeted him, and she giggled like a loon. "Who's there? Well, obviously not me, and since Billy can't answer the phone, ha ha, you gotta leave me a message. Talk sweet to me, and I'll talk sweet back." More giggling as if it were a fine joke.

Callen didn't leave a message because a) he wanted an answer now and b) he didn't want anyone interrupting his day by calling him back.

He scrolled back through the contacts and pressed Judd's number. Last he'd heard, Judd had moved into the cabin right next to Buck's house, so he would know what was going on.

"Yes, it came from a chicken's butt," Judd growled the moment he answered. "Now, get over it and pick it up."

In the background Callen thought he heard someone make an *ewww* sound eerily similar to the one Havana had made earlier. Since a chicken's butt didn't have anything to do with a phone call or wedding invitation, it made Callen think his brother wasn't talking to him.

"What the heck do you want?" Judd growled that, too, and this time Callen did believe he was on the receiving end of the question.

The bad grouchy attitude didn't bother Callen because he thought it might speed along the conversation. Maybe. Judd didn't like long personal chats, which explained why they rarely talked.

"Can somebody else gather the eggs?" a girl asked. Callen suspected it might be the same one who'd ewww'ed. Her voice was high-pitched and whiny. "These have poop on them."

"This is a working ranch," Judd barked. "There's poop everywhere. If you've got a gripe with your chores, talk to Buck or Rosy."

"They're not here," the whiner whined.

"There's Shelby," Judd countered. "Tell her all about it and quit bellyaching to me."

Just like that, Callen got another ass-first knock back into the time machine. Shelby McCall. Buck's daughter. And the cause of nearly every lustful thought and unplanned hard-on that Callen had had from age fifteen all the way through to age eighteen.

Plenty of ones afterward, too.

Forbidden fruit could do that to a teenager, and as Buck's daughter, Shelby had been as forbidden as it got. Callen remembered that Buck had had plenty of rules, but at the top of the list was one he gave to the boys he fostered. *Touch Shelby, and I'll castrate you.* It had been simple and extremely effective.

"Buck got a new batch of foster kids," Judd went on, and again, Callen thought that part of the conversation was meant for him. "I just finished a double shift, and I'm trying to get inside my house so I can sleep, but I keep getting bothered. What do you want?" he tacked onto that mini rant.

"I got Buck and Rosy's wedding invitation," Callen threw out there.

"Yeah. Buck popped the question a couple of weeks ago, and they're throwing together this big wedding deal for Christmas Eve. They're inviting all the kids Buck has ever fostered. All of them," Judd emphasized. "So, no, you're not special and didn't get singled out because you're a stinkin' rich prodigal son or some such shit. *All of them*," he repeated.

Judd sounded as pleased about that as Callen would have been had he still been living there. He had no idea why someone would want to take that kind of step back into the past. It didn't matter that Buck had been good to them. The only one who had been. It was that being there brought back all the stuff that'd happened before they'd made it to Buck.

"Is Buck okay?" Callen asked.

"Of course he is," Judd snapped. Then he paused. "Why wouldn't he be? Just gather the blasted eggs!" he added onto that after another whiny *ewww.* "Why wouldn't Buck be okay?"

Callen didn't want to explain the punch-in-the-gut feeling he'd got with Rosy's *Please come. Buck needs to see you*, and it turned out that he didn't have to explain it.

"Here's Shelby, thank God," Judd grumbled before Callen had to come up with anything. "She'll answer any questions you have about the wedding. It's Callen," he said to Shelby. "Just leave my phone on the porch when you're done."

"No!" Callen couldn't say it fast enough. "That's all right. I was just—"

"Callen," Shelby greeted him.

Apparently, his unplanned hard-ons weren't a thing of the past after all. Even though Shelby was definitely a woman now, she could still purr his name.

He got a flash image of her face. Okay, of her body, too. All willowy and soft with that tumble of blond hair and clear green eyes. And her mouth. Oh man. That mouth had always had his number.

"I didn't expect you to be at Judd's," he said, not actually fishing for information. But he was. He was also trying to fight back what appeared to be jealousy. It was something he didn't feel very often.

"Oh, I'm not. I was over here at Dad's, taking care of a few things while he's at an appointment. He got some new foster kids in, and when I heard the discussion about eggs, I came outside. That's when Judd handed me his phone and said I had to talk to you. You got the wedding invitation?" she asked.

"I did." He left it at that, hoping she'd fill in the blanks of the questions he wasn't sure how to ask.

"We couldn't change Rosy's mind about using that picture of Billy in the veil. Trust me, we tried."

Callen found himself smiling. A bad combination when mixed with arousal. Still, he could push it aside, and he did that by glancing around his office. He had every nonsexual thing he wanted here, and if he wanted sex, there were far less complicated ways than going after Shelby. Buck probably still owned at least one good castrating knife.

"I called Rosy, but she didn't answer," Callen explained.

"She's in town but should be back soon. She doesn't answer her phone if she's driving."

Callen couldn't decide if that was a good or bad thing on a personal level for him. If Rosy had answered, then he wouldn't be talking to Shelby right now. He wouldn't feel the need for a cold shower or an explanation.

"Rosy should be back any minute now. You want me to have her call you?" Shelby asked.

"No. I just wanted to tell them best wishes for the wedding. I'll send a gift and a card." And he'd write a personal note to Buck.

"You're not coming?" Shelby said.

Best to do this fast and efficient. "No. I have plans. Business plans. A trip. I'll be out of the state." And he cursed himself for having to justify himself to a woman who could lead to castration.

"Oh."

That was it. Two letters of the alphabet. One word. But it was practically drowning in emotion. Exactly what specific emotion, Callen didn't know, but that gut-punch feeling went at him again hard and fast.

"Shelby?" someone called out. It sounded like the whiny girl. "Never mind. Here comes Miss Rosy."

"I guess it's an important business trip?" Shelby continued, her voice a whisper now.

"Yes, longtime clients. I do this trip with them every year—"

"Callen, you need to come," Shelby interrupted. "Soon," she added. "It's bad news."

CHAPTER TWO

SHELBY JABBED THE end-call button before Callen could repeat his no. Before he could insist that he wouldn't be coming back for the wedding. Which she was certain he had been about to do.

Callen had no trouble turning his back on everything in Coldwater, and he apparently still wanted to keep things as usual. Well, she wasn't going to make it easy for him. Not the way it had been when the back turning had first happened.

When Callen had left all those years ago, that morning of his eighteenth birthday, he had taken a battered suitcase with his things from the house. He'd said a goodbye to Buck, Rosy, his brothers and her.

Just a goodbye, nothing else.

No one, not even Shelby, had called Callen on that, had reminded him that the four years he'd lived there with them warranted more than a hasty farewell. They'd just let him go.

Then Callen had climbed into an old, rust-scabbed truck that he'd bought with the money he'd saved from his summer jobs. He hadn't even looked in the rearview mirror as he'd driven away. Callen had taken that Texas-sized chip on his shoulder with him.

A chip Shelby suspected still sat on his broad shoulder.

Hanging up on him hadn't been a very mature reaction, but at the moment it was the best she could manage since she couldn't think of an argument better than *It's bad news*.

Besides, she had other obstacles to face, what with Rosy driving up and the three teenagers eyeing her. One of those teens was peering down at her from the upstairs window. The hollow-faced, frightened Lucy Garcia. One from the barn—Lucy's brother, Mateo. The other, Rayna Hooper, from the vicinity of the chicken coop.

Of course, the one by the coop probably wasn't eyeing her with the notion of sussing out what was wrong, but in her own way Rayna would need to be reassured. Along with giving her hand sanitizer to go with the egg-gathering chore that the girl obviously wanted to shirk.

Shelby knew a little about duty shirking since she was about to take step two of that process. Just in case Callen hit Redial, she crossed the yard to Judd's cabin and tossed the phone on the seat of the porch swing. It was best to regroup and then figure out the best way to deal with Callen.

When Rosy got out of her truck, Shelby made sure the worry that she was feeling was tamped down enough, and she smiled. Rosy smiled, too, but then she usually did, no matter what the situation. Her name certainly suited her.

"I got the second batch," Rosy said, giving a squeal that would have been worthy of a schoolgirl rather than a woman on the back side of seventy. The box she was cradling under one arm was already open, and she waved the freshly printed wedding invitation at Shelby.

Before Shelby even got to her, she could see that the second batch also included another Billy picture on the front of the card. This time, the armadillo was dressed like a groom, complete with a poinsettia boutonniere on the lapel of his photoshopped tuxedo.

"Delia Cranshaw saw them when I opened the box at the post office, and she said it was morbid," Rosy went on as they walked up the steps and into the house. She shrugged, kept on smiling. "But what does she know?"

Well, since Delia was a mortician's assistant, she probably knew a lot about that particular subject, but Shelby didn't want to get into another discussion about morbidity or the invitations.

"Miss Rosy?" Rayna called out. "I need to talk to you like ASAP." The blond-haired girl was coming around the side of the house, making a beeline for them. She had a wicker basket in her hand, and hopefully from the way she was swinging it, it was empty. If not, eggs would soon be flying.

"How'd Dad's appointment go?" Shelby asked Rosy before Rayna could reach them.

Just asking the question required more worry tamping, and Shelby cursed herself for letting Buck talk her into not going with him. Yes, someone needed to stay with the foster kids, but she should have found someone else to do that so she could be there with him.

Rosy went with her usual rosy tone. "Fine, of course. The doctor's going to do a teeny exam and do some routine lab work. Buck says it's a lot of fuss about nothing, that he's fit as a fiddle, and I agree."

Shelby held back from asking if fiddles were actually fit. Besides, she didn't doubt that her father had told Rosy that—both about the fiddle and the teeny—but Shelby knew bone deep that it wasn't true. She hadn't lied to Callen when she said it was bad news.

Bad with the potential to get a whole lot worse.

Over the past couple of weeks, Shelby had seen her father's face lose some of its ruddy color. Had seen the dark circles beneath his eyes, and he'd developed a cough. And just the day before when she'd come over for Thanksgiving dinner, she had walked in on him catching onto the stairs. She hadn't missed the white-knuckle grip he'd had on the newel post, and when she'd asked him what was wrong, he'd given her a smile, a hug and a dose of BS.

"Wedding jitters," he'd said.

Considering that Rosy and he had been "dating" for years and were in love, Shelby didn't have any trouble recognizing a dodged question. He'd dodged the next one, too, when she'd asked point-blank if he was sick. That was when he'd mentioned he had his annual checkup today with Dr. Breland. Shelby couldn't cry BS on that because he did indeed have annual checkups, but she knew he'd scheduled the appointment because something was wrong.

"Miss Rosy." Rayna, again. She blew at a strand of her curly hair that had fallen onto her forehead. "I need a new chore. Eggs have chicken poop on them, and I touched one. Now I have poop smell on my hands."

"There's a big bottle of sanitizer on the back porch," Rosy said without missing a step. "Use it, and we'll talk."

They stepped into the massive old house, and even though Shelby no longer lived here, it was still home. Always would be. And maybe it was the worry about her father that had her taking a long look at it. The scarred wood floors, the nothing-special furniture that was somehow special. The fireplace mantel loaded down with photos of some of the kids Buck had fostered—and saved—over the years.

Callen was one of those saves.

Maybe when he remembered that, he would finally come back. Maybe it would help. Her father must have thought it would because when he'd given Rosy the invite list, Callen's name had been at the top.

"You've gone all pale and pasty again," Rosy said. Dropping the box of invitations on the entry table, she hauled Shelby into her arms for a python-tight hug. Rosy might only be a hundred pounds soaking wet, but she had some upper-body strength. "You're down and mopey about Gavin again. I don't know what got into that boy with him dumping you."

Shelby sighed, and then wiggled out of Rosy's grip when oxygen and potential internal organ damage became an issue. "I'm okay about Gavin."

Of course, Rosy wouldn't believe her. No one would, including Gavin Sweeny himself, who was her ex-fiancé. Everyone in town thought she was in a pity puddle now that Gavin had ended their five-year romance. But the pity puddle was reserved for her father.

Shelby pulled off her coat and hung it on one of the wooden pegs by the door. Plenty of the pegs were empty now because they only had three fosters staying with them, but there were times when the pegs were jammed. She didn't want to think that peg jamming might be a thing of the past.

She spotted Lucy at the top of the stairs, and Shelby made it a point to give her a smile. Lucy didn't smile back. Not a surprise. Lucy hadn't realized yet that she was safe here. However, the girl almost certainly knew that something wasn't on the up-and-up.

Rosy shrugged out of her coat, too, hung it next to Shelby's and picked up the box of invitations again as they made their way through to the kitchen. Rayna was already there, smelling of hand sanitizer while she looked at the chore chart fastened with magnets to the large double fridge.

"I'd rather fold laundry," Rayna said. "Or dust upstairs like Lucy. But I don't want to clean out the barn with Mateo. There's even more poop out there. I don't like the way it smells."

"Honey, nobody likes the smell of poop." Rosy took out a pair of plastic gloves from under the sink. "Use these. Get at least three of the eggs so I can bake that chocolate cake for dinner. And when Mr. Buck gets home, I'll talk to him about moving the chores around."

Rayna eyed the gloves as if they were the dreaded poop, but with a huff and some muttering, she took them and headed back out the door. Good. Maybe it'd take her at least five minutes, giving Shelby time to talk to Rosy.

"Callen called," Shelby said at the same moment Rosy said, "I've decided on the pink one."

They stared at each other a moment. "The pink wedding dress?" Shelby questioned as Rosy said, "Callen's coming for the wedding, right?"

Shelby shook her head. "He's got business to take care of. Not in Dallas, where he lives. He said this was a trip."

Some of that rosiness faded. "Oh, that's too bad. Buck was really looking forward to seeing him. Top of the list," Rosy added, tapping the invitations. She went to the dishwasher and started unloading it.

"Yes," Shelby said. She went closer to help Rosy.

"Why? Why is it so important that Dad see Callen?" she clarified when Rosy glanced at her.

"I'm not exactly sure. But he really wants Callen to come. He said so a couple of times. You know he's always had a soft spot for Callen and his brothers."

That was true, but Shelby suspected—no, she feared—that it was more than that. Her father was still in contact with all but a handful of the kids he'd fostered over the past thirty years, but this felt like more than that.

It felt like he was trying to say goodbye.

"I don't suppose you'd be willing to call Callen back?" Rosy pressed. "Or maybe go up to Dallas to see him?"

Shelby remembered him not looking in his rear-view mirror. "I'll call him, but I'm not going to Dallas."

Rosy shrugged. "I just thought it would be good for you to see an old friend. I mean, since you're trying to get over Gavin and all."

"I'm not going to Dallas," Shelby repeated, and she shifted the conversation. "Did you stay with Dad during the appointment?"

Rosy nodded. "Well, I stayed in the waiting room."

Shelby tried not to huff. "You said you'd go in with him."

"I was about to, but then Buck pointed out that he might have to strip down to his birthday suit for the checkup. That wouldn't be fitting for me to see that until after we're married."

No, but it would have been informative.

"I stayed until Buck came out of the appointment," Rosy went on, "and when he came out, he told me that he needed to get the routine lab work done, and then he was going to do some errands. He wanted me to come back here in case you had to get home. He said he wouldn't be long." She paused. "I have seen Buck in his birthday suit, you know."

Shelby was certain she didn't want to hear this, but she refrained from slapping her hands over her ears. "Well, you've known each other a long time." It was such a puny thing to say, but she was lucky she got out actual words.

Rosy glanced at her when she reached up to put a plate in the cabinet. "Buck and I have had sex."

Now Shelby did put her hands on her ears, and she turned away or rather she tried, but Rosy took hold of her arm. The woman had anaconda hands, too.

"I know this is hard for you to hear because you loved your mother, and you don't want to think about your dad having sex with anyone but her."

"I don't want to think about it at all," Shelby insisted. Not with her mother. Not with Rosy. Heck, she didn't want to think about her father or Rosy thinking about it.

But Rosy only nodded and kept going. "It happened three years ago. I'm not sure why, but he kissed me when he was helping me change the covers on one of the upstairs beds, and it just happened. We didn't even use a condom," she added in a whisper.

No words.

None.

Shelby just stared at her.

"After that, we'd bump into each other once a week," Rosy went on. "You know, like when the kids were at school or if there weren't kids here at all. Our favorite day was Tuesday."

"Uh," Shelby managed. "So, you decided on the pink wedding dress?"

The beaming smile was back. "Yes. Didn't you just love it?"

Not really. The wads of shiny pink fabric looked like blobs of bubble gum still wet with spit, but that wasn't what Shelby said. "You'll look perfect in it."

More beaming. Then the smile faded. "Buck hasn't touched me in a month," Rosy whispered. Her voice shook a little. "I mean no sex." She mouthed the last two words. "Do you think that means he wants to switch to a different day? Or maybe he's getting tired of me?"

"No. Of course not." Now it was Shelby's turn to dole out a hug, and she did that even though she was holding a cup and Rosy had a plate. The dishes clanged together between them. "I'm sure it's just wedding jitters. Or maybe he wants to hold off until your wedding night so that it can be special."

Shelby wanted a shovel to dig a hole deep enough

that she could climb into it. But it worked. It got Rosy beaming again.

"You think so?" Rosy asked.

"Of course," Shelby lied. And while she hated the notion of even considering parental sex, it only confirmed that whatever was going on with her father, it was bad.

"Thanks for listening to me chatter on." Rosy went back to putting away the dishes. Shelby held on to the cup in case her hands were trembling. She was pretty sure there could be trembling involved.

"Say, before you go, could you talk to Lucy, just to make sure she's settling in okay?" Rosy asked.

Part of Shelby was thankful for the change in subject, and it wasn't unusual for her father or Rosy to ask her to check on one of the kids—or, like today, watch them when they were off from school. But what with the worry about her father and the chat with Callen, she was feeling emotionally spent.

Shelby wouldn't give in to that, though. Checking on the kids was important, and Lucy had been here only a week. Coming into a new place was hard, but it had to be even harder over the holidays.

"Sure. I'll talk to her," Shelby agreed. "How about her brother, Mateo? And Rayna?"

"Rayna's fine. She'll only be here three or four days while her mom's in the hospital. No other family to take care of her. Mateo…" Rosy lifted her shoulder. "I was hoping Judd might try to bond with him a little."

Hope might spring eternal, but there was no chance of Judd doing that. He wasn't only carrying a chip on his shoulder. It was a mountain. He just hadn't driven that mountain out of town in a pickup truck the way Callen had.

"Mateo and Lucy are going to need some TLC and chocolate cake," Rosy insisted. "Chocolate cake fixes a lot of things."

In Rosy's world, it did. But Shelby knew it was the love that went along with that cake that did the trick.

"Don't worry—I'll save a piece of cake for you," Rosy went on. "You can get it tomorrow unless you've got too much work to do to come by. Say, how's the training going on that palomino, the one that the rich fella from Austin is boarding at your place?"

She was indeed training a new horse, and Shelby wouldn't have minded a little talk about that if she hadn't heard the vehicle approaching the house. Now she let go of the cup, practically slapping it onto the counter and hurrying to the door.

Her dad.

Buck pulled up in his red pickup that was as familiar to her as her own hand. Ditto for the weathered Stetson that had aged to a rich cream color. As usual, he wore jeans. She'd never seen him in anything else except for Sunday, when he wore his one and only suit. His buckskin coat covered a blue plaid flannel shirt.

"Please don't mention that I said anything about sex," Rosy whispered, coming up behind her.

Shelby would have voluntarily sat on a vat of hot pokers before doing that.

"Wasn't sure you'd still be here," her dad greeted her. "Thanks for staying with the kids."

"Anytime." Even though it would likely be a big red flag of concern, she went onto the porch and down the steps to hug him. She'd hugged him plenty of times, of course, but not when he'd only been gone an hour or so. The red flag probably flapped a little harder when she held on longer than she normally would have.

"How'd the appointment go?" she asked when she eased back from him.

Oh yes. He'd noticed her concern. He might look a little frail, but he was still sharp. And about to lie to her.

She was sharp, too. Shelby could see the lie forming in his green eyes, which were a genetic copy of her own.

"Everything went fine," her father said with his arm hooked around her—which meant he was no longer looking her straight in the eyes. Easier to maintain the lie that way.

"Told you," Rosy insisted from the doorway. "Buck's right as rain."

Because, of course, rain was right.

Except when it wasn't.

"Callen called," Rosy told him when they stepped inside. "Shelby talked to him."

Buck paused in the process of taking off his coat, and his gaze shifted from Rosy to Shelby. "Is he coming to the wedding?"

Shelby shook her head, and she instantly saw something deflate inside her father. There was no other word for it. His chest fell. His shoulders sagged a little. And the sigh that left his mouth was as weary as it could get.

It broke her heart.

"Miss Rosy?" Rayna called out from the kitchen. "I accidentally dropped the eggs, and they broke. You don't want me to pick them up off the ground, do you?"

Rosy gave a rare eye roll. "I'll be back." And she scurried away toward the kitchen.

Shelby figured her father might want to try some scurrying, too, but he stayed put. "I just need a few more tests at the hospital," he said, fixing the lie he'd told her earlier. Still not the straight truth, but it was a start.

"What kind of tests?" she asked.

"Just a shadow that showed up on an X-ray." He brushed a kiss on her forehead. "Don't start worrying about it until we know. And don't mention it to Rosy."

She could agree to the second but not the first. That was because she was already worrying.

"Too bad about Callen not coming," Buck said, walking away from her. "I really wanted to see him."

Shelby sighed. Then cursed.

She was going to Dallas.

CHAPTER THREE

"Hey, LITTLE GIRL. Have you been naughty?" Santa Claus called out to Shelby when she walked out of the parking garage and onto the sidewalk.

Santa—and that was just a generic label, of course—came toward her, his lumpy stuff-filled suit shifting and waddling with each staggered step that he took. She thought he might be grinning at her, but it was hard to tell since his beard had shifted and angled across his face instead of his chin. He spoke through the matted tufts of the sideways polyester hair.

"Would ya like to see something naughty?" Santa added, and his wink got stuck when some of the stray beard hair pasted his eyelashes together.

That didn't stop him from turning his backside to her and mooning her.

As asses went, it was big and blinding white. She'd seen far better on some of the horses she boarded, but it was a reminder that she was in a big city where things like a mooning Santa could happen. A reminder, too, of why she lived in and loved Coldwater.

There was still a risk of a mooning Santa in Coldwater if Gopher Tate got liquored up enough and found something red to wear, but Gopher was more likely to flash than moon, and he wouldn't actually be naked beneath whatever coat he was wearing. And besides, Gopher fell into the "colorful" category. This guy was just a drunk perv.

It was all about perspective.

Shelby debated if she should just ignore the perv or dole out an insult, suggesting that he purchase some butt rash cream at the local pharmacy, but she didn't have to make a choice. Two uniformed cops came running up the sidewalk toward them.

"Bob!" one of the cops called out. "What have we told you about pulling stunts like this?"

A mooning Santa named Bob. It didn't hold a candle to a flasher named Gopher.

"Sorry about this," the cop said to her. He latched on to Bob and hiked up the Santa pants. "Did Bob bother you?"

Shelby shook her head. She was only bothered by one thing right now, and Bob wasn't it.

"She's gonna be naughty," Bob slurred as the cops hauled him away.

Well, that might work better than being nice—which was her default approach to anything that might not go her way. Like this meeting with Callen. Heck, being nice was her default approach, period. She had plenty of mean thoughts—naughty ones, too—but they rarely made it to her mouth in any kind of impressive, cohesive way. And that was the reason everyone thought of her as a nice, good girl.

Perspective, indeed.

Just once, she'd like to be the mooning Santa or the naughty one. For now, though, she'd settle for convincing Callen that he needed to return to the town that he hadn't even glimpsed in his rearview mirror. Buck wanted him there, and whether she had to go naughty, nice or somewhere in between, Shelby would make it happen.

Because of the shadow.

Shelby no longer thought of that as something mysterious, not when it came to medical tests. She'd looked up the term on the internet and had learned that it was often associated with a tumor.

And with cancer.

There weren't many things that could have caused her to drive four hours to Dallas to see Callen, but that did it.

Thankfully, his address hadn't been hard to find. Neither had info about him. She'd got fourteen pages of hits with her internet search on him. Photos, too. Callen owned and operated Laramie Cattle and had been darn successful at it.

Something she'd already known.

Shelby had no intention of telling Callen that she'd kept cyber tabs on him over the years. Even when she'd still been with Gavin, she hadn't been able to resist typing Callen's name in the search engine and poring over the details of his life, both business and social.

He apparently preferred brunettes.

Ones who shopped in the 34D section of fancy underwear stores.

No, best not to mention that. She would just plead her case to try to get him to change his mind about coming to the wedding, and then she would take her 34Bs and go back home.

Shelby went up the street to his office building and, following the directions she'd jotted down, she took the elevator up to the fifty-first floor. She'd taken some time to dress for the occasion. Nothing fancy, but she'd put on her good black jeans, a red sweater that'd been a gift from Rosy, and she had made sure there wasn't any manure on her boots.

When she stepped off the elevator and onto his floor, she realized she would have still been under-dressed had she worn a pricey designer suit. This place was high-end with its white marble floors veined with the silver that was mirrored in the sleek reception desk and wall art.

Since it was Saturday and the weekend after Thanksgiving, there weren't as many people milling around as there likely would have been, but there was a woman at the desk. A busty brunette in a winter-white dress and silver high heels. Perhaps it was some kind of strange requirement that her clothes match the decor.

"I'm here to see Callen Laramie," Shelby greeted her.

"Is he expecting you?" According to her name tag, she was Tiffany, and Shelby didn't miss the stink-eye and once-over the woman gave her. Tiffany also turned up her perky nose, making Shelby wonder if she'd been completely successful with the manure removal from her boots.

"Yes, he's expecting me. I made the appointment through his assistant."

Which had been intentional on Shelby's part. Yes, she could have called Callen herself since she had his number, but she'd been worried that it would be too easy for him to say no—again—over the phone. This time if there was a no, he'd have to say it to her face.

Tiffany tapped the keys on the laptop in front of her—also silver—and she motioned to the hall off to the right. "Suite 5101."

Steeling herself up and still debating how to pull off a naughty approach, Shelby made her way there. The door was open but no Callen. However, there was an orange-haired woman in a flamingo-pink suit seated at a desk. The moment she spotted Shelby, she got to her feet.

And she smiled.

Not a trace of stink-eye, but the woman's lids were covered with what could have been a kilo of green shadow and liner.

"I'm Havana, and you must be Shelby McCall," the woman said.

Shelby nodded and would have maybe shaken hands with her if she hadn't continued.

"Daughter of Buck McCall," Havana went on.

"And someone from Callen's past." She came closer, leaned in. "Callen moans out your name during sex."

"What?" Shelby jerked away, ready to go a couple of steps past stink-eye, but then Havana laughed.

"Just kidding," Havana insisted. "I have no carnal knowledge about my boss. I'm just trying to break the ice a little from the frost Tiffany would have no doubt given you."

Well, she had indeed felt some of that frost, but Shelby wasn't sure she liked Havana's attempt at humor, either. *Callen's still moaning over me? I haven't moaned over him in years*, was what Shelby wanted to say, but she settled for, "I'm here to see Callen."

"Yes, I know. He's on the phone right now, but I'll take you in as soon as that little light turns green." She tipped her head with the piled-up hair to the landline on the desk. The light was red.

"So, of course I did a quick background check on you," Havana went on. She helped Shelby out of her coat. "In the six years that I've worked for Callen, you're the only visitor he's ever gotten from his hometown. Needless to say, I was curious about you."

She recognized the questioning inflection in Havana's voice that invited her to spill why she was there. Shelby had used such inflections herself, but for this she stayed quiet.

"I figure this is about the armadillo wedding invitation," Havana threw out there.

So she'd seen it. Hard to miss it, and, yes, this visit was sort of about the invitation since that was what had triggered her father's saying he wanted to see Callen. But the shadow trumped the armadillo.

"Callen said he'd send the wedding gift himself," Havana continued. "Know how many times in the past six years he's actually sent a gift himself?" She didn't wait for an answer but instead made a zero with her thumb and index finger. "Again, that's why I was curious about you."

As she'd done with her Bob the Santa response, Shelby debated what she should say. Something snarky, maybe about how small Havana's nose was for her to be sticking it in so many places. Or perhaps it was time for another moaning reference.

Or she could go with a Bob tactic and moon her.

But then Shelby saw it. The concern in Havana's eyes. Concern that Shelby detected even beneath the unnaturally violet-colored contacts and magenta mascara.

"Whatever you're here to do, I'm on your side. Six years is too long for anyone to hang on to bah humbug," Havana said, verifying the concern and lining the path to the possible beginnings of a lifelong friendship with a woman she'd just met.

On the desk, the light on the phone flashed to green.

"Showtime," Havana announced. She patted Shelby's back as she led her toward the massive double doorway. "Be brave, and never underestimate the power of a good French kiss between old friends."

With that, Havana pulled open the door and nudged Shelby in. It felt a little like being thrown to the wolves. Well, one wolf, anyway.

Callen was standing at the massive floor-to-ceiling windows that had an incredible view of the downtown. His back was to her, but then he turned.

And she turned into a melting puddle.

Good thing Callen wouldn't get a visual of that because she doubted it was pretty, but Shelby could feel the flush of heat make its way from her mouth to the center of her body.

Oh my. He still had it, all right, and that "it" included but wasn't limited to everything she saw. Because Shelby was reasonably certain that Callen would look just as good out of those clothes as he did in them.

He wore cowboy clothes. Jeans, a casual white shirt with the sleeves rolled up, cowboy boots. But this was no ordinary cowboy with that thick black hair and those smoky gray eyes. And the face. Yes, there was another "it." A strong jaw, nice angles, complete with some dark desperado stubble. He would have looked at ease at a poker table in a Wild West saloon. Maybe a high-noon shoot-out.

And he would have looked especially good naked in her bed.

There was a reason she'd spent so much time fantasizing about him.

Shelby tried her best not to look as if she was still weaving her fantasies and got her mind back on what it should be on. Convincing Callen to come home. She had just about regained her mental footing when he pulled out a big gun in his hotness arsenal.

A smile.

Not a full-fledged one. Too ordinary for a man like him. No. Only the corner of the right side of his mouth lifted. Just a slight hitch that caused a dimple to flash in his cheek. And the puddling returned.

"Shelby," he said. Of course, he didn't just say it. No ordinary accent for him, either. It was a Texas drawl so smooth that it could have qualified as long, slow foreplay.

"Callen," she managed to say right back. Nothing smooth about her voice. Too much breath, which was somewhat of a surprise since it felt as if she'd forgotten how to suck air into her lungs.

How could this happen after all this time? Yes, the heat had been there when she'd been sixteen, but she was a grown woman now. Strangely, that seemed to make the heat even worse. Her sixteen-year-old self wouldn't have known what to do with Callen Laramie.

She knew now.

Shelby shook her head to clear it, squared her shoulders and prepared to launch into the argument she'd practiced on the drive. Callen disarmed that, too, with more of that drawled foreplay.

"You ventured to the big city," he said.

Yes, and met a mooning Santa and a clever assistant who likely knew the depths of both their souls. Shelby settled for a still-too-breathy yes.

The silence came. Not exactly awkward since his gaze was skimming her entire body. Heck, hers was still skimming his, too, and she figured it was too much to hope that he wouldn't notice.

Callen finally broke the gazing, half-smiling silence by motioning to the chair. "Have a seat. You want something to drink?"

Probably best not to ask for a shot of whiskey and ice packs to cool her down. "Water if you have it."

He went to the far side of the room to a wooden panel, tapped it, and when it slid open, she could see a full bar. Callen grabbed a bottle of water, a glass and a napkin and came to her side to set the items in front of her.

When his body brushed against hers, she caught his scent and dragged it in as if she were a starving woman. "You smell...expensive," she muttered, her voice dreamy now. But since this wasn't a dream, she quickly yanked herself back. "Everything in here smells expensive," she amended. "You've done well for yourself."

There. That was the grown-up, nonsexual thing to say.

He nodded. No smile, though, and it was as if it took some effort for him to tear his gaze from hers. He turned and went behind his desk to sit. She doubted he'd missed the symbolism of putting some distance and a barrier between them, but she couldn't figure out why.

Unless he still thought of her as hands-off.

She considered mentioning that she'd known about her father's threat to de-ball any boy who touched her, but it was best if she steered away from the old sexual stuff and any mention of severed male anatomy.

"So, what's it like to be Callen Laramie these days?" she asked.

"Good." No hesitation. He jumped right into that answer, something he'd had a knack for even during his teenage years. Of course, maybe he was fast on the reply because it didn't take much effort to give an answer that didn't really say anything. "How about you?"

"Good." She frowned because she hadn't intended to play his quick-fire verbal game. And besides, it wasn't true. If she'd been "good," she wouldn't have driven here to see him.

"Married? Engaged?" he went on.

She shook her head and took a much-needed gulp of the water. Shelby nixed mentioning that she had been engaged as recently as three months ago. She didn't want to deal with the sympathy she'd see in Callen's eyes when he found out she'd been dumped.

"How about you?" she said. "Married or engaged?"

"No." He didn't offer any details, but considering

her response had been a headshake, she supposed that made him the chatty one here.

He didn't continue the chat. Callen just kept those made-for-sin eyes on her. Waiting. And now that her nerves had quit jangling like a tambourine, Shelby geared up to do what she'd come here to do.

"You mentioned on the phone that you'd gotten Buck and Rosy's wedding invitation," she said. "That's why I'm here."

He made a sound that indicated he'd figured as much, but Callen couldn't have known about why she'd actually come to see him.

"Is something wrong with Buck?" he asked.

Okay, so maybe Callen did know. She considered asking him why he thought that, but instead Shelby nodded and tried to put reins on all the emotions that she crowded together in her head, heart and body.

"He won't tell me specifically what's wrong with him, or how serious it is," she explained. "I asked. He gave me a thin reassurance that it was just something that showed up on an X-ray. Nothing to worry about, he said."

Callen stayed quiet a moment. "Maybe he's telling the truth."

"I don't think so." Since reined-in emotions made her feel jittery, she got up and went to the window. Plus, this way she didn't have to look at him while she talked. "I believe it's serious, and I think that's why he proposed to Rosy. And why the timing of this wedding has become so important to him."

"You're considering that he wants to…what? Get married while he can? Spend some time with his fosters? Say goodbye?"

Maybe all of the above. But Shelby prayed it wasn't the last one. "The only thing I know for certain is that Buck wants you there. It could be for a goodbye. Or possibly because he's always had a soft spot for you." That was Rosy's theory, anyway.

She waited for him to snort or make some other sound that the soft spot wasn't true, but he didn't. "Buck's not a liar, and he's not one to play games. If this wedding is some kind of gathering because of a health scare, he'd come out and say it."

"You'd think," she agreed. "But he's pale these days. And he has this cough. I'm pretty sure he's also having dizzy spells." She turned back around to face him. "Could you just reschedule your business trip and come to the wedding? Or if you can't reschedule, just come to Coldwater and see him?"

There. The ball was in his court. His silent court. She could see his jaw muscles stirring around that fashionable stubble, but he wasn't saying anything. Despite his lack of words, she guessed what was going on in his head.

Going back to Coldwater wouldn't be easy for him. In fact, it would probably sling him back to all those dark places inside him.

Six years is too long for anyone to hang on to bah humbug, Havana had said, but it'd been a lot longer than that. Broken and beaten, Callen had come to them. However, Buck had been good to him. He'd been a wonderful father to Callen. Just as he had been to her.

"I'll call Buck," Callen said. "If there's something he wants to tell me, then he'll have a chance to do it."

Buck didn't want to tell him. He wanted to *see* him.

She went back to the chair, sat and faced him. "You might think it's selfish of me to put his wishes above yours, but I can be selfish when it comes to my dad. Buck wants you there. You don't want to go. I'm asking you to go."

And she waited.

And waited.

The seconds started crawling by. Silence had a special way of making her crazy. Usually she started babbling, trying to spur the other person to do their part in this two-way conversation. If Callen was going to say no, then she just wanted him to get it out there so she could start changing his mind.

He was definitely going to say no.

She could see it. Practically hear the words coming out of his perfect mouth. "Would a French kiss make you change your mind?" she threw out there.

Callen blinked.

Shelby shrugged. "My attempt at levity. *Failed attempt*," she amended when he just stared at her.

In her rehearsed argument, she'd said a lot of pleases, smiled at him a lot and reminded him of things like "it's just one day" or "you wouldn't have to stay long" or "do it for old times' sake." In her re-hearsed argument, she'd been downright eloquent and persuasive. That made her French-kiss offer sound even more ridiculous.

Maybe Havana and she wouldn't become lifelong friends after all since Callen's assistant had been the one who'd put that crazy suggestion in her head.

Sighing, Shelby stood. "All right. Call Buck, then." She turned, ready to leave, hoping she didn't get an-other Santa mooning. Or cry. God, she hated crying. Hated failing even more.

Callen didn't say anything else until she'd made it all the way to his door. "I'll be there Monday," he said. Then paused. "You can give me the French kiss then."

CHAPTER FOUR

STUPID.

That was the most common word repeating through Callen's head as he took the turn off the interstate to Coldwater. Stupid to have made a trip that could be resolved by a phone call.

Probably resolved, anyway.

Stupid to have rearranged important business meetings to fly to San Antonio, and then rent a car to drive the half hour to a place he didn't want to be. And since he was tallying up the "stupids," Callen could top the list with that French-kiss remark to Shelby.

Her visit hadn't been a joking matter. Then again, maybe the offer of the kiss hadn't been, either. In that incredible stupid moment, he'd just wanted to say something to get her to turn back around.

Hell, who was he kidding? He'd actually wanted to kiss her. Still did. But first he needed to get to Coldwater, talk to Buck face-to-face, kiss Shelby and then get back to the airport to make his six o'clock flight.

Head 'em up, move 'em out.

Then he could go back home and hope that the nightmares didn't follow him. Nope, no joking matter.

Even though Callen knew the way, he still had on the GPS just in case some of the roads had changed or been closed. After all, Coldwater wasn't exactly on anybody's beaten path. It was a small ranching town, technically part of the scenic Texas Hill Country, but no one would consider it exactly scenic. Well, other than the acres and acres of pastures dotted with livestock.

As a cattleman, Callen found that somewhat appealing, but with every mile he drove, he did battle with the memories of the first time he'd come here. He'd been fourteen. A cast on his arm and leg. Three broken ribs. He had been alone in the truck with Buck since his younger brother, Nico, was still in the hospital, and his two older brothers had been in a different home, waiting for the paperwork to clear so that Buck could foster all of them.

And that was all he allowed himself to remember before he buried it and kept driving.

The town sign was new. Red, white and blue, sporting not only the Texas flag and the town's name and population—an even thousand, which he figured was padded—but there was also a slogan on the sign.

"Welcome! If you're here, you might be lost, but consider staying anyway," complete with a smiley face.

Callen figured there'd been long discussions and

poor judgment when they came up with that particular slogan.

Main Street wasn't far from the welcome sign, but he'd have to drive all the way through town to reach Buck's place. Not a long trip, only about a mile, but it would be at the poky thirty mph speed limit.

At first glance Callen didn't see anything else new. Same old grocery store, bank and two churches. A bakery—that was new. Patty Cakes, and they were apparently having a sale on Root Beer Cupcakes. The police station that was right across from the Gray Mare Saloon, which he supposed deterred drinking and driving.

He kept driving, past Rosy's taxidermist shop—Much Ado About Stuffing. Callen slowed to try to get a glimpse of her, but there was a Be Back Soon sign in the window.

Next up, he drove past the town's jewelry store/gift shop simply called Ted's. He wasn't sure how it'd stayed in business because it seemed to have the same display as it had years ago. Callen was certain he recognized the gold necklace on a headless mannequin surrounded by even creepier Russian nesting dolls. The only new addition was a For Sale By Owner sign just behind the biggest of the dolls.

"Good luck with that," Callen grumbled.

Next up, Callen passed the library, school and diner—before he ran into a roadblock of sorts. There was a longhorn bull in the middle of the road, and several people were trying to shoo it off to the side.

The longhorn looked bored and totally uninterested in moving, and because the street was so narrow, it was impossible to get around him.

The sports car right behind Callen got in on the horn honking. Finally, the driver got out. A woman wearing a bright red coat walked past Callen and the two other cars to the bull and tried her hand at shooing. The longhorn ignored her, and when the woman looked around, probably for help, her attention landed on Callen.

Silla Sweeny.

Callen had expected to run into people he especially didn't want to see, and Silla was one of them. Former cheerleader, daughter of a well-to-do rancher and a snob. Callen had also had sex with her when they'd been seventeen. When the "romance" had run its course, Silla had turned batshit crazy on him, complete with stalking, spreading rumors and generally making herself his own personal pain in the ass.

It was somewhat cowardly, but Callen eased down the brim of his black Stetson in the hope that Silla wouldn't recognize him. That didn't happen. She came toward him, squinting and peering until she reached his rented Jeep Wrangler.

"Well, I'll be. It's Callen Laramie." She didn't add the other labels she'd given him after he'd ended things with her. Breaker of Hearts, Stone Cold SOB. And Dookie Head—the one he'd hated the most because it was just so dumb.

"Silla," he said as a way of greeting, and he wondered if he could physically pick up the longhorn and get it out of the way. Backing up was out because there were now two other trucks behind Silla and him.

"Is the bull likely to be there for long?" he asked.

She shrugged, causing her coat to dip off her shoulders, and she kept looking Callen over. "He belongs to Esther Benton, the librarian. He's always breaking fence and getting out. I've already called your brother Kace, so he oughta be along soon to get it moving."

Callen didn't want to imagine the duties that were normal for the sheriff of a small ranching town, but Kace was someone else he didn't want to run into just yet. If at all. It was possible that Callen could get his business done with Buck and kiss Shelby if he couldn't muster up enough willpower to stop himself. Then he could get out of town without getting a lecture from Kace or risking castration from Buck.

"I heard you got all rich and stuff," Silla went on. She leaned against the Jeep, and while she did smile, it was as if it had an oily film over it. Maybe she was plotting revenge.

"And stuff," he answered. She would either see it for the snark that it was or ignore his attempt at bad humor.

She didn't have a reaction either way. "So, you headed out to Buck's?"

He nodded and got out to see what he could do about the longhorn. Silla trotted along behind him, her very high-heeled boots clomping on the asphalt. "You're here to help Shelby?" she added.

That didn't cause him to stop, but Callen did look at her from over his shoulder. "Shelby needs help?"

Silla gave a hollow laugh as if the answer were obvious. "Well, yeah." She stretched that out a few syllables. "Broken heart and stuff. My brother, Gavin—you remember Gavin, right?"

Another nod. Gavin had taken it upon himself to try to beat the crap out of Callen for wronging his sister. Gavin had failed, but then most had. When you had two older brothers as Callen did, you had a lot of experience with adolescent fistfights.

"What does Gavin have to do with Shelby?" he asked. And broken hearts?

"Gavin and Shelby were engaged, and he broke it off with her a few weeks ago. Poor girl, she's just crushed. I'm not sure she'll ever get over it."

Callen hadn't seen anything in Shelby's expression to indicate a broken heart. Worry, yes, for Buck. But she hadn't mentioned a word about Gavin and an engagement. That was even more reason to skip the much-thought-about French kiss. Even if it was done for pure fun and pleasure, which he was sure it would be, it was best not to interfere with heart mending.

Though it riled him that Shelby had planned to marry the likes of Gavin Sweeny.

Callen approached the longhorn and gave it a swat on the butt with his Stetson. The longhorn tossed him a look of mild annoyance before it started to amble away. The handful of people who'd gathered for the bovine roadblock all cheered and got back in their vehicles.

All except Silla.

It was clear she intended to carry on a conversation that Callen hadn't wanted to start in the first place. Callen wouldn't say he panicked, not exactly, but he did get the engine started and quickly hit the accelerator. Thankfully, the vehicles ahead of him did the same, and while he wasn't especially proud of it, if there'd been any dust on Main Street, he would have left Silla in it.

All right, he was a little proud of it, and leaving her standing there, gawking, was some petty revenge for her spray painting Dookie Head on his locker.

Callen was smiling as he sped away. But the smile pretty much ended when he heard the siren and he saw the police cruiser coming up fast behind him.

Hell.

He'd blown that thirty mph speed limit to smithereens and by doing so had drawn an audience. One that was even bigger than the one waiting for the longhorn to move.

Cursing, Callen pulled to the side of the road, the cruiser coming to a quick stop behind him. And then Callen saw yet someone else he'd hoped to avoid seeing.

Judd.

"Welcome home," Judd snarled as he approached Callen's window.

And his brother proceeded to write him a speeding ticket.

WITH JUDD'S SIGNATURE still wet on the speeding ticket, Callen pulled into the driveway of Buck's ranch. His *head 'em up, move 'em out* plan hadn't got off to a smooth start, but maybe now he could get back on track.

The pint-size blonde on the porch had him slightly concerned about that, though.

The girl was about twelve or so and had her arms folded over her chest. She wasn't actually tapping her foot, but Callen was pretty sure that was impatience he saw on her face. Maybe with a dash of annoyance.

"Did you really beat up a cow?" the blonde demanded the moment Callen was out of the Jeep.

"Uh, no." He approached her with caution, the way he would a crazy person.

"Well, Jenny said you did. I don't know her that well. I just met her yesterday, so she's not like a bestie, but I don't think she'd lie. Her mom owns the diner in town, so she was there, watching, and Jenny said you hit Miss Benton's cow-thingy."

Oh, that. And Callen seriously hoped that cow-thingy didn't refer to balls or such. He didn't want talk about that getting around. "The longhorn. I swatted it on the butt with my hat so it'd get out of the road."

The girl's mouth opened in outrage and sputtered out a few garbled sounds before she actually formed words. "First, all the poop. Then the bedsheets. Now this. What kind of place is this?"

Apparently, she didn't expect him to provide an answer to that since she threw her hands up in the air, turned on her heels and stormed inside.

Callen didn't follow her. Instead, he stood there and posed the same question to himself. What kind of place was this? Well, it was a big-assed trip into that time machine, that was what it was.

Like Main Street, there'd been few changes here. A fresh coat of yellow paint on the large two-story house. When he'd lived here, it'd been white. Other than that and the addition of a second barn, the place looked the same. Ditto for the small cabin just a stone's throw away. Callen scowled at it because he knew his ticket-writing brother lived there.

There were some horses milling around the white-fenced pasture. That was also the same. Buck always liked having horses around to give the foster kids the responsibility of taking care of them. Riding them, too. That made the chore of mucking out the stalls in the barn more tolerable.

Callen walked closer and spotted a dark-haired boy probably around the same age as the blonde girl. Apparently, he'd got egg-gathering duty since he was by the chicken coop.

When Callen reached the porch, he saw that some-one had already started hanging Christmas decorations. There was a wreath with red berries and holly hanging on the door.

A door that immediately flew open.

"You're here!" Rosy squealed, and the woman was a blur of motion when she launched herself into Callen's arms. Her own arms came around him to give him something else that hadn't changed—a very hard hug.

"You're here," Rosy repeated when she let go of him and stepped back. Her eyes were a little wet with tears, making Callen feel both guilty and welcome. Rosy had a way of doing that.

"Come in," Rosy insisted, tugging at his hand to pull him inside the house, and Callen immediately got slammed with the smells of roast beef, onions and fresh bread. Yet something else that hadn't changed. Rosy always had some good stuff going on in the kitchen, and he thought that under the roast beef and bread he could smell dessert.

Chocolate cake.

His favorite.

He glanced around, getting another shot of the guilt when he saw the framed picture on the mantel. Buck, him and his brothers. It wasn't tucked into the rows of the others on the shelves that flanked the fireplace. It was front and center. A place that Buck had reserved for family since it was right next to one of Shelby and him.

Callen was cynical enough, though, to wonder if Shelby had moved it there as a way of showing him just how important this visit was to Buck. If so, the maneuver hadn't been necessary. Callen had already figured that out. Buck wanted to see him, and now Callen could figure out why. Then he'd do what he could to help and head back to the airport to catch his flight.

However, Callen thought the image of that perfectly placed picture might stay with him for a while.

"Sorry that I didn't hear you drive up," Rosy went on, helping him out of his coat. "I had on headphones, listening to music choices for the wedding, and had the volume up a little high. I didn't know you were here until Rayna came stomping in saying the cow-abuser was here." She patted his arm. "I know she's exaggerating."

"She's pissed at me. And about poop and sheets, too."

Rosy sighed. "Fitted sheets. She couldn't figure out how to fold them. Best not to get into the whole poop thing. Don't worry—Rayna's going home tomorrow, so she won't be around to complain. She won't spoil your visit."

Callen was about to clarify that his visit would be a short one, definitely not lasting into tomorrow, but before he could say anything, a chicken ran into the room. A gangly dark-haired girl was right behind it.

"Oh, for Pete's sake." Rosy huffed. "Rayna," she added in a grumble. "She let the chicken in the house again because she thinks it's too cold for them outside."

Since the chicken was heading right toward him, Callen scooped it up so he could hand it off to the girl. But the girl came to an awkward stop, bobbling to keep her balance. She took one look at him and slunk toward the stairs. There was no other word for it. She slunk.

And Callen knew slinking when he saw it.

Heck, he'd done it himself when he'd first come here. It was a good way of not having to interact with anybody that might look at you and see the hell and back you'd been through.

"Lucy," Rosy said with another sigh. "Wide berth, time and peanut butter cookies."

Callen figured that was Rosy's prescription for helping the girl get over whatever the hell it was she needed to get over. Judging from the slinking and her stark expression, the *whatever* was bad and there'd been lots of it.

Rosy took the chicken, tucking it under her arm and catching onto his hand to lead him to the kitchen. He'd been right about the cake and spotted it under a glass-domed lid on the counter. Rosy put the chicken out the back door and motioned for him to sit at the table.

"Cookies and milk?" she asked, making him wonder if that was her prescription for him.

"Coffee, if you've got it." Though he would have preferred a beer or some other form of alcohol to steady his nerves, but unless things had changed, there wouldn't be booze of any kind in the house. Buck's rules. He hadn't wanted something like that around for the fosters to sneak.

Rosy poured him a cup of coffee—and cut him a big slice of the cake, setting both in front of him. "Don't let the sugar spoil your appetite, though. I want you plenty hungry for dinner."

Again, he was about to tell her that dinner was out and ask to see Buck, but he got another distraction.

Shelby.

She came rushing in the back door. "I just thwarted another attempt from Rayna trying to get the chicken back in the house. And I gave her a new chore. I told her to learn how to knit little sweaters for the hens."

Shelby's cheeks were pink from the cold, and she had a big smile on her face. A smile that just sort of evaporated when she saw him. Like the slinking, Callen recognized that look, too.

Lust.

Oh yeah, and he didn't think he was projecting since he, too, was feeling some high levels of lust.

Hell in a handbasket. He didn't need this, and he especially didn't need the "I know what's going on here" glances that Rosy was giving both of them. Callen suddenly felt fourteen again and braced for Rosy to rattle off chores for him to do. Chores were Rosy's cure for lust.

Shelby saw those looks as well, and she put her hands on her hips.

"Why does he get cake?" Shelby asked. "You said you weren't going to cut it until dinner tonight."

Rosy eyed them again as if she might not buy the cake distraction ploy, but then she smiled. "It's a special occasion. Callen's home. Now, why don't you sit with him while he has his snack, and I'll go and find Buck."

"He's in his workshop in the barn," Shelby provided.

"I'll get him." Rosy wiped her hands on her apron and gave them another glance. "You two behave while I'm gone." Not her scolding tone. More of a tease.

That made Callen feel even more uneasy than a good scolding would have.

Shelby was smiling a little, too, when she sat in the chair across from him. And, yeah, the lust was still there mixed with something else. Relief, maybe.

"Thanks for coming. I wasn't sure you would," she said, sounding oh-so serious while she had that little gleam in her eye. Lightning fast, she reached out to snag the cake.

Callen was faster, as he'd always been, and he stood, shifting the plate to his side so that it was out of her reach. "I know what you're thinking," he said. "Am I going to have to French-kiss him to get that cake?"

She frowned. "Actually, that *was* what I was thinking. I never seem to be able to say things like that, though, before someone else gets the chance."

That made sense to him. He had always been able to see the wheels turning in her head even when she wasn't speaking. But her being on the same French-kissing page with him wasn't a good thing.

Callen silently repeated that to himself.

Flirting with Shelby was more than just playing with fire. Especially now that he knew about her broken heart because of Gavin. It didn't matter that he couldn't actually see signs of that brokenness. If there was any chance it was indeed there, he didn't need to be playing around, flirting or lusting. That was why he put on his adult face and handed her the cake.

She frowned again. Then eyed both him and the cake with suspicion. For a moment, he thought she might refuse it and launch into a lust-deflecting conversation that he didn't want to have. But she shrugged, picked up his fork and started eating.

"Mmmm, that is so good," she said, making him wish that he'd opted for the French kiss instead of surrendering the cake. But her mmm-ing and eating paused when she looked at him again and then made a sweeping glance around the room.

"A lot of memories here for you, huh?" she asked. She took another bite of the cake—a huge one—and then slid the plate back across the table to him.

He made a sound of agreement and occupied his mouth with finishing the cake instead of getting into details he didn't want any more than the lust-deflecting conversation.

"Dad kept your memory box," she went on. "He's got it in his workshop." She helped herself to a gulp of his coffee.

The gesture seemed, well, sort of intimate—sharing a cup, sharing a fork. The shift in conversation just sounded like one more thing he didn't want to talk about. But, yes, he knew what box she meant. It was something Buck did for all his fosters. He built them a small wooden box and gave it to them with one simple instruction.

Put only good memories in it.

Sappy but thoughtful, and Callen figured it was supposed to be some kind of healing/therapy tool. It probably worked a lot of the time, too, but Callen had never been able to open his.

A therapist would have had a field day with that. Callen, however, knew the answer was much simpler. Good memories were rare, and he hadn't wanted them in a damn box when they worked just fine in his own head. And now he was face-to-face with one of those good memories.

Shelby, the reason for lustful thoughts and unplanned hard-ons.

Maybe it was the sugar high he was getting from the cake or the fact that she was sitting right there across from him, but Callen wondered if—once she'd got over her broken heart, that was—well, he wondered if—

The back door opened, and the lustful thoughts of getting Shelby in bed vanished when Buck and Rosy came in. Callen automatically stood, shoving his hands in his jeans pockets. A therapist would have a field day with that, too, saying it was his way of avoiding a hug. If so, that didn't deter Buck. He went to Callen, gave him that hug and patted his back.

"I'm glad you're here," Buck said, and no one could have doubted that it was genuine.

Callen, however, had never understood it. He was so far from being special and lovable that he wasn't even on the special meter/lovable scale, had there been such a thing. Yet Buck had always looked at him as if he'd seen good things that no one else did.

Not even Callen.

Heck, maybe Buck did that with all his fosters. Maybe that was why he was the best of the best at fixing kids that others had so carelessly broken. Well, the best of the best except with Callen. Buck had never quite been able to fix him.

When Buck stepped back, Callen gave him the once-over. Not in a blast-from-the-past kind of way but to see if he could pick up on any of those concerns that Shelby had mentioned. His stomach tightened when he saw it. Buck's paler skin. The tired eyes. Of course, maybe the paler skin was just because he was getting older. And for that matter, the eyes could be because he was indeed tired.

Callen's gut told him otherwise, though.

"I'm fixing all of Callen's favorites for dinner," Rosy announced, and she began to rattle off things that made his mouth water, along with jogging his brain about what he needed to tell them.

"I have a six o'clock flight back to Dallas," Callen explained. "I'll need to leave for the airport by four."

He looked at his watch even though it wasn't necessary. He knew the time. It was just past two. But he wanted to give himself a second to brace for the disappointment or whatever else he'd see in their eyes.

And the disappointment was there, all right.

Rosy made an *uhhh* sound. Shelby frowned, sighed. But Buck just smiled.

"Good. Then you've got time to come out and see the new mare. Her name is Georgia."

That was all that was needed for Rosy to volunteer to get Callen's coat, and she hurried back toward the living room.

"Shelby trained Georgia," Buck went on. "She was going to sell her to some fella up in Austin, but I took one look at her and figured she'd be a good one for my kids."

My kids. Not fosters. Not something less than the highest label that a father could give.

Callen put on his coat when Rosy brought it to him, and he headed out the back door with Buck. Rosy stayed behind, no doubt sensing that this needed to be a private conversation. Perhaps hoping, too, that Buck would be able to change his mind about staying. Shelby didn't go with them, either.

The wind had a bite to it. Not unusual for this time of year. Of course, nothing was usual weatherwise for late fall and winter in central Texas. They could get anything from an ice storm to eighty-degree temps.

Today, it was cold and crisp, and Callen took in the scent of the pasture grass, the livestock and the old leather from Buck's jacket.

"He beat up a cow," Callen heard Rayna call out. She was behind the house and had a chicken tucked beneath her coat.

Buck's eyebrow winged up when he looked at Callen. "Did Esther's longhorn break fence again and muck up traffic?"

He wasn't sure how Buck managed to deduce all of that from Rayna's cow-beating accusation, but Callen merely nodded. "I got it moving, and then Judd gave me a speeding ticket."

Callen hadn't meant for that to sound sort of whiny, but hell, that stuck in his craw. Nobody could hold a grudge like Judd.

"Maybe you can see your brothers while you're here," Buck went on as they walked toward the barn. "Not Nico, though. He's off in Abilene for the rodeo. But Kace'll be at the police station until five or so."

Callen just nodded again, though both of them knew Kace wasn't on his visiting list. No grudge holding for the oldest Laramie brother, but there was that whole lecture thing that Callen intended to avoid.

"So, exactly how did Shelby convince you to come back?" Buck came out and asked.

Best not to mention the French kiss.

"She said she thought it was important that I talk

to you, that it might do you some good," Callen settled for saying.

He waited for Buck to press him for more on that. He didn't. In his slow, calm way he just kept walking to the barn, and Callen got another look at the teenage boy he'd seen earlier. His dark features were enough like the slinking girl that he suspected they were siblings.

Something stirred in Callen. Not lust or a sugar high. But a slam of the memories so bad that he got an instant reminder of why he'd left. Why he'd avoided coming back here.

"That's Mateo Garcia," Buck said, following Callen's gaze to the boy who was sitting on the corral fence and feeding a bay gelding a carrot. "He'll need some time."

Callen truly hoped that time was all that it would take, but just as he'd recognized the slinking, he noticed the damaged look on the kid's face. It didn't help, either, that this Mateo was probably around fourteen or so. The age Callen had been when he'd first come here.

"Mateo's sister is Lucy," Buck added. "Two years younger than he is. She's just as spooked."

They kept walking, the ground beneath his boots wet with what had almost certainly been frost that morning, and they finally stepped into the barn. So few changes here, too, and he got confirmation of that as they went through to the back doors and to the fenced-in pasture where Callen spotted the four horses.

"Georgia," Buck said, tipping his head to the blue-black mare. It was what folks called a nonfading since the color was pure without any brown fading caused by the sun.

"As in 'Midnight Train to Georgia'? Or 'Georgia on My Mind'?" Callen asked.

Buck smiled, pushed his battered hat back on his head. "The first one. You remembered that I named all the horses after songs."

He did. That was why during Callen's time at the ranch, there'd been Wichita for "Wichita Lineman," Sue for "A Boy Named Sue," Maggie for "Maggie May" and the somewhat embarrassing "Achy Breaky."

"Georgia's a gentle one but a little skittish," Buck went on. "I figure I can eventually get Lucy to start taking care of her. That'll help both of them."

Callen wondered if Buck knew that this was as much therapy as Rosy's chocolate cake and peanut butter cookies. Probably. He suspected there wasn't much that got past Buck. Which meant he might know about Shelby's kiss offer.

Buck leaned against the barn and continued to look out at the horses. "How much aggravation would it cause you to change your flight and stay the night?"

The knot tightened in Callen's gut. He had steeled himself up enough to hear whatever bad news Buck might dole out, but this... Well, this was a rock and a hard place. It would be an aggravation, a little one, because Callen would have to reschedule some meetings, but Callen suspected the staying the night would fall way out of the aggravation zone and into things he wasn't sure he wanted to deal with.

Buck was probably going through the same thing— dealing with things he didn't want to deal with. Things that had made Buck tell both Rosy and Shelby that he needed to talk to him.

Buck gave him another pat on the back. "If you can swing it, stay for the night. I think it'll do all of us some good."

Callen silently cursed. Added some silent groans, too, and a not-so-silent sigh that he wasn't about to swallow. He wasn't so sure about that "doing us all some good," but Callen took out his phone to call Havana.

Apparently, the time machine was going to be on pause for a while.

CHAPTER FIVE

FIRE IN THE HOLE.

For some stupid reason that was the thought that had continued to go through Shelby's mind. During the dinner with Callen, Buck, Rosy and the kids. Throughout her chores and tending the horses. And even now that she was back home and in her own bed with her pudgy black cat, Elvira, sprawled out next to her.

Fire in the hole.

A warning that some kind of big explosion was about to happen.

Callen probably wouldn't like that he was part of that particular metaphor, but he was. Because he wouldn't have agreed to stay the night unless something was truly wrong with her father.

Of course, she'd known something was wrong, but she'd hoped—*God, she'd hoped*—that she had blown it out of proportion. But now it was right there in her face, as glaring and disturbing as the mooning Santa had been.

Elvira opened her green, already-narrowed eyes and made a feline grunting sound that smacked of *give it a rest already and go to sleep.* Shelby would. As soon as she managed to turn off her brain and not replay every second of the past hours.

Had Buck told Callen what was wrong? she wondered.

Maybe. If so, then Callen had the most pokered of poker faces because he hadn't given her any hints whatsoever. Then again, they hadn't had a minute to themselves so she could pump him for information, either. She could thank Rayna and her constant whining for that, and Rosy, who'd decided to pull out all the stops and create even more of a dinner feast— one that she'd wanted Shelby to help her prepare while Buck and Callen went out riding with Mateo.

She could thank her father for the horseback riding suggestion that had also robbed her of any pumping time with Callen. Buck had claimed he wanted to show Callen the mineral springs that weren't far from the ranch. Springs that had been there for eons and that hadn't changed in the fourteen years since Callen had left. But those eons-old springs had apparently become so riveting that Buck had insisted on the ride. The fact that Callen had agreed likely meant he knew whatever bad gloom and doom stuff that Buck hadn't been willing to tell her.

Tomorrow, before Callen could drive away again, she would go back for another pumping attempt.

In the darkness, she frowned. Why the heck did that suddenly sound so sexual? Maybe because of all the lingering lust that hung between Callen and her, that was why. The info she needed from him was critical, top-of-the-list kind of thing, but maybe it wouldn't hurt if she gave him that goodbye kiss that she'd been storing up for fourteen years. Maybe this time, he'd give her a glance in the rearview mirror.

Yes.

Nothing could go wrong with that.

"Fire in the hole," Shelby whispered as she drifted off to sleep.

SHELBY WAS GUZZLING her third cup of coffee when she heard the vehicle approaching her house.

Her first thought was Callen.

Of course, he had pretty much been her first or second thought throughout the entire restless night, so that wasn't much of a surprise. That was why she'd already tended to the horses and got dressed so she could drive over and have that chat with him. But maybe he'd come to her.

Or not.

When she sprinted to the door and looked out, she saw Rosy sitting behind the wheel of her truck, motioning for Shelby as she rolled down the window. "Hurry. We have to decide between the cowboy-cowgirl, the matching bunny rabbits or the rearing horse."

Shelby was certain she gave Rosy a blank stare. That was before she remembered that today was the day they were supposed to make a final decision on the wedding cake—and the plastic or floral topper.

And to do that they needed to see Jaylene Winters, the owner of Patty Cakes.

If the decision had been left up to Shelby, it wouldn't have been any of those choices Rosy had just mentioned, but at least she'd managed to talk Rosy out of using a figurine of Billy the Armadillo. The sight of the likeness of the stuffed critter would have squelched even the heartiest of appetites at the reception.

"Hurry," Rosy repeated, causing Shelby to finish the last gulps of coffee, grab her purse and go out to meet the woman. "I got a late start," Rosy added, "and Jaylene can only give us a half hour or so. She's running a special on snickerdoodles, and she'll have to get started baking."

Shelby got in the truck and managed to hold off a good twenty seconds before she asked, "How's Callen?"

"Right as rain. I'm not sure if he got much sleep, though, because he was working on a laptop and talking on the phone when I got there this morning. It seems to me that he'd been working most of the night. Buck said Callen had some business stuff to take care of, and he didn't come down for breakfast, so I left him some French toast and bacon warming in the oven."

While Rosy drove into town, Shelby took her time to figure out how to best word her next question. "Did Buck and Callen get to spend any time together? You know, talking?"

"Well, sure. You were there when they went out to the barn."

Yes, but that would have been only time enough for Buck to drop some health bombshell on Callen. It wouldn't have been a long enough discussion for her father to get off his chest whatever was bothering him.

"And they'll get to spend some time together today," Rosy continued. "Callen said he wouldn't be going back until later this afternoon."

Good. That would give Shelby the chance to interrogate him. If that failed, then she was going to have to press her father. Of course, Buck wasn't going to give up anything that he didn't want her to know— which he'd already proved by dodging her questions about anything being wrong. That meant her best shot was with Callen.

Since it was only seven thirty, there weren't many people on Main Street, but they were delayed because they got behind the old school bus that belched out exhaust and creaked when the driver took the turn toward the school. Once it was out of the way, Rosy hurried to the parking spot directly in front of Patty Cakes.

It wasn't a big place. The bubble-shaped glass display cases divided the kitchen from a small seating area that would soon be packed with others jamming around those cases. It smelled like what Shelby figured heaven was like. Sugar, yeast and butter. Some cinnamon and chocolate, too.

Shelby dragged in some long breaths, figuring each breath was at least a pound that would cling to her thighs.

Jaylene Winters—who had bought the place from Patty Mervin, hence the name—was there, taking out a large tray of cookies from the gleaming stainless oven and then effortlessly sliding in another tray. She shot them a smile, emphasizing the copious amounts of killer red lipstick that she preferred. She definitely didn't look like a baker with her Marilyn Monroe figure—the younger years—and her platinum blonde hair. The woman was a genius when it came to high-calorie, fat-saturated yummies.

"Hi, Shelby, Rosy," Jaylene said. "Let me get those toppers you wanted me to order for you. I can send back the ones you don't like." And she scurried off into her office.

"I'm sorry," Rosy whispered, catching onto Shelby's hand. "When I asked you to come with me, I wasn't thinking things through. Does this place give you bad memories? Because it reminds you of your engagement to Gavin?" Rosy added when Shelby gave her what had to be another blank stare.

Oh, that.

Shelby recalled asking Callen something similar about being back in Coldwater, but that was because she knew he had actual bad memories. He'd brought them with him from whatever circle of hell that he'd escaped. But Shelby had no such memories of Gavin and this place.

"Gavin and I never got around to choosing a cake," Shelby said. They'd never got around to choosing a lot of things. Like a wedding date, for instance.

"Good. I know you're down—I can see it all over your face—and I just didn't want to make it worse."

The downer was for Buck, but since Shelby wanted to reciprocate and not make things worse for Rosy, she just stayed quiet.

"Here they are," Jaylene said. She was carrying a box that she set on one of the tables. "Option one." She took out an overly cutesy cowboy and cowgirl in wedding clothes. The cowboy was bowlegged. The cowgirl appeared to be giggling with her non-bouquet-holding hand pressed to her mouth.

"I vote for that one," Shelby commented, knowing there would be nothing better coming out of the box.

She was right.

"Option two." Jaylene pulled out a bunny bride and groom. Not plastic. They were furry and reminded Shelby of the critters in Rosy's shop. The bunny eyes were opened as if they'd been stapled in place, giving them a semi-zombie feel.

"Option three," Jaylene continued, and her blush let Shelby know that this one wasn't going to get Jaylene's vote.

It was what Rosy had referred to as the rearing horse. Well, it was rearing, all right. The black stallion was standing on its hind legs, its forelegs high and pawing the air. The pose gave an unobstructed view of the genitalia, proving that it was indeed a stallion. A well-endowed one. Rosy either didn't notice the endowment or else ignored it as she gave it a careful study and didn't blush.

"Oh, this is such a hard choice," Rosy declared.

"I vote for option one," Shelby repeated, only to get what was definitely some hemming and hawing from Rosy.

Since Rosy appeared to be settling in for even more hawing and possibly some hemming, Shelby went over to the window. As she looked out, her gaze practically collided with Judd's. Looking more cop than cowboy right now, he used two fingers to motion for her to come outside.

Well, Judd was better than eyeing the disturbing cake toppers again, but not much. At least he was easier to look at. Of course, she could say that about all the Laramie brothers, who had apparently been created by the gods as some kind of benchmarks for hotness.

Like his brothers, Judd had got the black hair, the handsome face and the mouth that made women sigh. Not her. She'd never had a single sigh over Judd. For whatever reason, Judd had never done it for her the way Callen had.

Judd was scowling when she stepped outside with him. Then again, he usually scowled, and this morning his eyes were bloodshot. She hoped that was because he was coming off the night shift and not because he'd gone to bed with a bottle of the single malt he preferred.

Callen wasn't the only Laramie with demons.

"Why is Callen back?" Judd demanded.

He sounded like a cop, too. Not a surprise since he had been one for about ten years now, but since this wasn't an official interrogation, she gently brushed her hand down his arm to remind him that she was in every way that counted his sister. And that she wasn't going to take any crap from him.

"Buck wanted him here, so I went to Dallas to talk him into coming," she explained.

For such a simple answer, it caused Judd to give her a long, pensive glare. "The wedding's not for nearly four weeks," he pointed out.

"Buck wanted him here before the wedding," she pointed out right back to him. Then she sighed. "I'm worried about Buck. And, no, I don't have any details. For now, just call it a big cloudy ball of worry, and I thought Callen could help."

"Help? How? He washed his hands of us. He left," Judd spit out.

She heard the hurt in his voice, but he would have chowed down on Billy the Armadillo before admitting it existed. Or that it ate away at him like acid. Once, Callen and he had been so close. Thick as thieves, Rosy would have said. Whatever that meant. But Callen had tossed aside that closeness to try to outrun those demons.

Of course, Judd had tried the outrunning approach, too. Or so Shelby suspected when he'd become a cop in Austin. It hadn't lasted, though, and he'd come home. Probably after realizing that demons had a nasty habit of going wherever you went.

"Callen's leaving later today," she added. "So, if you want to see him, you should do it soon."

"I've already seen him. I gave him a speeding ticket. Forty-one in a thirty zone."

She patted his arm again and considered going snarky. Something like *thanks for keeping us safe from all those dangerous criminals*. But Judd didn't look as if he'd appreciate snark today, even from someone he tolerated more than others.

"Is Buck sick?" Judd asked, and there it was. The worry.

"Maybe." Probably. "Maybe" sounded more optimistic, she thought, and she needed to hang on to that a while longer. "I don't know for sure."

Now it was Judd who ran his hand down her arm. "Keep me posted," he said as he walked away.

She would. Ditto for Nico and Kace, and she made a mental note to call them on the outside chance that they knew what was actually going on with Buck.

Shelby glanced in the bakery window to see that Rosy was still in the throes of making a decision. Thankfully, Jaylene had taken the stallion and was holding it partially behind her back. Maybe it was the baker's attempt at out of sight, out of mind.

Since Jaylene was no doubt eager to get back to those snickerdoodles, Shelby turned to make her way inside to see if she could hurry Rosy along. The sound of someone calling out her name stopped her.

And she groaned—not silently this time. Because it was Gavin.

It wasn't the first time she'd seen him since he'd ended the engagement. She'd caught glimpses of him in town and on the road. However, it was the first time he'd sought her out, she realized, as he made his way over to her.

For someone who seemed awfully interested in talking to her, Gavin clammed up once he reached her. He looked at her, and, yes, there was sympathy in his eyes, before he glanced at Rosy. It likely only took a glance for him to figure out what was going on inside and that he didn't especially want to be part of it.

Gavin wasn't stupid. That was one of the things that she'd always liked about him. Plus, he was good-looking in a blond hair, blue-eyed sort of way. Definitely not the Laramie tall, dark and edgy. He was more the Nordic-god type. You almost expected him to sling mythical lightning bolts while wearing a toga only long enough to cover his manhood.

"Uh, is it hard for you to be here?" he asked, tipping his head to the bakery. "To deal with Rosy and Buck's wedding plans, I mean."

Yes, it was hard, but not in the way he probably thought. She didn't want to look at the zombie bunnies on a wedding cake.

"It's okay," she said, because that was the grown-up thing to say. And because they had drawn a small audience.

She couldn't miss the movement behind the glass front windows in the shops and businesses along Main Street, and Hattie Dapplemore was using binoculars in the parking lot of the diner. This encounter with Gavin, even when it was grown-up conversation, would generate plenty of gossip.

Plenty more sympathy for her, too. Something Shelby absolutely didn't want, but she was damned if she did, damned if she didn't. If she stayed quiet, folks assumed she was sulking and moping. If she smiled, then she was putting up a brave front to hide her broken heart.

Which had barely been dinged.

She had no broken heart. No sulking. Darn sure no moping. She was tough. She ran her own horse boarding and training business and was totally undeserving of the kid-glove treatment.

"You know, I can load hay bales on the tractor bed all by myself," she snarled.

"Huh?" That came from Gavin.

It was a reasonable reaction, considering it'd seemingly come out of nowhere, but Gavin hadn't been privy to the conversation going on in her head about her being more than capable of surviving a broken engagement. That had morphed into blurting out the totally irrelevant skill set of being able to lift seventy-five pounds, more or less, and hoist it onto a flatbed.

"I just wanted to point that out," she mumbled.

He nodded as if that'd made sense and glanced

around at their audience before his attention came back to her. "Silla said Callen was back. The wedding's nearly four weeks off. Why'd he come back to town so soon?"

When Judd had posed that very question to her just five minutes ago, it hadn't bothered her, but it bothered her now. "How the heck should I know? Why don't you ask Callen?" The words came out with a heavy dosing of anger. *Heavy.* And it seemed as if they had taken on bullhorn volume.

Gavin actually dropped back a step and held up his hand as if about to break into singing "Stop! In the Name of Love." "I was just curious, that's all." He stared at her a moment longer. "Get some rest, Shelby. You sound and look...tired."

She wanted to smack him, or better yet throw a hay bale at him, but she reined in the un-grown-up, mean-girl things going on in her head and glared at him until he walked away.

"Oh dear," Rosy said as she came running out of the bakery. She had a small box in her hand. "I'm sorry. If I'd known you'd run into Gavin, I wouldn't have asked you to come with me." She slid her arm around Shelby and started leading her back to the truck. "Are you okay? Are you going to cry?"

"Yes. No," she answered, and hoped that Rosy could figure out the order of those responses. "I really am okay," she added.

Rosy muttered another "oh dear," to indicate that she wasn't buying it. She got Shelby in the truck and strapped on her seat belt as if she were a kid and not the strong hay-bale-lifting woman that she truly was. Then Rosy hurried to get behind the wheel to drive them away from prying eyes.

"Here, I got you some snickerdoodles." Rosy passed her the box. "Eat them. Then maybe a good cry would help you."

"No, it'll just make my eyes puffy." But the cookies weren't off-limits. She plucked one from the box and bit in.

God. A baked treat orgasm. It didn't actually help, but that would have been asking a lot of flour, butter and such.

With the hopes of changing the subject and deflecting a lecture from Rosy, Shelby asked, "So, which topper did you choose?"

Rosy gave her a sheepish smile. "I bought all three. I figured one for the wedding cake, one for the groom's cake and another can be table decoration."

Shelby hoped the stallion or bunnies didn't end up at her table, but in the grand scheme of concerns and worries, either of those wouldn't be a biggie. Ditto for Gavin. Everything else, though, was a biggie.

"You're sighing again," Rosy said as she drove toward Shelby's. "And you look so sad." She paused. "Say, have you thought about a diversion?"

That got Shelby's attention. "What kind?"

Rosy smiled as if what she was about to suggest was a fine idea. "Rebound sex. I could even help you set it up," Rosy continued, probably not noticing Shelby's gaping stare. "And I know just the right person." She patted Shelby's hand. "It's hours before Callen has to leave for the airport, and I've seen the way he looks at you. He'd jump you in a New York minute."

Shelby started to blurt out some probably garbled protest that would address all the parts of that stupid idea. But then she stopped. And she let it come to her slowly. Quietly.

As ideas went, it might be exactly what she needed.

CHAPTER SIX

AS IDEAS WENT, Callen knew now that it had been a bad one to sleep in the same bed he'd had when he'd been a teenager. Clearly, his back had been a lot stronger as a teen, but his thirty-two-year-old body hadn't fared as well. He was achy, sore and had had a sex dream that'd left him grouchy and on edge.

Definitely not a good way to start what would likely be a hard morning.

Still, he tanked up with some more coffee and went in search of Buck. Callen needed to have the "big talk" and get the man to spill his troubles. That way, he could try to figure out what he could do to help fix things. If he couldn't, then he'd feel shitty about it but would leave. If there was something he could do, Callen would do it, then leave—and feel shitty about it.

Since he was apparently going to have a shit day no matter what, he kept looking for Buck and wasn't surprised when he found him in the corral with Georgia. Buck was leading the mare through a few fancy steps while Mateo looked on from his perch on the top fence rail.

Buck waved when he saw Callen, motioned for Mateo to take the mare's reins, and once the boy had done that, Buck headed his way. Callen had got good at reading people. A skill he'd had to cultivate since he was basically a salesman, and judging from Buck's face, Callen wasn't going to have to prod and poke to find out what was wrong. Buck looked like a man ready to spill all.

Callen hoped he was ready to hear it.

Buck joined him about fifteen yards or so away from the corral. A spot that wasn't near the house or Judd's place. In other words, nobody else was going to listen in on this.

"You want to work your way up to what you need to say?" Callen started.

"No." Buck kept his attention on Mateo and softly repeated that one-word response. "But I want you to swear that you won't repeat to anyone what I'm about to tell you. Swear it," Buck added, and there was a fatherly order in it.

"I swear," Callen agreed, even though he knew it was going to come back to bite him in the ass.

"The doc found a tumor on one of my lungs," Buck said a moment later, "and it could be cancer."

Even though Callen had known something bad was coming, it smacked him hard to hear it spelled out like that. Cancer. Yeah, Shelby had been right about there being something wrong.

"I'll need surgery," Buck went on, "and if it's cancer, I'll have chemo and maybe some other treatments. But I want to put it off until after the wedding."

"No," Callen snapped, and he didn't have to give that any thought to know it was the right answer. He pushed aside the shock, the worry, the hard twisting knot in his gut, and he stepped in front of Buck so they were facing each other. "That's stupid. If it's cancer, you need to get the diagnosis right away. You can't wait nearly four weeks."

Buck shook his head. Not a weary "I'm mulling this over" kind of shake, either. It was a "digging my heels in" kind of one. "I love Rosy, and I want to give her the perfect wedding."

"Your love for Rosy will be the same whether you marry her on Christmas Eve or wait until you've taken care of yourself." Callen cursed, earning a stern warning glance from Buck. Callen gave him one right back. "You need to get the biopsy or whatever the hell needs to be done so your doctor can treat you."

Since that argument clearly wasn't working, Callen went with the optimistic approach, one that Rosy would probably use had she been in his place. "Besides, this could turn out to be nothing. Tumors are often benign. If you have a biopsy, you could get a clean bill of health. Think how much happier the wedding would be if you had that weight off your shoulders."

Buck moved just enough to the side so that Callen was out of his face. There was no more eye contact.

Buck put his attention on Georgia and Mateo. "It's cancer," he said, his voice quiet, almost a whisper, but it was practically a shout in Callen's head.

"You don't know that," Callen snapped.

He glanced at Callen, smiled. Yeah, Buck did know that, and Callen could feel the knot getting tighter.

"You'll never be able to keep something like this from Shelby," Callen tried again. "She already suspects something's wrong."

Buck gave a quick nod. "That's why she went to Dallas to talk you into coming. I'll tell her that I'm a little anemic, that I just need a tonic or something."

Callen groaned. "You're going to lie to her."

"I am anemic. The doctor said so, and he told me that's one of the reasons I've been getting so tired."

Despite the warning he knew he'd get, Callen cursed again. "Shelby will know if you're lying."

Buck lifted his shoulder, kept staring out at the corral. "I've kept other things from her. Well, one thing, anyway." He paused. "Something even bigger than cancer."

Callen couldn't imagine bigger than that, but he'd bite. "What?"

Buck didn't say anything for a long time. "You remember Shelby's mother, Anita?"

"Sure. She died about a year after me and my brothers came here." But that was seventeen or so years ago. Callen didn't know what it had to do with now.

"She was killed in a car accident," Buck explained, then paused again. "Anita was on the road that night and in that car because she was leaving me. Leaving us," he amended.

Callen nearly blurted out "bullshit," but then he picked back through the old memories to see if that was possible. Maybe. He hadn't had a lot of interaction with Anita, who'd worked at the bank in town. She'd been kind but also sort of distant. Definitely not hands-on like Rosy.

"Anita said it wasn't another man," Buck went on, "that she just didn't want to be married to me any longer. That she just didn't want the life she had here. So she packed a suitcase, got in her car and died about thirty miles up the road when a semi lost control and hit her."

Buck had spoken all of that like a student giving a book report, but when he turned and looked at him, Callen saw the emotion swirling in those faded green eyes.

Hell.

It must have torn Buck apart, but Callen couldn't recall a single incident where Buck had been so overcome with grief that he hadn't still managed to be there for his kids or to run his ranch.

"Shelby knows about the accident, of course," Buck went on. "But she thinks her mom was going on a short trip to meet up with some friends. She didn't know Anita had no plans to come back. Or to say goodbye to her."

Well, that explained why Shelby had never brought up the subject. "Anita could have changed her mind. She could have come back." Though he doubted that would give Buck much comfort now.

Buck shook his head. "I could see she meant it when she told me she was leaving. I could tell she was done with me and this life."

That stirred something else in Callen. Something he would have preferred left untouched. "Was she done because of us, because of the foster kids?"

"No," Buck quickly said.

But Callen put his BS meter to work and figured that was at least a partial lie.

"It wasn't you," Buck insisted as if reading his mind. "Not the rest of the kids. It was more the... whole package. Anita wanted a bigger life, one that didn't remind her of here." He smiled a little. "You know something about that."

Yeah, he did, and that "bigger life" hadn't been just a want but a need. Still was. A bigger life outran the shitty little one that he'd had for his first fourteen years.

Well, in theory it did.

Buck hadn't outrun anything. Nor had he wanted to do that. After being in foster care himself when he was a kid, Buck had decided to play it forward and give a good home to those who needed it. Callen and his brothers had certainly needed it.

"Shelby can't know any of what I've told you about her mom," Buck said a moment later. "She'd had a big argument with Anita that night, and Shelby might blame herself."

Crap. Crap. Crap.

Callen couldn't recall an argument between Shelby and the woman, but, yeah, Shelby would blame herself for what happened to her mom.

"Sorry to dump all of this on your shoulders," Buck added, looking away from him again.

Callen gave that some thought, too. "Why'd you tell me? Why me? Judd's just next door—"

"Judd's dealing with some stuff right now. Old stuff," he amended when Callen just stared at him. "You deal with this sort of stuff better than he does."

Like hell. But then Callen rethought that, too. He honestly didn't know how his brothers handled the crap they'd been through, but since Judd was older, it meant he'd gone through that crap a year longer than Callen, before they'd got to Buck's. Plus, Judd and he hadn't always been in the same foster homes, so God knew what kind of hell his brother had experienced in those places.

Or on the job.

Not here in Coldwater but before, when Judd had been a city cop. He'd heard rumors of something going wrong there. Since Callen didn't know the details, he wasn't certain if it had actually affected Judd or not, but it could have been bad layers on top of the already-bad stuff.

"I failed with Anita," Buck went on, drawing Callen's attention back to him. "I couldn't figure out what she needed or how to give it to her. It was the same with you. I failed you, and I'm sorry about that."

For the third time during this conversation, or maybe it was the fourth, Callen cursed again. "Not you. You didn't fail me. But everything else that came before you did."

Even though Callen started slapping up those mental roadblocks, the memories bulldozed over him. Watery ones of a father who'd walked out on the family, leaving his kids with their junkie mother. Callen didn't even want to think her name. Didn't want the image of her clear enough to remember the rest. Ironic that he'd thought it had been crappy enough with her, but it'd got a whole lot worse once his brothers and he had been fed into the system.

Callen knew there were wonderful foster homes out there. Buck's was one of them. But until Buck, Callen figured he'd managed to get sucked into the hellhole ones that had left him needing to outrun everything.

"My failure is the reason I wanted you to come," Buck went on. "Call it an old man's dream, but I wanted a second chance with you. A chance to make things right."

Callen had to swallow the lump in his throat before he could speak. "You made things right enough."

Buck gave him another of those thin smiles and a pat on the back. "Bullshit, but thanks for saying it." He paused again and seemed to be swallowing a lump or two of his own. "When Shelby and Rosy do find out about the tumor and the treatment that I'll need, they'll be upset."

"Damn right they will be."

Buck made a sound of calm agreement. "That's where you come in, and I'll warn you in advance. What I'm about to ask you is big. A lot bigger than you're gonna want to take on."

This time, the tight knot moved to Callen's chest. He didn't ask. He just stood there with the winter chill seeping through him and waited for Buck to continue.

"Shelby and Rosy need help with this place," Buck finally said. "Not the physical labor but finding someone who can take over things. It'll need to happen pretty soon, right after the wedding."

Less than four weeks. Yes, very soon. Sooner if Callen could talk Buck into going ahead with the biopsy and treatment. He wasn't giving up on that just yet.

"I'll also need help with the kids. Lucy and Mateo," Buck added. "It won't be easy to find, but they'll need a new place to live. The right place. They're…troubled."

Callen had picked right up on that. "Abused?"

A muscle flickered in Buck's jaw. "Yes. In some very bad ways. It can't be left to the system to find them the right place. I'm asking you to help with that."

"I don't know anything about finding a home for foster kids," Callen quickly pointed out.

"Shelby can work with you on that. Rosy, too."

No, they wouldn't because they'd be too worried about what was going on with Buck. Hell, *he* was worried about what was going on with Buck because this felt a whole lot like a man making final plans before he died. And he just might if he delayed treatment that could save his life. One way or another, he had to convince Buck not to wait.

"Will you help?" Buck asked him. Direct, simple and very much to the point.

Callen wanted to say no. Well, not really. He wanted to help the man who'd given him the chance to survive, but Callen knew that meant extending his stay here. It meant getting involved, which would almost certainly include—but not be limited to—dragging up the past.

"Take some time to think about it," Buck offered but then stopped when they heard the approaching vehicle. Or rather vehicles. Callen spotted Rosy's truck, and Shelby was behind her in her own vehicle.

"They're back from doing wedding-cake stuff," Buck said. He looked at Shelby when she stepped out. "I'm worried about my girl."

Callen looked at her, too. "Because of her crushed heart from Gavin."

"No. Because her heart didn't get crushed when the man she was about to marry broke up with her."

Callen frowned. Shelby really didn't look upset over a failed relationship, but what the heck did he know?

Buck patted his back again. "That whole thing

about castrating you if you touch Shelby… That's off the table now."

With that, Buck walked away, strolling toward the women.

Callen stayed put. Not actually by choice. His feet had somehow become glued to the ground. He stood there, trying to gather his thoughts, which were all over the place.

What the heck had just happened? Spilled secrets. Not one but two, what with the Anita confession to go along with the health stuff. Favor requests to keep said secrets and do things that Callen didn't know how to do. He didn't know how to fix broken kids. Or broken adults for that matter.

And now the castration threat was gone and Shelby didn't have a broken heart.

For shit's sake, what was he supposed to do?

He was still mumbling that question to himself, still cursing both himself and Buck, watching Buck greet Rosy and Shelby, as if it'd been days instead of hours since they'd been together. There was love, no doubts about that, and Callen knew that the love extended to him. He just didn't know why. He'd never been able to figure that out.

Rosy went inside first, but Buck and Shelby lingered a moment longer before Shelby started toward Callen. As she got closer, he could see that she had the same dumbfounded expression that he almost certainly had on his own face. She hiked her thumb in the direction of the house.

"My dad just said he won't castrate you if you touch me. What the heck kind of conversation did you two have?" she demanded.

"A very complicated one," Callen settled for saying—though hearing that Buck had told Shelby that was another punch in the gut.

And somewhat distracting.

Of course, Shelby was the ultimate distraction since she was now standing right in front of him, and she smelled amazing. Like sugar and cinnamon.

"Did you just eat a cookie?" he asked, obviously surprising her. But then she'd likely expected him to say something that was at least remotely connected to the castration/complicated one comments.

"Yes," she confessed. "It was a tough trip to Patty Cakes, and I needed a fix. Now, tell me why my dad gave you permission to nail me."

Callen frowned at the "nail me," but then he shrugged. Permission was exactly what Buck had given. Of course, it wasn't anything that Callen's own brainless body hadn't already suggested he do to Shelby, but it was awkward to have such a frank discussion about it. Especially since there was a second part to this particular subject.

The why.

Shelby knew a concession like that from Buck wouldn't just come from the goodness of his good heart. Nope.

"Taking castration off the table comes with strings," Callen said. "He's worried about you and thinks if you have mindless sex with me that it might help. Or at least that's how I'm interpreting it."

She stared at him. Specifically at his mouth, and Callen didn't believe she was considering sharing a cookie with him. No. That was lust again.

"He's worried about me?" she asked.

Callen didn't groan, but it was close. That was what she picked out of what he'd just told her? Well, that wasn't lust in her eyes after all.

"He's worried about me because of Gavin," she concluded a moment later. Then she huffed. "I can lift my own hay bales, you know."

He couldn't see the connection here. Unless that was some kind of sexual reference.

Which intrigued him far more than it should have.

She fired a few glances around and settled for kicking a rock. "He doesn't need to be worrying about me. Not with him going through whatever the heck it is he's going through." She kicked another rock, her gaze snapping back to him. "What's wrong with him, anyway? And don't lie because I'll know it."

She probably would know. He dragged his mind away from hay bales and castration to consider what he should say. If anything… No, it had to be something. Shelby wasn't just going to let him walk away from this.

"Buck's anemic," he told her. Not his best effort at responding, but sadly, it wasn't his worst, either. And it was true.

She blinked. Opened her mouth, then closed it. Before the breath of relief swooshed out of her. Sugar, cinnamon breath, and there was so much of it that it must have made her a little light-headed because she sagged against him. Callen caught her in his arms because it seemed as if she might slide right to the ground.

"Anemic," she repeated. The relief was in her voice, too. She repeated it a couple more times, paused again, and then she looked up at him. "You're not lying to me, are you?"

"No." He managed a straight face, too. "Buck really is anemic."

She kept looking at him, processing that and probably trying to decide if it was true. "If it's just anemia, then why did he want you back here?"

Okay, this would take some even-deeper semi-lying. He'd been right when he thought swearing himself to secrecy would come back to bite him in the ass. It would have been a much more pleasant experience if Shelby had been the one doing the ass biting.

Something that he wished hadn't popped into his head.

Callen steeled himself up, looked her straight in the eyes. "The anemia is causing Buck to get tired. His doctor said so," he added. Well, at least that much was true. Of course, he was withholding the biggest truth of all. A tumor. Possible cancer.

She kept staring at him as if trying to climb into his head. "Really?"

He nodded. "Buck wanted me here to help out with things," Callen went on. Good. So far, the things coming out of his mouth had been the truth. That might quell Shelby's BS meter. "He's worried, what with the fatigue, that he's not able to keep fostering Mateo and Lucy, and he wanted me to help find a good placement for them."

Now her staring went up a whole bunch of notches. "I could have helped with that."

Callen nodded again and carefully considered how to put this. "He's worried you already have a lot on your plate." And he left it at that.

"Gavin," she snarled. "He thinks it's because of Gavin." She kicked another rock. Stopped. Paused. Stared some more. "Did you actually agree to help Dad? *Here?*"

The addition of *here* didn't help the tornado that was going on in his head since it was a reminder that *here* was the place he didn't want to be, doing things he especially didn't want to be doing.

But Callen nodded.

Best not to try words right now since they might come out like a croak with his throat clamped shut like it was.

"You're staying," she said on a rise of breath.

Another nod. "For a short while." And, yes, he croaked a little.

If she noticed the break in his voice or that he'd

just told her a smidgen of the truth, Shelby didn't show it. She smiled, and before he could suss out exactly what the smile meant, she came up on her toes and kissed him.

His brain turned to mush. Hot mush. And he sank right into that cinnamon-flavored kiss. Sank, and just kept on going until... Yeah, he made it French.

Oh man. It was good. The kind of good that could get him in trouble very, very fast. He didn't remember that he was standing out in the open with their mouths fused together and their tongues playing around. Hell, he didn't remember his own name.

But Shelby obviously did because she said it on that same silky rise of breath. "Callen." Her mouth was still against his.

The next part wasn't so breathy or silky, though, when she eased back. "We have an audience."

Once he got his eyes uncrossed he glanced around and confirmed that Shelby was right. Rosy was watching them from the kitchen window. Rayna from upstairs. Mateo from the corral. Heck, even the mare was watching.

"Welcome home," Shelby whispered, and she smiled again as she strolled away.

CHAPTER SEVEN

THE KISS HAD stayed with her. In one of those itchy, "I want more" kind of ways that she hadn't been able to act on for the past three days.

But the itch scratcher wasn't there.

Shortly after the well-witnessed kiss, Callen had headed back to Dallas to clear up some business stuff and gather some things for the next wave of his homecoming. A homecoming to help her father.

Or so Callen and her dad had said.

She'd leave it at that for now. Or at least until Callen had settled into the Lightning Bug Inn, where he not only intended to sleep—something about a lumpy bed at the ranch—but where he was also setting up a temporary office that, according to the gossip, he'd be using until the wedding.

Well, actually not gossip. Shelby had called Havana in Dallas and had got the scoop from her. Havana had confirmed that Callen was indeed committed to helping Buck even though it meant returning to a town he'd vowed never to step foot in again. Foot stepping aside, he was back, or at least on his way back, and Havana had added something about hell freezing over at the prospect of her boss voluntarily spending time in Coldwater.

Shelby hadn't told Havana that the *voluntarily* should have an asterisk next to it since she figured her father had applied his own version of arm-twisting to get Callen to do something that others could have done.

Her, included.

That meant Buck was dealing with much more than anemia and he wanted Callen around to help him pick up the pieces when the truth came out. Or Buck was possibly matchmaking. The second option sounded a lot more fun and might get her itch scratched, but the first option loomed over her like a cloud filled with broken glass, ready to rain down on her and everyone else who loved Buck.

That brought on a heavy sigh and would have even spurred a tear or two if she hadn't been on Main Street, where plenty of folks could see her. Any visible tears now wouldn't be connected gossipwise to Buck but rather to her breakup with Gavin.

Callen could help with that, too. That was why she'd driven to the Lightning Bug to see if he'd made it back yet. Just being with him, even in a superficial kind of way, would turn the gossips in a different direction. She'd no longer be Buck's *bless-her-heart, poor thing!* daughter, who'd got dumped by Gavin. She'd be the *bless-her-heart, poor thing!* woman who was nailing Callen in what folks would see as a rebound affair.

Baby steps. Rebound affair vs. poor pitiful Shelby.

It wasn't even a close decision. Especially not after that kiss. And especially since it wouldn't actually be a rebound. Still, she wouldn't stand a chance convincing anyone of that.

She drove to the teeny parking lot of the inn only to find it full. The rental Jeep Callen had used on his last visit wasn't there, but there were some unfamiliar vehicles. A candy-apple-red Mustang, a gleaming silver luxury SUV that had almost certainly come with some serious sticker shock and an old dark blue Ford truck. Like the SUV, the truck gleamed a little, probably because of a good wax and paint job, but it looked...

She froze.

Considered.

It looked like the truck Callen had driven away in fourteen years ago.

No. It couldn't be. He wouldn't have hung on to something like that. Would he?

With that question in her head and now joining the itch in her body, Shelby took a spot just up the block and got out of her truck. She frowned at the sleet that pinged down on her as she dragged on her gloves. With the yucky, cold weather, she obviously wouldn't be able to say she was out for a stroll and popped in to see how things were going. Callen, if he was there, wouldn't have believed that anyway.

She had nearly made it to the inn when a man popped out from the alley. He moved so fast that at first, he was a blur. Then he wasn't as he stopped in front of her. It was Gopher Tate, and he threw open his heavily lined raincoat to flash her.

He had a blue bow tied around his wrinkly junk that was covered by a pair of whities that weren't so tight. They were at least three sizes too big, and the elastic in the waist was shot.

"Really?" she griped. She would have thrown up her hands if she still hadn't been putting on the gloves. "Flashed and mooned in less than a week. Sheez, am I lucky or what?"

"Lucky?" Gopher said, sounding both hopeful and uncertain.

Shelby gave him a glare that was colder than the sleet pelting his thinly covered privates. "Close your coat, Gopher, before you have to explain to the ER folks why you got frostbite on your wanger."

She walked off, figuring Gopher would put a speedy end to his flashing since she could see the cruiser coming toward them. Kace. He gave her a nod in greeting before aiming what she could only believe was a huffing scowl at Gopher. Shelby didn't wait around to see the arrest. She hurried the rest of the way up the block to the inn and ducked inside.

There was some chaos going on in what was usually a quaint, quiet place with its antiques, flowers galore and the undercurrent of lemon furniture polish. There were two men, strangers, who, according to their shirts, were from Shetland Deliveries, and they were talking with Ozara Proctor, the silver-haired clerk who was seated at one of the inn's prize antiques. A Victorian desk that Shelby had always thought looked too fragile and puny to have survived all these years, but then she could say the same thing about Gopher's junk.

Some things were just a puzzle never meant to be solved.

And speaking of puzzles, she spotted one. Callen. He was in the small café tucked just behind the reception desk. He appeared to be having coffee, smiles and conversation with a redhead whose breasts strained against a sweater that was nearly the same color as the Mustang in the parking lot. Maybe her car, but Shelby was betting she'd come in the overly priced SUV.

She found herself frowning again. Heck. She hadn't asked Callen if he was involved with anyone. She'd brought up the marriage/engaged question in Dallas but not the *are you nailing anyone on a regular basis* one. So maybe she wouldn't get that itch scratched after all.

With that dismal thought ruining her already-sour mood, Shelby turned to leave and nearly ran into Havana, who was coming down the stairs on the other side of the tiny foyer.

"This man with a very saggy weenie flashed me this morning," Havana greeted her. She hugged Shelby as if they were the old friends that Shelby had imagined they might become.

"Gopher. He flashed me, too, but don't worry— the sheriff arrested him."

"I hope he tacks on being stupid to the charges.

Anyone who flashes in this weather is about as sharp as a bowling ball."

She nodded. That described Gopher, all right.

Shelby tipped her head to the delivery guys. "Callen's?"

"Yep. He brought in some furniture to use as a makeshift office. That's to complete the makeshift life he's creating here. I gotta hand it to you. I didn't think you could talk him into coming back."

"I didn't. That was my father's doing." Shelby studied Havana to see if she knew something about that, but her face was blank. At least it was until she looked in the dining room.

"I see Miss Thunder-Tits found her way here."

Shelby arched an eyebrow. "I'm guessing that's not her real name?"

"No, it's Charmaine Wokingham. Old money and now in charge of her daddy's big ol' ranch." She slipped right into an exaggerated Texas drawl. "And, of course, she'll only do business with Callen. They're not lovers," she added as if taking a peek into Shelby's green-eyed thoughts. "But she'd sure like to be."

Shelby didn't doubt that. Not the way Charmaine was leaning in with those thunder-tits. "He must know that she's throwing herself at him."

Something that Shelby knew a little about since she had planned to do the same thing to Callen. She just wouldn't be leading the charge with massive breasts.

"Oh, he knows, all right," Havana assured her,

"but Callen never mixes business with pleasure. If Charmaine ever figures that out, she'll quit buying cattle from him, and then try to jump him. Even then, he'd turn her down." She paused, gave Shelby a sideways glance. "How'd that French-kiss suggestion work out for you?"

Shelby smiled, suddenly feeling in a much-better mood now that she knew the redhead wasn't her competition. "It worked out well, as a matter of fact. Thanks."

Havana gave her an elbow nudge. "Now, to get to the part when he moans out your name during sex."

Shelby turned, looked at her. "Are you, uh, always inappropriately interested in Callen's personal life like this?"

"Always," Havana said in a whisper just as Callen and Charmaine stood to walk out into reception.

Callen spotted her, of course. She would have been impossible to miss in the eight-by-eight-foot space. And Charmaine noticed her, too, and she slid chilly blue eyes from the top of Shelby's sleet-frizzed hair to her suspiciously stained boots. Shelby had considered gussying herself up a bit, but she hadn't wanted to be too obvious.

As opposed to being a little bit obvious, which she'd done just by coming here.

"Shelby," Callen greeted her. He glanced at the deliverymen, then Havana. "Is everything set up?"

"Just about. I'll give them a push so they'll hurry. Apparently, there's some concern about where to store the things they removed from the room so they could get your desk in there." Havana stepped away, giving Shelby a thumbs-up as soon as she was behind her boss.

"Shelby, this is Charmaine Wokingham," Callen said. "Charmaine, this is Shelby McCall."

Shelby had never thought her name sounded, well, plain, until it was said in the same breath as the redhead's.

"Callen and I are old…friends," Charmaine purred, offering her hand for Shelby to shake. Shelby hadn't missed the perfectly timed pause before *friends*, which, of course, was meant to make her believe they were much more than that. "And Callen and you are…?"

She wanted to say that Callen and she had once lived together. Not a lie. They had lived under the same roof. But Shelby doubted that Callen would want his childhood secrets smeared around all for the sake of her winning a one-upmanship competition.

"We're friends," Shelby said, but the compromise of holding back on the snark had her feeling even more snarky.

Apparently, it had the same effect on Charmaine's jealous eye because her snooty expression jumped a couple of rungs higher on the ladder. "Well," Charmaine said, managing to give Shelby a condescending, dismissive glance as well before she turned to Callen and brushed a kiss on his cheek.

The woman let her mouth linger there a moment,

maybe to make sure Shelby had caught it, or perhaps she was hoping Callen would shift a little so she could turn it into a real kiss. Callen didn't fall for it, though, which was perhaps why Charmaine's next glimpse at Shelby went all the way to the top on the mean-expression ladder.

"I can lift a hay bale by myself," Shelby blurted out as the woman glided away.

"I've never known anyone so proud of an accomplishment like that," Callen said as he moved to Shelby's side to watch Charmaine leave.

"Well, you take the accolades where you can get them," Shelby mumbled, and was pleased when it caused him to smile. One day she'd tell him that his smile was foreplay. Maybe she could tell him when and if he ever moaned out her name.

"So, you're setting up a temporary office here?" she asked to shift the conversation—though she couldn't think of a good segue to kissing and such.

He nodded, checked his watch. "Some of my clients are willing to come here. I'll have to go to others, but I'll try to stick to business as usual while I help Buck."

At the mention of her father, she eyed him until he looked directly at her. Then she eyed a few more seconds. "Just checking to make sure you told me the truth about my dad and anemia."

"I did. Did you ask him about it?" Callen countered.

"Many times. He's taking iron supplements and probably some other meds that he's hiding from me.

He knows with my mad Google skills that I'd look up any meds to see what they're for."

Callen made a sound of agreement, tipped his head to the stairs. "Come with me. I need to check out the office space, and you can continue to try to use your brain-piercing radar to see if I'm lying to you."

He smiled.

Well, shoot. That was playing dirty. Hard to use brain radar when your own brain had gone to mush.

"Did you come to talk about that kiss?" he asked as they went up the stairs.

"No. Possibly," she amended. "Do you want to talk about it?"

"No. Actually, I want to do more of it, but it's not a good time. I have another client coming any minute now. Best not to do business with the taste of you clouding my senses."

And there it was. The melting puddle. Her, not him. He looked so cool, not capable of self-melting, only being the cause of it for others. It bothered her more than a little that he could do that to her. It bothered her, too, that she wanted him to do it.

He led her to the room at the top of the stairs, where all the bedroom furniture had indeed been moved out, and in its place was a sturdy desk already loaded down with a laptop, in and out baskets, and file folders.

Shelby slid her hand along the smooth wood of the desk before she went to the window. And the view of the parking lot. Definitely not the flash and glitz of the Dallas skyline. However, the SUV was gone, which meant she'd pegged it right—it did belong to Charmaine.

"You can control the financial universe from here?" she asked.

"I only need to control a country or two. And it's only for a couple of weeks. I figure I can leave shortly after the wedding."

Shortly. Now, that was an interesting word. Not just *after* the wedding, but he'd left it with the possibility of tacking on a day or two. She doubted that was for her benefit but wondered if it was for her father's. She just couldn't shake the feeling that there was more going on.

Callen came to the window and looked out at what had held her attention. "The truck," he said.

"It's the same one," she pointed out.

He nodded. "It's hard to explain why I kept it."

Shelby shrugged. "You wanted to be in control of what you chose to keep from your past. A reminder of what you'd come from so that you wouldn't go back."

"Maybe not so hard to explain after all," he muttered.

She turned, met his gaze, which only sped up the melting again. "The next time you drive out of town, make sure you look in your rearview mirror. You might be surprised what you see."

Judging from his raised eyebrow, she had intrigued him. Or maybe just confused him.

"I could be standing there naked," she added, because she wanted to see that smile again.

It worked. She got it. And she even got a quick brush of his mouth over hers. She was reasonably sure that had she been wearing toenail polish, it would have melted, too.

His phone buzzed, and tearing his gaze from hers, he looked at the screen. "The client just arrived."

That was her cue to state her business and then get moving. "I came to invite you to dinner. My house. Just the two of us," she added. "Well, and my cat."

"You and the cat?" He nodded. "I could do that. But not tonight. Another business meeting." The softly mumbled profanity under his breath let her know that it wouldn't be a fun one. He scrolled through the calendar on his phone. "And late tomorrow I have an appointment with a social worker."

That caught her attention. "For Mateo and Lucy?"

He nodded and continued scrolling. "That meeting might run late, and I have to go back to Dallas just for the day on Saturday. So how about Sunday night about seven or so. Does that work for you?"

After that mini kiss, anything would have worked for her. "Sure. I'll see you then." And because she heard footsteps coming up the stairs, she started out.

Callen went with her to the door, turning her so fast that it made her head spin. Spinning it even more when he dropped an amazing kiss on her lips. It was quick and dirty and thorough before he turned her back around to send her on her way. Somehow, she managed to walk despite the bones that the kiss dissolved in her legs.

Great.

Just great.

She was so going to get a real broken heart out of this. Then again, some more good kisses and maybe incredible sex, too. Just what was the right price to pay for a broken heart, anyway?

Shelby figured she was about to find out.

CHAPTER EIGHT

JUST WHAT WAS the right price to pay for keeping a promise to someone who'd been damn good to him when he was a teenager? Callen was finding that out, and it wasn't going especially well.

Buck, he'd learned, was muleheaded.

For the past two days, since Callen had set up shop in Coldwater, he'd visited and called Buck multiple times. The one visit he'd made an hour earlier had ended with Callen having to take hold of Buck's arm to stop him from falling after having a dizzy spell. Maybe it was a result of the anemia, but Callen was betting it had more to do with the tumor.

It had done no good—none—to remind Buck that the dizziness could have happened when he was driving. Or on a horse. He could have been hurt, and that was the reason he needed to tell Rosy and Shelby what was going on. But no. Not the muleheaded Buck, who had not only refused to do that but had reminded Callen of the promise he'd made about keeping the secret that should have never been a secret in the first place.

With problem one—Buck's medical crisis—nowhere

near solved, Callen was tackling problem two. And he wasn't tackling it very well. The report his PI had made on Lucy and Mateo looked plenty thorough, but Callen hadn't been able to get past the first page.

His attention kept landing on words like *multiple contusions. Fractured hand. Malnourished. Neglect. Extreme.* For most of their lives, the kids had been put through that, and it hadn't been abuse from the system but their own mother.

He put the file aside when he heard Havana's voice coming up the stairs. Another somewhat-familiar voice, too. Lizbeth Gafford, and a moment later Havana showed the woman into Callen's office. Not a friend exactly, but she'd had a longtime relationship with one of his business associates, so Lizbeth and he had seen each other socially plenty of times.

This wouldn't be social.

"Thanks for coming," he told Lizbeth once Havana had walked out and shut the door.

She didn't look like a social worker with her perfect hair and clothes. There was a good reason for that. She was actually an heiress, who had likely disappointed her real-estate mogul parents to become a lowly social worker. Callen had heard that she was a good one, too. One who cared and had yet to reach burnout. And that was why he'd called her.

"I was a little surprised to hear from you," she said, sitting when he motioned to the chair in the seating area by the window. Callen sat next to her, and he poured her some of the green tea that Havana had learned the woman preferred. "Surprised, too, to learn you were here in this small town. I didn't think you'd do business anywhere but Dallas."

"I hope it wasn't too much of a hassle for you to come all the way out here. I would have gone to you." He skipped any explanation about why he was here in this particular small town, though it was possible that as a social worker Lizbeth had access to his old records.

"No hassle. My grandparents have a place not too far from here. A ranch. I can check on it for them after we chat. Two birds with one stone, and I'll earn some brownie points for being a good granddaughter." She paused, sipped some of the tea. "I looked up the kids you asked me about. Lucy and Mateo Garcia. They're placed here in Coldwater. A good placement, too, from everything I read. That's why I'm a little puzzled as to why you'd ask about them."

He was going to have to walk on eggshells here. Callen didn't want to say anything about Buck's health that might alarm her. If he did, Lizbeth might be duty bound to remove the kids ASAP. Or at least ask questions that might get back to Rosy and Shelby.

"I've met the kids," he explained, feeling some of those eggshells crunching beneath his boots. "I just thought it might be good if they could find a solid family. Something permanent." Since there was no way in hell they were going back to their mother.

Lizbeth smiled a little. "I see. Are you considering adopting the children?"

"No." Callen couldn't say that fast enough, and he reined in his sharp tone when he continued. "I just want them in a good place, together. One where they won't get shuffled around or get separated."

The smile was gone, but she did give him one of those sympathetic looks like the ones nurses give to sick or hurt kids. "Look, I can't get into anything personal about the children, but since you obviously know their foster father, Mr. McCall, you know that he often takes kids who are hard to place."

Yeah, he knew all about that. Callen had been one of them. "But from what I understand, Buck McCall's age comes into play here. Kids don't get permanent placements with him. Not anymore. He mainly gets kids now who basically have nowhere else to go, and they only stay with him a short while before they're just moved on to the next place."

"That's right." But Lizbeth was hesitant to say more. "Again, without getting into specifics, the Child Protective Services office that handles this area will look for a suitable, safe, permanent home for the kids— where they can stay together." She had more tea, and in doing so dodged his gaze. "Finding one, though, might be a problem."

"Because of Mateo's juvie record." Callen had got a glimpse of that in the PI's report.

"Mr. McCall told you about that," she concluded, her eyes a little wide with surprise. And Callen let her believe that was how he'd heard about it. "Well, his record doesn't help things."

"Mateo stole… He got into fights. He acted out because he was getting the hell beaten out of him at home." Some of that was deduction, but Callen knew plenty about what the kid had been through. "When the cops had had enough, they sent him to juvie."

"Because they had no choice," Lizbeth reminded him.

"The choice should have been to get him and his sister to a safe place," he snapped. Obviously, he was failing big-time at the whole reining in sharp tones. That had been a snarling bark.

She gave him that sad-nurse look again, coupled with a weary sigh. "The system isn't perfect, and if we don't know about the abuse—which the servicing CPS office didn't—we can't fix it. I'm sorry. It's just the way it is. Sometimes, even when we can fix it, we can't make it completely right."

Yeah, yeah. Sometimes life sucked.

"Callen," Lizbeth said, leaning in closer. "I'm glad you're looking out for these children. Heaven knows, they need it, and I promise I'll go above and beyond to find them a permanent home. Trust me on this."

That soothed some of the sharp edges of his frustration and temper. "Thank you."

Her smile returned, and she set her teacup aside as she rose. "I'll make some calls, ask some of my colleagues, and I'll get back to you."

He thanked her again and walked her out of the office and down the stairs.

"This is a beautiful place. Pretty town, too, from

what I've seen of it," Lizbeth added. "How long will you be here?"

"Not long." He meant it. Of course, he had to get past those promise obstacles, but he could always keep up searching for a home for the kids once he was back in Dallas. And if Buck's treatment, surgery or whatever lingered on, he could make trips back for that, too.

He walked Lizbeth out the front door to see her off, and once he'd done that, he turned to go back in. Then he spotted Kace coming toward him. His brother aimed an accusing finger, but Callen realized it wasn't for him. It was for Gopher, who was loitering on the sidewalk just up from the inn.

"Go home, Gopher," Kace warned him. "You'll freeze your balls off here."

"I'm just taking in the scenery," Gopher said as innocently as a suspicious-looking guy in a trench coat could manage. But he turned and skittered away.

Callen figured Kace would just leave, too, but he stared at Callen, then huffed. "Let's get a cup of coffee and talk." That sounded like an order from a cop.

Kace didn't wait for him to agree to that coffee or the order. He threw open the inn's door and made a beeline for the diner.

"Afternoon, Sheriff," the clerk said, and the two people in the diner and the cook all issued the same greeting. Kace nodded greetings back to them and made his way to the table in the corner.

"Just pour me a cup of coffee, Dave," Kace called

out to the cook. "Do you still drink coffee or are you a mochaccino kind of guy now?"

"Coffee's fine." And Callen motioned for Dave to pour a second cup.

Kace didn't say anything until the burly cook had set the cups on the table and then moved away. "What the hell is going on?" Kace demanded. "Why are you here?"

Callen nearly made a comment about the friendly welcome that Judd and now Kace had given him, but he let it pass. "Buck asked to see me."

Kace gave him that cop's stare. "Seeing Buck and moving into the inn are two different things. Why are you here?" he repeated.

Well, hell. Here was that rock and hard place again, the one where he had to walk on eggshells. Callen dragged in a breath first and had some of the coffee. "Buck doesn't want it getting around, but he's anemic and has been having dizzy spells. He wanted me to come in and help with the ranch and look for permanent placements for his current kids."

Another long stare from Kace, followed by a "Shit. Why didn't Buck come to me with this? Or Judd?" But he immediately waved off the Judd suggestion. "*Me*. He could have come to me."

Callen just couldn't help himself. "I guess Buck figured I was more special than you."

"Yeah, you're special, all right." And Callen thought only about 90 percent of that was purely negative. The other 10 percent was big brother who was trying to get his goat.

Callen had some more of his coffee before he continued. What would come next would be the truth minus an even-bigger chunk of the truth that he couldn't tell Kace, even if it might help bridge some distance between them. "I think Buck just wanted to see me, and this was as good an excuse as any. He said he feels guilty that he wasn't able to fix me. I guess he believes he fixed Nico, Judd and you."

"Shit," Kace growled again. "None of us is fixed, but Buck did the best he could. He's got nothing to feel guilty about."

"That's how I see it, too, but I thought I'd stick around for a few weeks to make sure Buck understands that."

Kace's mouth tightened. "Never took you for a do-gooder."

"It goes well with mochaccinos."

"Smart-ass." But Kace's mouth suddenly wasn't so tight, and he motioned toward Dave. "Got any of that apple pie left?"

"Naw. That went early. I got some of those fancy cookies from Patty Cakes."

Kace paused, considered, looked at Callen. "Are you going to make fun of me if I eat some froufrou cookies?" Kace asked.

"You bet," Callen assured him in his best little-brother tone.

That earned him another scowl, but Kace ordered

the cookies, and in under a minute Dave brought them to the table. They were decorated cutouts of flowers, drizzled with icing and colored sugar sparkles. They were the visual definition of *froufrou*, something that looked like they'd be served at a tea party, but they smelled good. Judging from the sound Kace made when he bit into them, they tasted good, too.

"Who's this Patty Cake, anyway?" Callen asked.

"Jaylene Winters. She moved here about five years ago and bought the place from Patty Mervin, old man Cooper Mervin's granddaughter, who couldn't make a go of the place." He popped another cookie in his mouth. "Just one of the things that's changed since you decided you didn't want anything to do with the town. With us," he added.

He figured that Kace was looking for some kind of apology, but Callen didn't have one. He'd needed to leave. No choice there.

"Lots of things have changed," Callen pointed out. "You're the sheriff. And Judd's your deputy. By the way, he gave me a speeding ticket."

"I heard. Let me see how I can put this." Kace paused, considering. "Judd's been in a bad mood for the past decade or so."

"Then what better person to have a gun and a badge," Callen remarked, and it wasn't all a joke.

"He's steady enough. The only person he harms is himself."

And just like that, they were talking about the

past again. Something that probably neither of them wanted to delve into too deeply. At least Callen didn't want that.

Kace studied him for several long moments and then handed him one of the cookies. The froufrou-est of the bunch. A yellow pansy. Callen ate it anyway and made one of those "man, this is delicious" sounds that Kace had made.

"So, is it true that you're richer than God?" Kace asked.

"No. God's got better tax write-offs than I do, but I do okay."

"So, rich enough," Kace concluded.

Callen smiled, washed down the pansy with some coffee. "There's no such thing as *enough* when it comes to money. There's always more to be made."

Kace shook his head, made a sound of disagreement. "You can't buy a clean past with money."

"No, but you make the present pretty damn sweet with it." Callen snagged the last cookie off the plate and popped it into his mouth.

"Enjoy it," Kace said. "Because you'll be getting the tab for this."

That seemed reasonable, considering this conversation hadn't been as unpleasant as Callen had thought it would be.

Kace went still, staring into his coffee. "I figure there's something you're not telling me about why you've come back. I've narrowed it down to two things. Either something is really wrong with Buck or else you're trying to get in Shelby's pants."

Since both of those were true, Callen went for a deflection. "I'm here to help Buck."

Kace's gaze came back to him. Cop's eyes. "Right," he said with mega skepticism. "You're here to get in Shelby's pants."

Callen wasn't sure he could deny it with a straight face, especially now that he'd kissed her and castration wasn't a possibility.

But there was a problem.

Shelby's potentially broken heart.

So, sex with her now would be of the rebound variety. Sometimes, that could help in a quick Band-Aid kind of way, but just as often it could lead to more problems. Like not working through feelings that needed to be worked through—or so Callen had heard. It occurred to him that he'd never been in the position to cure what ailed him with rebound sex. That made him lucky, he supposed. Maybe it had been fate's way of trying to even out all the other "unlucky" crap he'd been through.

He didn't want Shelby having regrets, not with what she would soon have to face with Buck. Callen didn't want her hurting any more than she already was, either.

Well, hell.

Had he just talked himself out of having sex with Shelby?

Apparently so. But he also knew that talk was

cheap and that it wouldn't be so easy to resist her if he kept up the kissing and the lusting.

Kace snapped his fingers in front of Callen's face to let him know he'd wandered off there. "Daydreaming about Shelby?"

"I've always had a thing for her," Callen admitted. Best not to lay out the argument he'd just had with himself about her and rebound sex.

"A thing you didn't act on because you skedaddled." And just like that they were back to the past again. It was like a rubber band that Kace couldn't seem to resist popping against Callen's hand.

"The past doesn't haunt you?" Callen came out and asked.

Kace lifted his shoulder, breathed deeply. "Not like Judd. Not like you. Not like Nico. Judd uses single-malt scotch. Nico uses women. *Sex.* Of course, he's got such a pretty face that women don't seem to mind being the cure for what ails him."

"Sex, booze and money," Callen concluded. They all had their drug of choice. "What do you use to get through it?"

"This." Kace tapped his badge, stood and downed the rest of his coffee.

"The big man in town," Callen concluded.

"The man who can fix shit when it goes wrong. Well, sometimes. Sometimes, shit's not fixable." Kace paused again. "As for Shelby, you'd better tread easy there. I don't want you coming in here and hurting her."

"I don't want to hurt her, either."

"Then rethink getting in her pants. Oh, and enjoy your dinner with her Sunday night," Kace added as he strolled toward the door.

"You know about that?" Callen asked before Kace could get away.

Kace glanced back at him, the corner of his mouth lifting into an easy smile. "Little brother, everybody knows about that."

CHAPTER NINE

SHELBY EXAMINED THE roasted chicken that she'd just taken from the oven. It was splotchy. Nearly white in some places and bubbled up with burned spots in others. It looked more like something Rosy would try to stuff and "pretty up" in her shop than a tasty dish she could serve Callen at dinner.

"Uh, it's not too bad," Rosy said, peering over her shoulder.

It was a lie and nowhere near convincing since Shelby had eyes—and a nose. The chicken didn't smell so good, either. Apparently, the "surefire" recipe that she'd got off the internet for mixed herb rub wasn't so surefire after all.

Rosy and Shelby weren't the only ones who were frowning over the unpleasant-looking, smelly poultry. The cat, Elvira, was perched on one of the kitchen chairs, and she eyed it as if it might jump off the roasting pan and come at them all with a carving knife.

"Maybe putting some sauce on it would help," Rosy suggested.

Shelby figured she'd have better luck torching it

with a flamethrower. It was definitely a reminder that she couldn't cook worth a darn. Something she tended to forget despite too many failures to count. When she asked what she could bring to a party, the host would always recommend paper products and soft drinks. She was that sort of person. Why she thought she could fix dinner for Callen, she'd never know.

But she did know.

This was to be a seduction of sorts. Dinner, wine, hopefully followed by some incredible sex for dessert. Too bad she'd put a lot more time into thinking about the sex than she had the meal. If she had put more thought into dinner, Shelby would have asked Rosy to cook it. Or at least heavily supervise the process.

"Maybe you could go meatless tonight," Rosy said.

Shelby practically snapped toward her. No way did she want another sex talk with her soon-to-be stepmother.

"Serve only side dishes," Rosy clarified. She lifted the lid of the Crock-Pot to peer at the apple-buttered sweet potatoes that the recipe had called the fail-proof, perfect side. The recipe had further touted "you can't go wrong with this yummy dish."

Well, Shelby had clearly gone wrong because it looked like orange goo, and the butter had puffed up like globules. Elvira and Rosy looked distressed over that, too, and it sent Rosy scurrying back to the stove to take a look at the steamed green beans.

They were green mush.

"Oh dear," Rosy declared. "I wish I'd come over earlier to help."

There was no need for Shelby to say it'd be nice if hindsight were foresight or something about her needing a better memory about her lack of culinary skills.

Rosy did more scurrying, this time into the pantry. "You've got a box of mac and cheese in here," she suggested after surveying the shelves. "Maybe you could doctor it up a little and serve that? You still have nearly an hour before Callen is expected."

An hour that Shelby had set aside to get dressed. Besides, mac and cheese, even the doctored-up stuff— whatever that meant—didn't scream romantic, seductive dinner.

Shelby took out her phone and called Bluejay's Pizza, the one and only pizza place in town. It wasn't half-bad, which meant it'd be a whole lot better than splotchy chicken served with orange goo and green mush.

"Hey, Shelby," Pete Harper greeted her when he answered. He'd obviously seen her name on his phone. Pete was not only the owner but also the cook. Sometimes, the delivery person, too. "Want your usual?"

Italian sausage, peppers, spinach, extra cheese. "Sure, and could you maybe do a side salad and some breadsticks?"

"I'm out of breadsticks, but I've got some cookies Jaylene brought over at closing time. She had extras."

"Bring them and anything else you think might make a real meal of this."

"The cooking didn't go so great for your dinner with Callen, huh?" Pete concluded. "Don't worry, Shelby. I'll fix it all up and get it right out to you."

Shelby thanked him and turned to the next step—getting dressed. Something that she was certain wouldn't leave her with mush and goo. She switched off the oven, the Crock-Pot and the steamer and headed to the bedroom. She'd already showered before Rosy dropped by to check on her, so that would leave her plenty of time for makeup and stuff.

"Oh, I forgot to tell you," Rosy said, following her. "My wedding dress came late yesterday. Only three more weeks until the big day."

Three weeks. Not long at all. And Shelby tried not to think that shortly after those three weeks Callen would be moving out of the inn and going back to Dallas. It seemed a little depressing to think about while she was primping for what would be their first date.

"Anyway, I was wondering if I could try it on for you so you can see if it needs any adjustments or embellishments?" Rosy asked.

"Of course." Shelby went to her closet and took her new dress off the hanger. It was Christmas red, not too flashy, not too tame. Hopefully, just enough for Callen not to think she was trying too hard.

Which, of course, she was.

"And remember Monday we're doing the final selection on the flowers," Rosy added.

Yes, she remembered. That would mean a trip into San Antonio since there wasn't a florist in town. "Maybe we can go after school and take Lucy with us," Shelby suggested. "It might do her good to get out and about. Maybe we could even have an early dinner or something."

When Rosy didn't say anything, Shelby looked out from the closet. Rosy was sitting on the foot of the bed, and there were tears watering her eyes.

"What's wrong?" Shelby immediately asked and would have hurried to her if Rosy hadn't waved her off.

"It's okay. I'm okay," Rosy insisted. "It just touches my heart the way you help Buck's kids. Lucy needs that, more than some of the others."

Definitely more than Rayna, who was thankfully already on her way back home. But, yes, Lucy and her brother needed help. Shelby just wasn't sure she could do much.

"I don't have the knack with them that my dad does," Shelby confessed. And she thought of Callen. Of his brothers. They, too, had needed more than some of the others, and Buck had given that to them. For the most part.

Pushing that thought aside, Shelby shucked off her jeans and top and shimmied on the dress, realizing that just the fact it required shimmying meant it was likely overkill. However, when Shelby saw Rosy's face, she knew that overkill was the way to go.

Rosy's face lit up, and there wasn't a trace of the earlier tears. Well, not sad ones, anyway. She might water up a little with the happy variety. "Wow. Callen's gonna trip over his own tongue."

She hoped not. Shelby didn't want any injuries tonight. But she wouldn't mind if the dress boggled his mind a little. She located a pair of shoes and then went into the adjoining bathroom to put on her makeup.

"How's Dad?" Shelby asked. "Is he taking his vitamins?"

"He is, and I've been fixing more foods with iron in them. You know, liver and such. He'll be fine and dandy in no time."

Fine and dandy. One could hope. And that was what Shelby was doing. Lots and lots of hoping and praying. Maybe, just maybe, it was just a small problem that could be fixed with vitamins and liver.

"I'm glad you're having dinner with Callen," Rosy said. "I really think you two can help each other right now."

Shelby peered around the jamb of the bathroom door and gave the woman a long glance to see what hidden meaning there was in that or if this was about sex again. Nope, not sex. Hidden meaning, which, of course, wasn't actually so hidden because Shelby knew what she meant.

Her nonexistent broken heart that Rosy was certain

existed and that dark, troubled look in Callen's eyes. And the earlier thoughts of him and his brothers that she'd pushed aside came back to her.

"Do you remember the day the Laramie brothers first came to the ranch?" Shelby asked. She tried to make it sound like casual chitchat so as not to sour Rosy's mood.

"Of course I do." Rosy stood now and came closer. "Such sadness. Not so much from Kace. That boy was born old. I suppose that's because he was the oldest. Judd, on the other hand, picked fights with everybody. And Callen…" Her words trailed off. She closed her eyes a moment and shook her head. "He came first, a couple of days before Kace and Judd, and I've never seen so many cuts and bruises on a kid. He looked like he'd been in a car wreck."

So much for not souring the mood.

Shelby also remembered that day. She'd been twelve, and her nose had been out of joint when her dad had told her that four boys, brothers, would be staying with them. There were already two girls there, and while Shelby had liked them, she hadn't been so crazy about having the place overrun by boys. In her experience, teenage boys were loud, rowdy and ate like pigs.

But not these boys.

Especially not Callen.

Shelby had taken one look at him, and even though she'd been too young to melt in the way that she did now, he had tugged at something inside her. Something more than just the hurt of seeing all those injuries.

"I hope the man who hurt Callen and his brothers paid for what he did," Rosy said. "His name was Avis Odell."

Yes, Shelby knew that. And because of internet searches, she also knew he'd gone to jail for five years. Not nearly enough time for what he'd done. But Avis Odell wasn't the only dirtbag responsible for those bruises and breaks. Callen's then foster mother had stood by and let it happen. And she hadn't paid.

Heck, Callen's own mother hadn't done anything, either, nor had she paid. That was because she'd died of a drug overdose shortly after the boys had been removed from her custody. In the mother's case, death seemed like an easy out.

"You want me to wait around until your pizza comes?" Rosy asked.

The question drew her back from her thoughts. Which was a good thing. Those memories were too dark to go back to tonight.

"No need." Since Shelby hadn't put on her lipstick yet, she brushed a kiss on Rosy's cheek. "Thanks for dropping by to check on me."

Shelby heard Rosy let herself out, heard some chatter, too, and with the mascara wand still aimed in the vicinity of her eye, she went into the living room, expecting to see someone delivering the pizza.

And it was.

But that someone was Callen.

"Pete's truck wouldn't start," he said, using his elbow to hold the door open for Rosy. "So, he brought the food to the inn and asked me to get it to you. He said I should get it to you while it was still hot."

And speaking of hot, Shelby was reasonably sure that she was the one in danger of tripping over her tongue. Great-fitting jeans, a gray shirt and black leather jacket. He looked like a hot cowboy-biker who'd stepped off the cover of a glossy magazine. Well, except for the cardboard pizza box he was balancing in one hand and the plastic bag he was holding in the other.

"I'll just be going," Rosy wisely said. She gave them a toodle-oo and a wave and headed to her truck.

Shelby headed to Callen. "My plans to cook didn't go as planned," she confessed, hearing the silk and the sex undertones in her voice.

"That's what I figured."

There was sex in his undertones, too, and in the long, slow gaze he slid over her. He didn't even raise an eyebrow at the mascara wand that Shelby had forgotten she was holding until she nearly poked herself in the eye.

She quickly capped the mascara and tossed it onto the counter so she could take the pizza and usher in her dinner date. Maybe she could talk him into staying for breakfast. First, though, they could have a little wine—

Callen spun her around and kissed her.

Even though he'd done the same thing at the inn just days earlier, Shelby hadn't seen it coming, but she certainly felt it now. And this one was better. Because it was long, deep and satisfying.

She wondered if he knew he tasted as expensive as he smelled. Something manly and rugged. Something that let her know that he knew what he was doing. She didn't mind that this kind of expertise had no doubt required much practice. Nope, didn't mind it a bit since she was on the receiving end of it now.

Shelby groped behind her to put the pizza box on the counter. Well, maybe it landed there. She wasn't sure and didn't care. That was because Callen rid himself of the bag, and with his hands free, he dragged her against him. He didn't have to put too much effort into that since she was already headed his way.

She made a sound of drunk pleasure because the kiss was already going to her head. The kiss had some help, though. With her pressed against his body, she could let her hand slide underneath his jacket and over all of his muscles. Muscles that stirred beneath her touch, causing her to stir, too.

The body pressing got tighter. The kiss got deeper. And Shelby started to believe that getting him to stay until morning wasn't going to be an issue. But then Callen pulled back, his gaze colliding with hers.

"Hello," he drawled.

"Hello," she drawled back, and smiled.

Of course, it was easy to give him a heated smile

since their arms were still holding each other in place. Hers on his back and his on her hips.

"Nice dress." More drawling while he looked at her with those sizzler, dreamy eyes.

"Nice body."

That caused him to smile. "I hadn't expected you to be able to feel so much of it, but I had a hard time resisting."

"I noticed." She shifted a little, giving the front of him a nudge with the front of her. It caused a husky sound to rumble in his throat, and his eyes went hot.

His body went hard.

Well, one specific part of it did, anyway.

It would have been impossible for her to miss that, what with her being plastered against him. She was about to go bold, something she never did, and lure him back into another kiss. Then to her bed. Or the floor since it was closer.

But then Callen stepped away from her.

And amid all that heat in his eyes, she thought she saw something that wasn't on the foreplay menu. Regret.

"Seems a shame to let the pizza go cold after you slaved over the phone to order it," he said.

So maybe he was hungry. That was fine. The plan all along had been to eat, drink and…do other things. The other things would have to wait.

"I talked to a social worker," he added as she took the pizza box to the table that she'd already set.

"About Mateo and Lucy?"

He nodded, brought the bag to her. There was indeed a salad in it. One still in a bag, but the cookies looked good. They were pretty flower cutouts with sprinkled sugar. Maybe Callen didn't have a sweet tooth because he frowned at them a little. Of course, the frown could be about what he'd learned from the social worker.

"It won't be easy to find them a permanent home where they can stay together," he continued, "but the feelers are out. I already heard back from someone who's interested in adopting Lucy. Just her. But maybe my social-worker friend can change the family's mind and they'll want Mateo, too."

Such a serious subject, and it cooled down some of the heat from the welcome kiss. "Mateo will be tough to place because of his juvie record."

"You knew about that," he said, peeling off his coat and draping it over one of the barstools at the counter.

She nodded, went to the bottle of red wine she'd set out and poured two glasses. "He shanked some other boy when he was in juvie lockup."

"Hell." Judging by Callen's reaction, he hadn't known that particular detail.

"I think the other boy was giving him serious trouble," she explained. "At least that's what I've been able to get out of Dad. You know how he is about not spilling a lot on his kids. He's good at keeping secrets."

Callen suddenly looked about as comfortable as

a steer's rump on a branding iron. Perhaps because he thought Mateo shouldn't be trusted around Buck.

"For what it's worth," she continued, "while Mateo's been at the ranch, he's been as good as gold…whatever that means. Why isn't it as good as platinum or diamonds since they're more expensive?" She shook her head when she saw Callen give her that funny look again. "Never mind. Not relevant here."

It took a moment to get back on track.

"Anyway, maybe there's a family out there who'll see that Mateo just needs a safe, loving environment and will give it to him," Shelby concluded.

An environment that her dad would have almost certainly given Mateo and his sister had it not been for his age. Buck was sixty-nine, and since Lucy was only twelve, it meant Buck would be well into his seventies before the girl even came of age. That was a lot to take on when he should be at a point in his life when he was slowing down. Especially since he might want to enjoy married life with Rosy. Rosy could have taken on some of the child rearing, but she was seven years older than Buck.

After handing Callen the glass of wine, she sat at the table across from him. Shelby didn't bother with the salad but slid slices of pizza onto both of their plates. Since it appeared they were going to have a meal, she went with some conversation.

"I heard you had coffee with Kace," she remarked. Best not to mention that she'd heard it from six different people. One, Loretta Lavenhouse, who had been at the table across the room from them and had tried her hand at lip-reading to find out what they were saying. According to Loretta, Callen had either confessed to murder or had mentioned his mother.

Shelby knew Loretta was wrong on the first one and hoped the woman was wrong about the mother mention. That wouldn't have been a pleasant chat.

"I know you're only back here for a few more weeks, but maybe Kace and you can reach some kind of...understanding," she said. Though that wasn't the right word. They understood just fine, but there was anger folded and blended into it.

"Did Kace really tap his badge when he was talking to you?" she asked. Because Loretta had insisted that'd happened.

"He did. It's a big-brother thing." He drank some of the wine after he finished the pizza slice. "What else did the gossips tell you?"

"Nothing much...other than my name came up."

Now his eyebrow lifted. "It did," he admitted. And he didn't say anything else for several moments. "My brain tells me it's not a good idea to kiss you, that it could lead to sex. And other things. Things you might not be ready for."

She groaned, pushed back from the table and finished her glass of wine. "I'm not brokenhearted."

"I believe you, but you're only a couple of months out of a long-term relationship."

Great. It was a one-two punch. Either she got accused of the whole broken-heart business or else she was rebounding. There was no getting around it.

Was there?

"Just how long does the rebound period last, anyway?" she asked. "I hope less than three weeks because after that, you'll be gone."

He stared at her, set aside his wineglass. "You could get hurt."

"I could get lucky." And since that was way more forward than she'd intended to be, Shelby added a smile, leaned closer. "What if I give you some kind of disclaimer, like a business contract? I agree not to hold you responsible for any hurt that might happen when you drive away again?"

She could see him working that out in his mind. Of course, that wouldn't stop her from getting hurt. Nor would it stop him from blaming himself. That was just Callen. And that meant he was probably going to babble off a couple of reasons why they shouldn't go at each other again.

He didn't.

Callen went after her again. He reached out, took hold of her arms and pulled her onto his lap. He kissed her again. Despite the quick maneuvering, the kiss was slow and easy, as if he was giving her a chance to change her mind. *As if.* He had her exactly where she wanted him to have her.

His arms came around her, not that she had plans to go anywhere, but his grip was as gentle as the kiss. He didn't urge her closer, didn't tighten what she was sure would be clever fingers on her waist and back. He just kissed her while she sat there.

Shelby sank into the kiss, letting the feel of his mouth light little flames all over her body. Of course, they didn't stay little, but that was his fault because he slid his mouth and tongue first to the spot just beneath her right ear. Then lower, to her neck. He might as well have struck a match and set her ablaze because the need quit merely pulsing and took on an urgency.

She was pretty sure Callen was in on that urgency, too, because finally his grip tightened enough to pull her closer to him. It was a safe kind of "closer," though, since she was sideways on his lap. Not touching the suddenly very needy center of her body to the center of his.

He cursed under his breath, and she thought he was cursing both of them before he buried his face in her neck. Thankfully for her that meant his mouth was buried there, too, and with his breath gusting some, it was creating a very nice sensation. One that sped that urgency along.

"I'm going to hell for what I'm thinking about doing to you," he said, intriguing her.

"That good, huh?"

And she made him laugh. That was an interesting sensation, too, with his mouth still against that sensitive part of her.

But she had plenty of other sensitive parts, and Callen found a couple of them when his hands went to work. One of his hands slid over her breasts, cupping her and swiping his thumb over her nipple. The other—the one with the naughtiest intention—skimmed up her thigh. She was hoping that thumb could soon do some clever swiping, too.

Shelby figured she was well on her way to experiencing that when his hand continued up, up, up…

And then his phone rang.

She wasn't sure who groaned the loudest, but Shelby thought Callen had won that particular title. Along with the groaning, he cursed and continued to curse when he dragged out his phone from his jeans pocket.

The cursing stopped when he looked at the screen. "Sorry, but I need to take this," he said before she could get a look at who was calling.

He eased her from his lap and got up. Not easily. That probably had something to do with his erection that was straining against his zipper. He walked back into the living room before answering the call.

Shelby had zero lip-reading skills, but she knew bad body language when she saw it.

And this was *bad*.

"I'm on my way," he told the caller, and he put his phone away before he turned back around to face her. "I'm sorry. I have to go." He grabbed his coat and put it on.

"Is there anything I can do?" she asked, and she meant it. He looked genuinely distressed.

"No, but thanks. I'll call you," Callen said, and then brushed a kiss on her mouth before he hurried out the door.

CHAPTER TEN

CALLEN HADN'T RUN out of curse words by the time he got back in his truck and drove away from Shelby's. However, he did put a pause on the profanity when he hit the button on his phone to redial the last number.

Buck's number.

But as expected, Buck didn't answer. Mateo did. Not a surprise since it'd been Mateo who'd called him right about the time Callen had been kissing and groping Shelby. Talk about a fast way to chill down some lust.

"You need to come. Mr. Buck's been hurt," Mateo had said.

Yep, that had got Callen's complete attention, and when he'd asked the boy if he'd called an ambulance, his response had been: "Mr. Buck said no ambulance, for you to come right now."

So, here Callen was on his way, but since it'd take him a couple of minutes to get there, he wanted to talk to Mateo and get more details. And then Callen would call the ambulance. It was bullshit if Buck intended for him to keep his condition a secret when something bad had happened.

"You're coming?" Mateo pressed Callen, and he could hear the fear and worry in the boy's voice.

"Almost there," Callen assured him, trying to keep those same emotions out of his own tone. No use scaring the boy more than he already was. "Now, tell me what happened."

"I think he fell or something. I saw him go into the barn, and when he didn't come out, I went to see if everything was okay. It wasn't. Mr. Buck's head was bleeding."

Callen latched right on to that, too. "Bleeding? How bad?"

"He said it's not bad."

Which could be just more bullshit. "Is my brother Judd in his cabin?"

"No. I started to go there first, but Mr. Buck said Judd had gone out with friends, that I should call you."

Yeah, because Callen had established a stupid-assed pattern of keeping things secret that shouldn't be secret when it came to Buck. "I'm pulling up now," Callen told the boy.

He ended the call so he could park, and the moment he was out of his truck, he started running. Despite his speed, it seemed to take an eternity to get there. Plenty long enough for Callen to think the worst and reconsider calling an ambulance despite what Buck had said.

The only illumination in the barn came from a single light dangling overhead, but Callen had no trouble spotting Buck. He was sitting on the ground, his back against a stall post, and Mateo was holding something to the side of his head.

"I'm okay," Buck insisted before Callen even made it to him.

Callen wasn't so sure about that when he saw the bloody handkerchief that Buck had clasped in his hands.

Hands that were trembling a little.

Beside him on the ground was a bottle of hydrogen peroxide and some paper towels. Some of them had blood on them, too.

"I just had a little dizzy spell," Buck went on. "Lost my balance and bumped my head."

"I got the bleeding stopped," Mateo volunteered.

Callen had a look for himself and noticed that Mateo was using a package of frozen turnips as an ice pack. Since Callen hated that particular vegetable, he thought this was the best possible use for it.

"I know how to stop bleeding," Mateo added, and alarm fired through his eyes. As if he'd said too much.

Callen eased back the turnips and had to agree with the boy. "Yeah, you do know how to stop bleeding." He used the flashlight function on his phone to have a closer look. "You could probably use a stitch or two."

"I'd rather just have a Band-Aid," Buck insisted.

"I bet you would, and that way you wouldn't have to tell anyone about this."

"I won't tell anyone about this. Neither will you." Buck was insistent about that, as well.

"Are you still dizzy?" Callen asked him.

"No."

Taking him at his word—even though it had a fifty-fifty chance of being a lie—Callen eased his arm around Buck and helped him to his feet. Mateo gathered up the turnips, peroxide and paper towels, and his steady movements told Callen the boy had likely done that a time or two, as well.

Callen led Buck to the house and onto the back porch, where Lucy was waiting and holding open the door for him. "I need a Band-Aid," Buck told her. "Could you get me one from the upstairs bathroom? There'll be a box in the medicine cabinet."

With her dark, hollow eyes, she walked away to do that. There was no alarm on her face, which gave Callen a thump in his heart. A bloody head should never be old hat to a kid.

"I have to go to the bathroom," Buck claimed when Callen started to lead him to the sofa.

Callen frowned, looked down at him to see if there was some ulterior motive other than a full bladder. If there was, Buck wasn't going to own up to it, and he moved away from Callen to head to the powder room just up the hall.

Both Mateo and Callen stood, watching the door as Buck closed it.

"Is he gonna be okay?" Mateo asked.

"Yeah." That was possibly a lie, but Callen figured

the boy had been through enough tonight. "You did a good job taking care of him. Thanks."

"You're not mad that I called you to come over? Mr. Buck said you were on a date."

One that would have almost certainly led to sex. Callen was sure of that because he was basically brainless and had no willpower when it came to Shelby. He needed to figure out how to change that.

And how to fix this situation with Buck.

Callen looked over at Mateo, who was giving him some side glances. "You're not pissed off like your brother Judd," Mateo said. "I thought you'd be pissed off."

"No. Just worried."

"Me, too," Mateo added quietly.

Lucy came back down the stairs, and she kept her head bent as she handed Callen the box of Band-Aids. "There are different sizes," she said, her voice as dark and hollow as those eyes. "I didn't know which one he'd need, so I brought them all."

"This is fine. Thanks." But Callen had no sooner got the words out than she was already back up the stairs.

"She's scared of you," Mateo explained. "She's scared of a lot of things." He paused, glanced at the bathroom door again and then at Callen. "You're not scared of me. You don't look at me as if you expect me to shank you. Neither does Mr. Buck, his daughter or Miss Rosy."

"Well, around here we tend to give folks the benefit of the doubt when it comes to shanking." And it had the intended effect. It caused Mateo's mouth to quiver a little. Not a smile but close.

"Are you okay in there?" Callen called out to Buck.

"Fine. I just need a minute."

A minute, no doubt, to figure out the argument he was going to try to use on Callen to get him to stay quiet about this. But Buck was wasting his time.

Well, maybe.

Callen wasn't brainless and lacking willpower with Buck, but the soft spot he had for the man made him more susceptible to doing stupid things.

"I didn't stop my sister from being hurt," Mateo said out of the blue. "That's why she's so scared around everybody. She's just a kid and I couldn't stop her from being hurt because I wasn't there. I should have been there."

Well, hell. That was more than a heart thump. It was an emotion-drenched punch to the gut. And the flood of memories came. He hadn't protected his brother Nico. And he'd been just a kid, too. The same age Lucy was now.

"That's why I'm trying to be real good here with Mr. Buck," Mateo went on. "You should know that. I swear, I'll be good. Because I can't get sent back to juvie or my sister could get hurt again."

Callen took the long deep breath that he needed. Well, more than just one breath. He had no idea what to say to Mateo to make him feel better about this.

Hell, if he knew what to say, he would have already said it to himself.

"Being good sounds like the right plan," Callen finally managed.

Though he knew that it didn't always work. Sometimes, nothing did. But it was something he could maybe pass on to Lizbeth, to let her know that Mateo had damn solid motivation for being "good." That might play in his favor for a family on the fence about taking both kids.

The bathroom door finally opened, and Buck came out. He looked a little shaky, but he didn't catch onto the wall. Probably because he thought it would only alarm Callen. However, Callen was already alarmed, and if Buck didn't know that, he soon would.

"Could you give Mr. Buck and me a minute?" Callen asked Mateo.

Mateo nodded. "What should I do with this?" he asked, holding up the turnips. "Should I rinse it off and put it back in the freezer?"

"No. Toss it." Callen had been eating some meals here at the ranch, and he didn't want Rosy serving it up.

"Put it at the bottom of the garbage bin so Rosy doesn't see it," Buck instructed.

The boy gave another nod and headed into the kitchen to do that. Callen chose a Band-Aid and got to work. "You do know this isn't going to stick so well because of your hair," Callen reminded him.

"It'll be fine. *I'll* be fine," Buck added a moment later.

Callen got the Band-Aid in place, and he went back around to sit on the coffee table so he could face Buck.

"No," Buck insisted before Callen could say anything. "It's only three weeks to the wedding. After that, I'll tell Rosy and Shelby, and then I can have the surgery."

"What's so hell-fired important that you have to get done instead of tending to your health?"

"I just need more time to work out some things," Buck said without hesitating. "Paperwork for the kids. Supplies for the ranch. And I want to get something special for Rosy for a wedding gift. I want to spend more time with Shelby and her before they start treating me like an invalid. Plus, I need to come to terms with it, too."

Until Buck had added that last part, Callen had been about to blow his argument to smithereens. But that was a good one. Not stellar, though.

Callen mentally tested out a couple of salesman ploys that might work. And he discarded them one by one. Because there was only one thing that was going to work now.

"You've got a week to get your things and yourself in order," Callen said, and he made sure he looked Buck straight in the eyes. "Tell them then, or I will."

CHAPTER ELEVEN

SIX DAYS.

That was how long it'd been since her dinner date with Callen. Or what she was calling the near-miss pizza get-together. He'd got a phone call and hurried out. She wasn't upset about that. He was a busy man, and there'd likely been some kind of work-related crisis. Still, that was no excuse for him taking six days to turn the near miss into a home run.

Of course, he'd called her, and they'd had some shallow conversations about how swamped he was. And again, that was probably true. He had been helping out at the ranch and had even made two trips back to Dallas to tend to some things there. But all the work and trips couldn't cover up the feeling in her stomach that something was wrong.

Something not sex related.

What, exactly, she didn't know, but she intended to find out, and that meant a trip to the inn. When she spotted his truck in the parking lot, she knew he was there. So was Havana, since her Mustang was parked next to the truck. That likely meant they were working, but since it was around lunchtime and a Saturday, she might be able to convince Callen to take a break.

Unlike her last trip here, there were plenty of people out and about. Main Street wasn't a shopping mecca, but the weather was clear, so that brought people out to ooh and aah over the Christmas decorations—which were extremely festive for such a small town. Thanks to Rosy, Buck and the city council. They had donated money so that every lamppost was decorated with lights and coiled gold tinsel that glittered like the real stuff under the winter sun.

And then there were the heavenly smells.

It'd been Rosy's idea to put scent diffusers outside all the businesses, and today the street smelled like a fresh Christmas tree. It went well with the sugar-cookie aroma coming from Patty Cakes. Just up the street, the grocer, Will Myers, was dressed in a Santa suit and was handing out cups of warm cider with cinnamon sticks to people who passed by.

This was one of the reasons she loved Coldwater, and all the decorations, scents and such nearly made her forget that it'd been six days since Callen had paid her a visit.

Nearly.

Today, there was a space in the inn lot, so she parked there and had nearly made it to the front door when someone called out her name. Someone who made her wish she'd got there just a minute earlier so she could avoid this meeting.

Gavin.

He was coming up the sidewalk toward her and had a cup of cider in each hand. Either he was very thirsty or he intended one for her.

It was for her.

Gavin thrust the cup at her as soon as he reached her. "Your favorite," he said as if pleased he'd remembered.

She muttered thanks but made sure it was lukewarm to discourage conversation. It didn't work.

"I'm glad I ran into you," he said. "I've been meaning to call you."

Oh crud. Now she couldn't keep things lukewarm. "Look, Gavin, there's no reason for you to worry about me. I'm fine. Beyond fine. I'm ecstatic." Which was probably a little overboard, but she was trying to make a point here. She got her "enthusiasm" under control before she continued. "I'm not sitting at home crying my eyes out or anything. I'm getting on with my life."

"I know." And with that rather cryptic comment, he took a long sip of the cider. What he didn't do was look her in the eye. Yes, the decorations were pretty, but they suddenly seemed riveting to Gavin, and she knew him well enough to know something was up.

Something she probably didn't want to hear.

"I'll just be going," she said, tipping her head toward the inn.

He stepped in front of her. Then he opened his mouth, closed it and repeated those steps enough times to make him look like a handsome guppy in need of life-sustaining water.

"What's wrong with you?" she came out and asked.

"You. Me," he immediately amended, and he settled on another "me" before he paused again. "I think it was a mistake to break up with you, and I want you to consider getting back together with me."

Shelby had a slight mouth malfunction, too. It took her a few seconds to get it working, before she said, "No"

At the same time, Gavin said, "Just consider it." Now he looked deeply in her eyes. "We were good together, Shelby. We had plans to make a home together—here, in the town that we both love. Think about that."

He brushed a quick cider-scented kiss on her still-startled mouth and hurried off just as Shelby croaked out another "No."

Sweet baby Moses in the basket. This was not something she wanted. Something she wouldn't have. But now instead of convincing Gavin that she didn't have a broken heart, she was going to have to convince him that she was done with him.

And convince a good portion of the town, too.

Shelby realized that when she looked around and saw that their conversation had got the attention of plenty of people. A kiss from him on Main Street was equivalent to a high-speed global-release bulletin.

Huffing and sipping the cider, she went inside and

spotted Havana coming down the stairs. Today, she was dressed like Santa's elf, complete with holiday red hair and a jingle bell hat.

"I'm hoping the Christmas spirit will rub off on my Ebenezer of a boss," Havana said, fanning her hand over her outfit. An outfit that included dangling candy-cane earrings. "His mood would have to improve just to qualify for the 'it sucks' label."

Oh. Well, this probably wasn't a time to confront him about why he hadn't attempted sex with her in the last six days. Not that Shelby would have worded it that way, but she'd intended to touch on the subject in a roundabout way.

"Callen ripped down the mistletoe that I'd hung over his office door and threw it on the floor," Havana said, and without taking a breath continued, "and he kicked a Santa."

Shelby's eyes widened, and she thought of the friendly Will Myers handing out cider.

"A *toy* Santa," Havana clarified. "It was one of those about yay high." She held up her hands to indicate about two feet. "It was motion-activated, so whenever you walked by it, it sang 'Grandma Got Run Over by a Reindeer.'"

Shelby could imagine that would get old, fast, but kicking it didn't seem like the healthiest solution.

"Any idea why Callen's mood is so bad?" Shelby asked.

"Phases of the moon is my guess. I hope you're here to cheer him up." Havana gave her a knowing wink.

Since there was no "knowing" between Callen and her, Shelby just shrugged. "I was hoping to talk to him."

"Have at it. You could probably borrow a flak jacket from the police station." But before Shelby could groan and reconsider this visit, Havana smiled and switched subjects. "Are you all ready for the wedding?"

Shelby made a so-so motion with her free hand and then tossed the cider cup in the trash. "With Rosy, the plans tend to be, well, fluid. She likes to tweak a lot here and there."

"Well, she can't tweak too much longer. The wedding date's coming up fast. Rosy mentioned you'd gone to the florist with her."

Shelby started to ask when she'd seen Rosy, but since her shop was just up the street, Rosy probably popped in here all the time. Probably did some matchmaking, too.

Which might explain why Callen was putting some distance between them.

"I did go with her to the florist," Shelby answered. "She, uh, made some unusual floral choices."

"Wouldn't expect anything less. She invited me to the wedding. Then she asked me to be a bridesmaid."

Oh. Well, that was a surprise, and yet more proof that Rosy had paid frequent visits here. "That brings the number to thirty-six now."

Havana's eyes widened. "Uh, that's an unusually high number even for Rosy."

"Agreed, but she asked most of the women who'd been Buck's kids over the years. Thirty-five said yes. But don't worry—the dresses don't have to be all the same. She just wanted us to all wear something red."

"Yeah. She mentioned that. She also mentioned her dress was pink. I really like an unconventional color scheme." That from the woman in an elf suit.

A woman that Shelby very much liked.

"My advice—don't sit at table three at the reception," Shelby told her. "That's where she's putting the zombie bunny centerpiece. Oh, and avoid table five, too, if you don't want to have to look at stallion junk while you're eating."

"Thanks for the tip. I'll remember that." Havana came down off the step and moved out of Shelby's way. "Good luck visiting Ebenezer."

With slightly less determination than she'd had ten minutes earlier, Shelby went up the stairs. In the hall just outside his office, she spotted the sprig of mistletoe and the stuffed Santa with a bashed-in stomach. It was still moving, the stiff outstretched hands twitching, its mouth clacking up and down like a nutcracker, but thankfully it wasn't singing.

Because Callen's office door was open, she got a glimpse of Ebenezer in his natural habitat. He was scowling and barking out an order to whoever had the misfortune to be on the other end of the phone line. Something to do with a delayed contract. Callen threw the *f*-word around multiple times and made an anatomically impossible suggestion for the person responsible for the delay. Then he jabbed End Call as if he'd declared war on the phone button.

And he looked at her.

Shelby somehow managed a smile, and the lecture she'd thought to give him just vanished. Why, she didn't know. He was obviously seething with leftover anger, maybe from the contract, maybe a phase of the moon.

Whatever it was, Shelby snatched up the mistletoe from the floor and marched in, going straight behind his desk. She whirled his chair around until he was facing her, dangled the mistletoe over his head, dropped down onto his lap and kissed him. That part didn't require any courage whatsoever because that mouth of his was magic.

He was still stiff, his muscles tensed to the point of snapping, but she kept it up until she heard the husky rumble in his throat and felt his arms slide around her.

Oh yes. Magic.

She eased back, met his eyes and smiled again. "Hi."

"Hi back." He didn't smile, but those muscles relaxed a little.

"Bad day?" She tossed the mistletoe over her shoulder, moved her mouth closer to his until she was only a breath away.

"Not anymore."

"Then my job here is done." She chuckled, started to move off his lap, but he held her in place.

Mercy, what a face, and it was right there in front of her to kiss. Which she did. She went in deep, sliding into the hot taste of him and instantly wanting more. She was coming to realize that she always wanted more with Callen.

"Are you here to chew me out because I haven't been over?" he asked.

She shook her head and got a nice little buzz when her breasts brushed against his chest. "I don't usually kiss people I'm about to chew out."

There must have been some kind of inflection at the end of her comment because his eyebrow rose. "But?"

Shelby looked deep into those amazing eyes, and they gave her the nudge she needed to blurt out that whole thing about how she'd expected him to come back to her for sex. However, the movement in the doorway stopped her.

So did the chuckle.

Not Havana. No such luck. The doorway was filled with the Laramie brothers. Kace, Judd and Nico. It was Nico who'd chuckled and spoke.

"Interrupting anything?" Nico asked, and he winked at her.

CALLEN FIGURED HE was going to get some lectures and ribbings about this. And grief, lots of grief.

"Wow," Shelby said, getting to her feet. Callen could see that her cheeks were flushed pink with embarrassment and that she was struggling with what to say. Finally, she smiled, lifted her hands and said, "Merry Christmas."

"Merry Christmas to you, too." Of course, that came from Nico, the only person with Laramie DNA who was actually smiling.

"I should be going." Shelby looked at Callen, maybe to make sure it was okay for her to leave, and he gave her a nod and a hand squeeze.

Nico did a whole lot more than that. When Shelby went to the door, Nico gave her a hug and a loud smacking kiss on the mouth. He whispered something to her that Callen didn't catch, but it had Shelby's face pinking up even more.

It was Shelby who initiated the hug with Judd and Kace. No kiss, but she did punch Judd on the arm. It was hard enough to get his attention but soft enough to still qualify as sisterly.

"Quit being scary Judd when Mateo's outside," Shelby warned him. "He thinks you'll arrest him or something."

Judd didn't argue with her. Didn't agree, either.

Shelby walked out, and Callen heard the deranged stuffed Santa make clicking sounds again. She'd obviously triggered the motion activation that he hadn't managed to completely destroy.

"Nico insisted we come," Judd grumbled.

And Nico was probably the only person on earth who could have talked Judd into it.

"Why?" Callen asked.

"Well, it wasn't so we'd catch you with Shelby on your lap." Nico grinned. "Actually, I wanted a picture so I could give it to Buck. I was just out at the ranch and he said he wanted a recent picture of us for Christmas. So come on." Taking out his phone, he walked behind the desk and motioned for Judd and Kace to join him. "It's group selfie time."

Nico caught onto Callen's shoulder, pulling him to his feet. Something that wasn't necessary because he had no intention of balking about the photo. He just wished he'd thought of doing it. With Buck facing cancer, a group photo seemed like a small thing to give him. In fact, he could do better than a selfie.

"Let me get my assistant up here," Callen offered. "She can take it."

Callen was about to call Havana, but then he saw her coming up behind Judd and Kace, who were still in the doorway.

"We need a picture," Callen explained. And he was reasonably sure that Havana heard him despite the goo-goo eyes she was making at Nico. Of course, Nico was making them right back at her.

"Keep your dick in your jeans around my assistant," Callen warned him in a whisper. Though he couldn't actually think of a good reason as to why Nico should do that. Well, other than he didn't want the image in his head of his kid brother naked and screwing a woman Callen had to see and work with every day.

Nico only smiled, which was in no such way an agreement. It was just as well. Judging from the intensity of the goo-goo, Havana had decided that Nico would make a tasty Christmas present to herself.

Havana took Nico's phone, and, yes, there was some finger brushing when she did that. Despite the distraction, she started doing one of the things she did best. She took hold of Judd and Kace, positioning them where she wanted to get a good picture. It took her a couple of minutes, shifting and doling out instructions of "move an inch to the left" and "don't forget to smile" before she finally snapped some shots. She studied them on the camera and clicked off a few more.

"Got it," she said, handing the phone back to Nico.

More finger touching, smiles, and Nico winked at her, causing Kace, Callen and Judd all to groan in unison. Soon, Callen would warn Havana that Nico was a player, but he suspected that would only excite Havana even more.

Nico flicked through the pictures to show them. Not exactly a bloom of happiness and Christmas cheer on their faces, but Callen and Nico were smiling. Well, Nico was, anyway. Callen had done his best.

Judd grumbled about having something to do, and he headed out. So did Kace, but not before he said, "I want a copy of that picture."

"You bet. It's what you're all getting for Christmas," Nico said with a chuckle.

Havana lingered a moment, and Nico and she must have exchanged some kind of silent conversation because she grinned and nodded but closed the door behind her when she went downstairs. Obviously, that silent conversation had led his assistant to believe that Nico and he needed a private chat.

"So." Nico glanced around the office. "You're back."

"It's temporary. I'll be leaving after the wedding."

Nico nodded and settled into the chair next to Callen's desk. Actually, Nico "lounged," stretching his legs out in front of him and crossing his boots at the ankles. He tucked his hands behind his head and gave Callen one of those grins. Callen figured they were about to have a frank chat about Shelby. Specifically, his kissing Shelby while she was on his lap.

"Buck said he's anemic and that you've been helping him out," Nico commented, throwing Callen off his stride. He'd already geared up for the Shelby lecture, which wouldn't feel like so much of a lecture coming from Nico.

Callen nodded but wanted to curse. Buck's week was almost up, and he'd hoped that the man would just go ahead and tell all. Including Nico. Apparently not, though. That meant first thing tomorrow, he'd have to go out to Buck's and carry through on the threat to spill the secret. Buck would almost certainly bargain for an extension, but Callen wasn't giving him one.

"I saw Rosy while I was there," Nico went on. "She's in the full throes of wedding mania and never looked happier."

So true. And it caused Callen to feel another pang of guilt. It would put a damper on her happiness when she learned that Buck had a tumor. But telling her might end up saving Buck's life if it meant his getting treatment sooner than later.

Or too late.

"I met the kid. Mateo. He thanked me for not looking at him like he was going to shank me. What the heck is that about?" Nico asked.

Callen considered an answer that would keep that easy expression on his brother's face. Instead, he went with the truth. "Mateo and his sister went through some bad stuff. Like us. They had their own personal version of Avis Odell."

Nico made a sound of regret, stayed quiet a moment and then smiled again. "But now they've got Buck. He erases the Avis Odells."

No. Nothing could erase that, but Buck had certainly helped with that as much as was humanly possible. And that was why Callen had smiled in the picture.

"Are Mateo's and his sister's parents still around?" Nico asked.

"Their dad left years ago. Like ours."

There'd been no need, though, for him to remind

Nico of that, but unlike Nico, Callen actually had a few memories of their father. The best word he could think to describe him was *disinterested*. Not just in his own kids but his drugged-up wife. He would come home from work, grab a beer and then eat his dinner in front of the TV.

"Their mother's the one who beat the hell out of them," Callen added, once he was sure he had control of the rage that rippled through him at just the mention of it. "Mateo ended up in juvie when he fought back and she had him arrested. And when he was away, the mother whaled on the sister hard enough to put her in the hospital. That's when the right CPS worker got involved and got her out of there—and Mateo out of juvie. The mom's serving two to four years in jail."

Not nearly enough time, and she'd likely get out sooner than that. Avis Odell hadn't served out his sentence before being released.

Nico's smile stayed easy. And genuine. "But now they have Buck," he repeated.

Yeah, but not for long. Callen kept that to himself.

"So, are you here to try to get into Shelby's pants?" Nico asked.

Callen wondered if Kace had mentioned he'd asked the same thing and used those identical words. Judging from Nico's grin, it was something he would approve of. Hell, Callen approved of it, too, but...

"I'm here for only two more weeks," Callen reminded him. "If I had sex with her, then what happens afterward?"

"More sex?" Nico chuckled. Then got as serious as Nico could manage. "You mean because she's grounded here and you're not. I see your problem. Hard to have sex when you're hundreds of miles away. Plus, there's that whole out of sight, out of mind thing, and with Gavin pressing her to get back together..."

"What?" Callen snapped.

"Oh, you didn't hear about him kissing her about a half hour ago? It happened right outside the inn. Rumor has it that Gavin's trying to woo Shelby back."

Well, shit. A kiss? Shelby sure as hell hadn't mentioned that. And he felt the wave of what he was dead certain was jealousy come down on him like an avalanche.

"The kiss could have meant nothing," Nico went on, making it sound as if it were something. "After all, I kissed her, too. Right here when I came in."

Yeah, but that was different. Nico was like a little brother to Shelby. Gavin was her ex-fiancé and the town's "darling." And like Shelby, he had deep roots here. He damn sure wouldn't have to go three hundred miles to get in her pants.

"Something troubling you?" Nico asked in such a way that Callen wanted to slug him.

"No." But he wanted to have a chat with Shelby. After he had the chat with Buck, that was.

Hell. A kiss!

Nico eased out of his lounging pose, sat up and leaned closer. He looked Callen straight in the eyes. "So, tell me the truth—because I'm not buying the anemia story. What's really wrong with Buck?"

CHAPTER TWELVE

SHELBY THREW A handful of tinsel at the tree. Not "on" the tree. But rather "at" it. The way a pissed-off pitcher would hurl a ball at a batter.

And that was her cue that she probably wasn't in the right mood for decorating the five-foot Douglas fir that she'd just hauled from her truck and into her living room. Before she tackled delicate glass balls and other breakables, she probably needed to settle down some. Not easy, though, with so many unsettled thoughts going through her head.

Callen was one of those thoughts.

Actually, he was several of them. For a man who seemed to enjoy kissing her, he wasn't moving on to the next step. And they were under a deadline, less than two weeks to go until he left for Dallas. But she'd already made the "last" first move yesterday by going to his office and kissing him. The next move—if there was one—would have to come from him, and that was why her mood was so sour.

Gavin was contributing to the sourness, too, and the proof of that was in her trash can. The dozen red roses that had been waiting for her on her porch when she'd got back from buying the Christmas tree. They'd sat there in a shiny gold box with a white satin ribbon.

"Just thinking of you," the card had read. "Much love, Gavin."

Shelby had put down the tree long enough to take the flowers to the kitchen and drop them in the trash. It riled her, eyelash to toenails, that Gavin was pulling this now. And she doubted it was because he actually wanted her back. No. It was more likely because he'd heard about her kissing Callen.

Maybe Gavin thought he could save her from Callen and a second broken heart, or perhaps he just wanted her now because he thought someone else did, but either way, the flowers had just added another layer to her crappy mood.

The cat, who'd perched itself under the tree, looked up at her with disdain. Most would have likely told Shelby that she was reading into that feline expression, but she knew her own cat. Knew that looks of disdain were Elvira's specialty. Along with eyeballed accusations of *you haven't fed me human food, which we both know is far superior to that slop currently in my bowl*.

Actually, that was the most common look from Elvira, and Shelby was getting it now, too, along with the disdain from the tinsel-tossing show of temper.

Taking her temper with her, Shelby went out the back door and to her barn to check on the horses. It wasn't a necessary chore; she'd already done it that morning and again in the afternoon, but she could take the mare she was training through a few routines. Maybe even go out for a ride. She nixed the ride, though, when she stepped outside and felt the icy chill. The clouds had gone dark, too, which meant more sleet.

Why couldn't it just snow and make everything pretty and white?

Why couldn't Gavin just leave her alone?

Why couldn't Callen just come over and have sex with her?

Clearly, she wasn't putting out the right vibes in the universe since she didn't have the answer to any of those questions.

Since the weather wasn't going to cooperate, she went into the barn and decided to add another layer of hay to the stalls just in case any of the horses came in search of a warm place for the night.

Shelby put on her worn leather work gloves, hooked her hands under the strong twine of one of the hay bales that she'd stacked against the wall. She was in the process of hauling it to one of the stalls when she saw the movement from the corner of her eye.

And Callen stepped in.

Since she hadn't heard him drive up, she froze there a moment, the weight of the hay straining against her muscles, and she considered if he was a mirage or a figment of her temper.

"You really can lift a hay bale by yourself," he said.

So, no mirage. The sound of his voice and the

sight of him—the real him—melted her temper and had her smiling. And dropping the hay bale.

Damn it.

It landed on her foot, and while her boot had protected her from a break, it still hurt like the devil. Plus, she'd blown her whole image as a hay-hoisting horsewoman.

"You okay?" He went to her and took her by the arm. Her first instinct was to shake off his grip since he was doing it because of her stupid injury, but she wanted his hand on her even if it was a pity grip.

"I'm fine." That was possibly true, but she was certain if she had to walk right now that there'd be a limp involved. "I didn't hear you drive up."

"I didn't. I rode up." He tipped his head toward her yard, and she saw the bay mare by the oak tree just outside her kitchen window.

"Sweet Caroline," she said, recognizing her. "She's one of Dad's horses, and she's not so sweet."

"Yeah, I found out as much. When I stopped by the ranch, Mateo mentioned that Buck had told him not to ride the mare. He also said she spooked easily, but that the horse hadn't been out in days and could probably use some exercise."

"So, you rode her here," Shelby concluded. And just like that, her mood improved considerably. There were plenty of places Callen could have ridden the horse, and he'd come here.

"Buck wasn't home," he said as they started out of

the barn, and, yes, she limped a little. "Rosy thought he was here."

Her mood dipped a notch. Callen was looking for her father. Still, he had come *here* looking for him, so she'd take that as a nibble. "No. I haven't seen Dad today. Why did Rosy think he'd come to see me?"

Callen lifted his shoulder, shook his head, and the double nonverbal response sent up a red flag. A flag she soon forgot about when Callen started jogging ahead of her. "Let me put Sweet Caroline in the barn so we can talk. Mateo wasn't sure if she'd go wandering off or not."

"She will," Shelby assured him. "Sweet Caroline is one of my training failures." But you couldn't train out what was essentially an untrainable pissy equine personality. Why her dad had wanted to buy the horse, she'd never know.

While Callen tucked the mare away in the barn, Shelby tried to work out the pain in her foot and had just about managed it when he made his way back to her. No kiss, but Callen did slip his arm around her waist when they went onto the porch and inside. Since he kept glancing down at her foot, he had likely done that to compensate for the embarrassing injury.

"I've got beer," she offered when they were in the kitchen. "I could attempt something more wintery like hot chocolate, but it'd be from a box."

"The boxed stuff is fine," he said, surprising her.

Hot chocolate was a "chat by the fire" choice of beverage as opposed to beer, which could have been a gateway to tipsy sex. Well, if they'd had the whole six-pack, it could be.

"There's a reporter from San Antonio at the ranch talking to Rosy," Callen continued as she went into the pantry and came back with the hot chocolate. She was pleased that it was the kind with double marshmallows. A sugar high might substitute for gateway tipsy.

"Yes, Rosy told me about that." She boiled some water in a glass measuring cup in the microwave. "The reporter's an old friend of Rosy's from the days when she used to do taxidermy shows and wants to do a story on all the foster kids coming in for the wedding."

Callen took off his coat, put it on the back of a barstool and strolled into the living room, which was only a few yards away. Since her place had an open floor plan, she didn't lose sight of him as he studied the Christmas tree. Specifically, the wad of tinsel that dripped like gold mucus from the tree and onto the floor. No one would assume the placement had been a voluntary decorating choice. Ditto for the gold flower box that she'd stomped and left on the floor next to the door.

"Exactly how many of Buck's kids will be coming?" he asked.

"Dozens. Only a handful can't. One of them is Cleo Delaney. Remember her?" She poured the hot water over the cocoa mix, stirred it up and brought the cups into the living room.

Callen smiled. "Yeah. Judd will be disappointed that she won't be there."

"So, you knew that Judd and Cleo once had a thing," she commented.

"Sex," he corrected, and he sent her a look from over the rim of his mug. "You were too young then to have known about such things. But you knew."

"I was thirteen or so. Not that young. And Cleo asked me to help her put makeup on the love bite that Judd had left on her neck. I filled in the blanks as to how it got there. I filled in more blanks when I saw one on the top of her boob."

Callen made a sound as if impressed by his brother's ability to leave suck marks. Actually, Shelby had been impressed, too, because that had been around the same time she'd noticed that Callen was a hot boy who could possibly leave suck marks on her—if he'd kissed her. Well, he could have if he hadn't been two years older and living under the threat of castration from her father.

They stood there, both now looking at the nearly bare tree with the same level of interest as if it'd been covered with eye-catching ornaments.

"How'd your visit go with your brothers?" she asked just as Callen asked, "Did Gavin really kiss you on Main Street?"

Well, crud. She hadn't expected the gossip to stay out of his ear reach, but Shelby hadn't especially wanted to discuss that particular mood-killing deed with him, either.

"Yes," she admitted on a huff. She downed a swig

of hot chocolate as if it were a whiskey shot and then slapped the mug on the coffee table. "Emphasis on Gavin being the one who did the kissing. Not me. I was just the shocked, pissed-off recipient."

He stayed quiet a moment. Tipped his head to the box. "The shocked, pissed-off recipient of the flowers, too?"

"No, by the time I got those, the shock had worn off, and I was just pissed. He's like a kid who wants what he doesn't have. And you know what the real kicker is? I'll catch the flak from some folks, including his family and snooty sister, who think I should give him another chance. I don't want another chance. And that's why I threw the tinsel at the tree and stomped on the flower box."

There was too much emotion in her voice—too much information, as well—and she tried to soften her tone when she added, "I don't want Gavin."

There.

She'd softened it, all right. It had come out like a sultry purr with a whole bunch of hidden meaning attached. Well, big hidden meaning, anyway.

I don't want Gavin because I want you, Callen Laramie.

"You don't want Gavin because you want me," Callen said, making her wonder if she'd blurted out her thoughts after all. It didn't seem to be a question or clarification.

Callen set his double marshmallow cocoa on the coffee table, and in the same motion, he hooked his arm around her and kissed her. Maybe it was the un-expected movement or just the sheer intensity, but she heard Elvira hiss and scamper out of the room.

Shelby did some scampering, too. Deeper into Callen's arms. Also deeper into the kiss.

Maybe because this wasn't her first rodeo with him in the kissing corral, her body went from "thank you!" to full throttle. It was all fire, fire, fire. And it was hot, hot, hot.

Callen seemed to be in the same mode because his grip was mighty tight, and that kiss was as hungry as they came. Maybe he was trying to hurry before he could talk himself out of this, but she didn't mind the speed. It was exactly what her overly aroused body was after. She wanted suck marks, groping and sex. What she got was her back against the wall as Callen moved her there.

Which wasn't a bad start since Callen went with her.

Sort of. He spun her around, putting the front of her against the wall, and that meant the kissing stopped. Shelby started to protest but hushed when he pushed aside her hair and kissed the back of her neck. And his hands started to slide down the front of her body. Down her breasts, to her stomach.

And lower.

She gave up any notion whatsoever of protesting.

Callen kept kissing her neck and used his tongue, and the front of his body gave her back and butt some sweet torturous pressure. But the best pressure—oh yes—came when he unhooked her belt, followed by unzipping her jeans, and he slid his hand right down into her panties.

She definitely wouldn't have protested even if she had been capable of speaking. She wasn't. That was because all the air in her lungs vanished and she turned to molten gold.

He gave her a few of those well-placed bumps with his body, to let her feel his erection, and he slipped his fingers inside her. She cursed him, though it came out garbled. Definitely not a sexy purr, but it seemed to urge him on anyway because his other hand went up her shirt and to her breasts.

Double touching her.

And bringing her very close to an orgasm.

While an orgasm with Callen greatly appealed to her, Shelby wanted more than his hands and nudges from his erection. She wanted him inside her and was pretty sure he wanted the same. That said, he seemed to be struggling with himself. Maybe trying to take off the sexual edge for her so they could have a conversation about why this wasn't a good idea.

Shelby reminded him just how good of an idea it was when she reached back, slipping her hand between them and over the front of his jeans.

Now Callen cursed *her*, and it didn't come out garbled. She used the moment to turn the tables on him. Or rather to turn herself, and she managed it while his hand was still in her pants. Quite an accomplishment, but Callen had an accomplishment of his own. He spoke clearly and without profanity.

"Get naked now," he ordered.

"Right back at you," she insisted.

And the race was on. That hot, hot, hot fire turned into a blazing plume, and Shelby promised herself that later she'd do some much-slower fooling around with the cowboy whose shirt she was fighting to get off him. For now, though, she just needed to soothe this pressure-cooker heat or she was going to go up like that blazing plume.

She got her boots off and then his shirt. He got hers off, and he did it so much better because he even managed to tongue-kiss one of her breasts as he pushed down her bra. And this time, he slid his hand in the back of her jeans, over her butt, and used his grip to align the front of her zipper to the front of his while he kissed her out of her mind.

Shelby wanted to tell him that the continued foreplay wasn't necessary, but she was caught up in the tidal wave/plume now and just had to go along with wherever he was taking her.

In this case, the couch.

Probably because it was right there. He eased her down, and those clever multitasking hands of his pulled off her jeans and panties while he barely missed a breath kissing her. Not just her mouth, either. But her breasts and stomach. He probably would have gone lower, but her hands weren't nearly so clever, and she was interfering with his mouth so she could get to his jeans.

He helped with that, and back to multitasking again, he took out a condom from his wallet before he hiked his jeans and shorts down over his hips and gave Shelby her first look at some very impressive Callen Laramie full frontal nudity.

Oh my.

He'd been worth the wait.

She only got a glimpse of the full frontal, though, which was fine for now since he moved on to other things. He ripped open the condom wrapper with his teeth, got that sucker on and moved onto the couch with her.

"Hard and fast for now," he said to her like a warning.

That sounded good to her because that *for now* meant she could play with him later. For now, he played her. In the best possible way, of course. Full frontal pushed into her.

Hard and fast, just as he'd promised.

And it sent her flying straight toward the moon. She hadn't counted on *fast* being this fast, but she figured she reached the moon in under a minute. Incredibly amazing, though, for just a short ride.

The orgasm rippled through her, doing its orgasm thing of first making her think she was going to die and then letting her know she had spent every ounce of available energy she had.

But Callen wasn't spent.

Still very hard and deep inside her, he stopped and looked down at her. "Hard and fast again," he drawled.

She nearly laughed and wanted to tell him that she wasn't a multiple-climax sort of woman. She was more the sort who had sex, cuddled and then crashed. But before she could say anything, he started to move inside her.

He kissed her again.

Then he slid his hand between their bodies. The journey was much easier now since they were slick with sweat, and he touched her. Adding some pressure in just the right spot while he continued those deep, long strokes.

The fire reignited. Not some puny little ember or flame, either. Full-blown. And she went from sated to wanting a whole lot more.

This time took longer. Maybe ten minutes, maybe six days. Shelby knew she'd lost her ability to measure time. But she sure knew how to measure something else.

That Callen could follow through on his "again."

Apparently, she was a multiple-climax sort of woman after all.

DRINKING COFFEE, CALLEN stood at Shelby's kitchen window and looked out at the frost that glittered on the ground. There was a soft white mist rising above it, just enough to let through the rays of morning sun.

It was such a calm, pastoral scene with the horse grazing in the background.

Completely opposite to the nonpastoral scene going on inside him.

He'd come here to go ahead and tell Shelby about Buck. And to give a logical argument about why they shouldn't be lovers. He'd accomplished neither of those things and instead had had sex.

Oh, and spent the night with her.

Best not to leave that off his list of things he'd screwed up. Now folks in town would notice that he hadn't come back to the inn, and everyone would know he'd been with Shelby. It didn't matter that his truck was at Buck's. People would still know. Callen didn't care about that for himself, but Shelby had to live here.

She'd have to live with this.

Plus, staying the night was a gazillion steps beyond just having sex. Couch sex could fall into the impulsive "we couldn't help ourselves" category. But carrying her to bed, sleeping next to her, snuggling. Those were steps beyond. Steps that could cause her to get hurt.

At least he hadn't gone back for another round with her when they'd been in bed. Callen couldn't take credit for that, though. He'd only had one condom, and even he wasn't stupid enough to drive Shelby's truck into town to buy condoms.

This might be the twenty-first century, but Coldwater could be backward when it came to things like that. As archaic as it sounded, Shelby's reputation could be soiled. This could also piss off Gavin and his family to the point where Silla might start another Dookie Head campaign—this time against Shelby.

When he heard the footsteps behind him, Callen braced himself to see Shelby come walking in naked. After all, he'd left her naked in bed when he'd got up, grabbed a quick shower and then come into the kitchen to make some coffee. But she was fully clothed in her jeans and shirt. No boots but she had on socks.

He hated that he felt the punch of disappointment that he wasn't going to get another gawk at her.

She smiled, went to him, and as if it were the most natural thing in the world, she stole his coffee and drank nearly all of it before she handed him back the cup. Then she kissed him.

He hated, too, that he also wanted more of that kiss, but he eased back and met her gaze. "I'll probably go to hell for this."

"Well, at least you'll go there with all your parts intact," she pointed out. "No castration."

"There is that, but hell is still hell."

She smiled, brushed her temptress mouth over his again. "Then you should make it worth it," she purred against his lips.

Callen didn't like to lie to himself, and he knew if he'd had a condom that he would have nailed her right there against the kitchen sink. After all, you could only send a man to hell once. He could go out with a bang—literally.

"I need to see Rosy this morning." She finally moved away from him and poured some coffee in a go-cup. "Wedding dress fitting. But you're welcome to stay. Or maybe you want to ride over there with me to get your truck."

He couldn't say no fast enough to that last part. It was early Monday morning, which meant Buck would be there. He didn't want to face him that way. Not with the aura of Shelby sex glistening around him like frost.

Nope.

He'd ride Sweet Caroline back, deal with Buck's reaction to what the man would almost certainly guess had happened. And then Callen would remind Buck that his deadline was up and that he was going to have to come clean to Rosy and Shelby.

In other words, a shit day.

Shelby put on her coat that he took from a peg by the back door, and she touched her fingers to the bunched-up part of his forehead. "There are no strings on this, Callen. In two weeks, give or take a day, you walk. I know that."

"Do you?" And he searched her eyes, looking for any signs that she was just blowing smoke.

She wasn't. Or at least she believed what she was telling him, and because of that, Callen wanted to believe it, too. It would help with the shit day looming.

"Buy some more condoms," Shelby said, her voice all husky and smoky. "I want to play with you later."

And with that hard-on-triggering comment, she smiled like a horny siren and walked out into the cold Monday morning.

CHAPTER THIRTEEN

Shelby tried not to have too much of a spring in her step. Hard to keep her feet on the ground, though, when she was feeling so darn good. It was amazing what a night with Callen could do for a woman's mood.

Two nights would likely make her downright giddy.

She couldn't wait to find out. All she had to do was make it through this day and then she could get Callen back in her bed. This time with more than one condom.

Smiling at that thought, Shelby pulled into the driveway in front of her dad's. Callen's truck was there, causing her to wince a little. He'd probably let Buck or Rosy know that he wouldn't be bringing back Sweet Caroline until this morning, but he would have needed some kind of explanation to go along with that.

The truth, maybe?

And if so, when had that truth telling happened? After Callen and she had made their way to her bed, she hadn't noticed him texting or calling anyone, but

One Minute" Survey

You get **TWO books** <u>and</u> TWO Mystery Gifts...

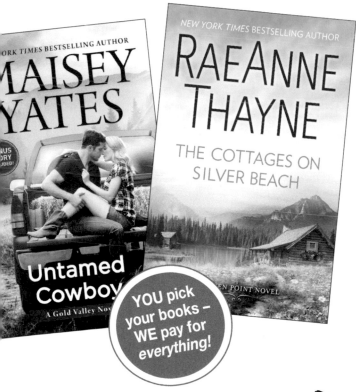
See inside for details.

YOU pick your books –
WE pay for everything.
You get TWO new books and TWO Mystery Gifts...
absolutely FREE!
Total retail value: Over $20!

Dear Reader,

Your opinions are important to us. So if you'll participate in our fast and free "One Minute" Survey, **YOU** can pick two wonderful books that **WE** pay for!

As a leading publisher of women's fiction, we'd love to hear from you. That's why we promise to reward you for completing our survey.

IMPORTANT: Please complete the survey and return it. We'll send your Free Books and Free Mystery Gifts right away. **And we pay for shipping and handling too!**

Thank you again for participating in our "One Minute" Survey. It really takes just a minute (or less) to complete the survey... and your free books and gifts will be well worth it!

We ↖
EVERY

Sincerely,

Pam Powers

Pam Powers
for Reader Service

"One Minute" Survey

GET YOUR FREE BOOKS AND FREE GIFTS!

✓ Complete this Survey   ✓ Return this survey

1 Do you try to find time to read every day?
☐ YES   ☐ NO

2 Do you prefer books which reflect Christian values?
☐ YES   ☐ NO

3 Do you enjoy having books delivered to your home?
☐ YES   ☐ NO

4 Do you find a Larger Print size easier on your eyes?
☐ YES   ☐ NO

YES! I have completed the above "One Minute" Survey. Please send me my Two Free Books and Two Free Mystery Gifts (worth over $20 retail). I understand that I am under no obligation to buy anything, as explained on the back of this card.

194/394 MDL GM32

FIRST NAME

LAST NAME

ADDRESS

APT.#

CITY

STATE/PROV.

ZIP/POSTAL CODE

◄ DETACH AND MAIL CARD TODAY! ►

© 2017 HARLEQUIN ENTERPRISES LIMITED
® and ™ are trademarks owned and used by the trademark owner and/or its licensee. Printed in the U.S.A.

then she'd slept like a rock. Yet another perk from great sex. Of course, she couldn't give Callen total credit for that since rock sleep was her usual mode.

She parked her truck and was about to go inside for the dress fitting with Rosy, but then she saw Mateo and Judd. They were by the corral where there were no horses in sight, and she could tell they were talking because their breaths were fogging up the cold air.

A trickle of alarm went through her, and she hoped Mateo hadn't got into trouble or something. Judd was all cop, and he didn't usually interact with the kids unless there was a problem.

She didn't exactly keep her footsteps light because she didn't want to sneak up on them, but they didn't pay any attention to her. As she got closer, she heard Judd dole out what was either a warning or a life lesson punctuated with some profanity.

"Sometimes shit just happens," Judd said to the boy. "Shit you can't prevent."

Mateo looked at Judd in a way that made Shelby think he was seriously considering that. "How do you get past it?"

"You don't." Judd's tone was his usual growl, but at least it didn't seem to be scaring the boy. "You just step over it and keep going until you find a pile of shit that doesn't stink as bad."

She stopped, continued to listen and hoped she'd soon learn what had started this conversation.

"But my sister might not be able to do that," Mateo said. "She might not be able to step over it."

"Yeah, she will," Judd assured him. "She'll cope. *You'll* cope. And you'll sure as hell quit worrying about me shanking you. I don't shank. When needed, I beat the shit out of people who mess with other people and do bad things."

"Like my mother?" Mateo asked after a long pause.

"No. She'll get what's coming to her in jail. I don't hit women because I have a dick. Men with real dicks don't hit women. Remember that."

It was good advice, but Shelby hoped the boy didn't repeat the cusswords. Of course, since Mateo had been in juvie, he'd likely already heard them.

"Are we okay?" Judd asked.

Mateo nodded and headed into the barn. Judd turned, and she saw his usual stern expression was a little softer today. Then it wasn't. He squared his shoulders as he came toward her.

Judd looked at her the way a cop would when examining a criminal suspect. "I covered for him," he said.

That gave her a quick jolt of concern. "Mateo?"

He huffed. "Callen. He texted me last night to say he wouldn't be coming back to get his truck. I told Buck that Callen had hooked up with some friends and wouldn't be back until morning. Yeah, I know. It reeks of BS, and my guess is Buck didn't buy it one bit."

The concern was still there. Not for Mateo this time, but because Judd was right. Her father wouldn't have bought that, and he wouldn't be pleased that Callen had put Judd up to lying for him. Well, sort of lying. Callen had indeed hooked up, but it hadn't been with friends.

She gave Judd's arm a quick squeeze. "I'll talk to Dad," she promised.

Now, that took some of the shine off her still-lingering sexual buzz. Nothing like starting the morning with a confession to her father that she'd had sex.

Shelby turned to go inside, but she stopped. "Thanks for covering for Callen. And for talking to Mateo."

Judd lifted his shoulder and made a sound that could have meant anything, but Shelby chose to believe it was a *you're welcome*. He headed to his cabin, and Shelby went inside the house.

And the first thing she heard was giggling.

She followed the sound of the giggles to the family room and found Rosy standing on the coffee table, already in her wedding dress. Or rather *a* dress. It wasn't the same one that Rosy had shown her about a week ago. That one had been a column of bubble gum–colored puffs that would have skimmed down Rosy's body.

This one was the opposite of a column. Yards of pink billowed like a massive cotton-candy cloud, and on top of the billows were thousands—maybe millions—of sequins. Also pink. And also shedding. Another million or so of those sequins were all over the floor.

And on the seamstress, a frazzled-looking Alice Murdock.

Alice was kneeling on the floor and appeared to be adjusting the hem, which was probably a good thing considering the dress hung well past Rosy's feet, past the coffee table as well and nearly touched the floor. Alice had her lips pinched over a line of red pearl-head straight pins, and Lucy was next to her holding an apple-sized stuffed thing with yet even more of them. There were pink sparkly sequins clinging to Alice's gray hair and some on her lipstick in between the pin stash. It wasn't a flattering look.

"Oh, you're here," Rosy said, motioning for Shelby to come closer. "I changed my mind and ordered a different dress. Don't you just love it?"

Shelby loved it only because Rosy obviously did. However, she did see an immediate concern. "Will you be able to get down the aisle?" Shelby asked.

Rosy's eyes widened a moment, indicating that she hadn't considered it. The party room at the inn was going to be at maximum capacity with all the guests, so widening the aisle was out. Still, Shelby hated that she'd put the troubled look in Rosy's eyes.

"I'm sure we can make it work," Shelby told her, despite not being sure of that at all. However, she made a mental note to be sure that no small children or feeble guests sat on the aisle because it was possible that Rosy could knock them down in that dress.

"Your dress is here," Lucy said, her voice as quiet as usual. She used the pincushion to motion toward the sofa where there were several boxes.

Shelby kept her "this is all good" look on her face even though she'd told Rosy that she would get her own dress. She'd done that figuring it would minimize her having to wear something more suited to Rosy's sometimes-unconventional taste.

"Mine's also there," Lucy added, her pretty mouth curving into a near smile. "Miss Rosy asked me to be a bridesmaid, too."

Shelby didn't have to feign a "this is all good" look this time. Because it was. Rosy was a sweetheart for doing this, and what was even more wonderful was that Rosy would be genuinely thrilled to have the girl in the wedding party.

"The bridesmaid dresses have pockets," Rosy told them. "I always cry at weddings, so I figured you'd want some place to carry a Kleenex or two."

Alice mumbled something. What exactly, Shelby didn't know, but Rosy appeared to be bilingual when it came to pin-impeded speech. "Alice said you both need to try on the dresses so she can see if they need to be altered," Rosy translated. "It'll be like a mini runway show."

Shelby tried to gauge Lucy's eyes to see if there was concern or excitement about that. Definitely excitement. That was good since it was a first.

"Why don't you let me hold the pincushion for Miss Alice," Shelby volunteered, taking it from Lucy, "and you can go ahead and try on the dress."

Definitely excitement, and Shelby was so thankful that if she could have actually reached Rosy and got her arms around her, she would have given her a hug.

Lucy picked up one of the boxes as if it were a fragile Fabergé egg and headed up the stairs. The silence came as both Alice and Rosy watched her go, clearly waiting for her to be out of earshot. Shelby was waiting for that, too, so she could gush to Rosy about what a good thing this was.

But Shelby didn't get a chance.

"You spent the night with Callen," Rosy blurted out before Shelby could say anything.

Alice babbled something, and judging from Rosy's nod, it was an agreement.

Well, crud. Shelby hadn't expected to keep her night under wraps, but she hadn't wanted it to be the topic of a group discussion.

"I tried to cover for Callen and you with your dad," Rosy went on. "I said something like Callen was probably over at Nico's or Kace's and the night just got away from him. But Buck gave me that look that let me know that he knew what was what. He said he'd talk to Callen and you this morning."

Oh joy. Shelby could hardly wait.

"Where is Dad, anyway?" Shelby asked, wondering if he was going to come in at any moment and contribute to this embarrassing situation.

"In town at the diner," Rosy answered. "I asked him to go because I didn't want him to see the dress."

Alice mumbled something else.

"She said we were going to do this at my place," Rosy translated, "but I didn't have the floor space for it. Alice needed to be able to move around to adjust the hem."

It was amazing that Rosy had got all of that from just a few mumbles.

"So, do you want to tell me about your night with Callen?" Rosy asked, giving Shelby a wink and a smile.

She'd rather get a quarter-sized zit in the middle of her forehead, but Shelby thankfully didn't have to come up with an answer that didn't sound so snarky. That was because Lucy came back down the stairs. Shelby had already prepped herself to say how much she loved the dress, but fudging or outright lying wasn't necessary. It was, well, perfect.

There were no gobs of anything, including sequins. It was just a beautiful dress with sheer long sleeves that matched the deep red color of the dress itself. It hung without clinging, and Shelby figured it would look good on a person of any age.

"It's beautiful," Shelby said as Rosy blurted out a teary, gushy, "You're a vision, Lucy. Simply a vision."

Alice mumbled something, and since Rosy was so enraptured by Lucy, she didn't translate it.

"Thank you," Lucy said, but her voice no longer

seemed so shy, and she made eye contact with Rosy while she continued to stand on the bottom step of the stairs. "I've never had a dress this pretty. Thank you," she repeated, and this time, Shelby was reasonably sure that it included more than just her gratitude for the dress.

"I couldn't get it zipped up all the way," Lucy added a moment later. "That's why I can't do the runway show. My, uh, back is showing some."

Shelby quickly put aside the pincushion and went to her to remedy that. "You really look amazing," she told the girl, and she motioned for Lucy to turn so she could get to the zipper.

Lucy didn't budge, and after a few long moments, she finally looked Shelby in the eyes. "I have scars," Lucy whispered. "Please, I don't want Miss Rosy and Miss Alice to see them."

Oh. Well, that put a ball of heat in Shelby's belly and thinned her breath some. Of course, she'd known that Lucy had been abused, but knowing she was about to see the proof of it made her feel a little ill. And angry. She made sure there was no anger in her voice when she spoke.

"Lucy and I are going in the powder room," Shelby told Rosy and Alice. "The zipper's stuck, and I'm going to put a little soap on it to get it working."

Shelby didn't wait for Alice to volunteer to fix it and not with soap but some seamstress skill that would get it done faster. She took Lucy's hand, moving her off the bottom step, and then Shelby got behind her when they went into the powder room.

"Thank you," Lucy repeated, still whispering.

Despite her thin breath, Shelby gathered as much air into her lungs as she could, and she looked at the girl's back. Yes, scars. Some new. Some old. And too many to count.

"It's okay," Lucy said when Shelby's hand hesitated on the zipper. "They don't hurt anymore."

Yes, they did. They would always hurt, and Shelby had to blink back tears as she covered the ugly marks by closing the zipper. Now the only thing visible was the beautiful red fabric.

Lucy stood on her toes, looking in the mirror, and she met Shelby's eyes in the reflection. Shelby managed to blink back the tears, but she couldn't stop herself from hugging the girl. She expected Lucy to go stiff or jerk back, but she just stood there, not actually participating in what was an overly emotional hug on Shelby's part. But she didn't stop it, either.

"I like you," Lucy whispered. "You're nice and you care."

"I like you, too. And I do care. Not so sure about the *nice* part, though."

"You're nice," Lucy repeated, and she lifted one hand to lay on Shelby's back. "I need to tell you something, and I think it's going to be hard for you to hear."

Shelby squeezed her eyes, trying to steel herself up to hear details of those scars. Details that were going to break her heart. Still, she'd hear them. "I'm listening," Shelby assured her.

Lucy took her time. "It's about Mr. Buck. He's sick. He doesn't want you to know, but he passed out in the barn and hit his head. Mateo found him. Mr. Buck wants everybody to believe he's okay, that he's just a little under the weather, but he's not. It's a big kind of under the weather."

Because Shelby had been waiting and bracing for more about Lucy's abuse, it took her several long moments for the words to sink in. Now it was Shelby who jerked back from the girl so she could see if Lucy was serious.

She was.

Oh God. Her dad was sick?

Shelby suddenly felt sick, too, and she had to lean against the sink. She'd known about the anemia and had felt that something else was wrong. But her father had assured her everything was okay.

"Mr. Buck was bleeding after he fell," Lucy went on. "And he made us all promise not to say anything about it to you or Miss Rosy. He made us all promise. All three of us."

Shelby's head whipped up. "Three?" she asked.

Lucy nodded. "Me, Mateo and Mr. Callen, of course. Mr. Callen knows how sick Mr. Buck is."

CALLEN FIGURED THIS was his lucky day. When he rode Sweet Caroline back to Buck's, he'd expected to face somewhat of a firing squad. Or at least some questions from Buck and/or Rosy. But no one was around, not even Mateo, when he led the horse into the barn and unsaddled her.

As parting shots to confirm her crotchety temperament, the mare flicked her long tail at him, aiming at his face, following it with an attempted head butt. But Callen had more luck when he managed to avoid both.

Callen continued to dodge and avoid as he brushed her down and made sure she had feed and water. Next time he got a wild hair to go visit Shelby, he'd drive there. Of course, he should be talking himself out of other visits. And buying condoms. But that wasn't going to happen. That siren grin she'd given him that morning sealed the deal.

Yeah, he'd go back.

Callen found himself whistling as he walked out of the barn. Still no signs of anyone, which meant all he had to do was get in his truck and drive to the inn. Havana might question him about why he hadn't come back to his room, but it was just as likely that she hadn't been in her room, either. Callen hadn't missed the heat stirring between her and Nico, and there was no way that Nico would pass that up.

He'd just made it to the back of the house when the door flew open. Shelby flew out right afterward, and her gaze shot around the yard before her attention settled on him.

There was fire in her eyes.

"You knew," she said, marching down the steps toward him.

This definitely wasn't sexy siren mode. She was pissed, maybe because she'd just had to go through a grand inquisition with whoever was inside.

She stormed toward him. "You knew about my dad. You knew he was sick, and you didn't tell me."

Oh, that. Well, Callen wasn't whistling now. However, he did groan because he'd known that this would come back to bite him in the ass.

"That's why you came back. That's why you stayed," she went on. Shelby didn't remain still. She started to pace, several angry steps one direction before cutting back with even more angry steps.

"Buck made me promise not to tell anyone." Callen groaned at his own words. They were the truth, but man, it sounded wussy saying them aloud.

"And you agreed to that?" she snapped.

He nodded, figuring that anything he said right now would sound bad except for "I'm sorry." He said it, but she certainly didn't seem to embrace the apology with heartfelt forgiveness.

"Shelby, are you all right?" Rosy called out. She was at the back door, and her entire body was surrounded by massive amounts of pink fabric.

"I'm fine," Shelby answered, not snapping, and she kept her face turned away from Rosy. That meant however or whatever Shelby had found out, Rosy didn't know. "Just finish the fitting. I just need to talk to Callen."

"All right, but bring him in for cocoa when you're done," Rosy insisted.

Callen didn't need to guess that there wouldn't be cocoa in his immediate future. Nope. He'd be looking at plenty of groveling, and then kicking himself for agreeing to keep this a secret in the first place.

Shelby stopped pacing, glared at him, but then her glare morphed into a hard sigh and a very distressed expression. "What's wrong with him? How bad is it?"

Despite his promise to Buck, the secrecy was going to end right now. "It's a tumor on his lung."

"Tumor," she repeated. "Cancer?"

"Maybe. Buck doesn't know, but he's aware that's a possibility."

Shelby groaned, shoved her fingers through her hair. "And he wanted to keep it a secret until after the wedding. He wanted to give Rosy her big day."

Callen nodded, and when he saw the tears shimmering in her eyes, he tried to pull her into his arms. She only batted away his hands.

"Buck promised me as soon as the wedding was over, he'd tell everyone and that he'd go in for the surgery." Callen followed her when Shelby started pacing again. "And, yeah, I told him that idea sucked, that he needed the surgery and the treatment ASAP, but he wouldn't listen."

"Why did he want you here?" she snapped.

Callen forced his chest to ease up so he could draw

in a long breath. "To find a good family for Mateo and Lucy. He also wanted me to help out on the ranch."

The look she gave him let him know that she wasn't just going to buy that. Because she no longer trusted him. Callen couldn't blame her for that.

"He didn't ask Kace or Judd to keep a secret like this because they would have told him no," Shelby spelled out.

Callen was certain that played into it. His brothers were part of Buck and Rosy's daily lives. Part of Shelby's, too. Plus, they were cops. Not exactly the best candidates to ask for what was essentially a lie. A lie because it was withholding the truth.

She paced some more. Cursed. Groaned. And lost the battle with a couple of those tears that slid down her cheeks. "Where is he?" she asked. "Is he actually at the diner like Rosy said?"

Callen had to hold up his hands. "I don't know."

Shelby did some deep breathing, too, and she whirled around and headed for her truck. No doubt she was on her way to the diner to have it out with Buck. He didn't blame her for that, but Callen didn't want her to have to do this alone. Nor did he want her behind the wheel right now.

"I'll drive," he insisted.

He figured she would argue about that or maybe spew some of that profanity at him. She didn't. Shelby was beyond upset and furious, but somewhere underneath all that fury, she must have realized she wasn't steady enough to make the drive into town.

She jumped into the passenger's seat, and Callen got them moving.

Almost immediately, Shelby's phone rang, and she yanked it from her pocket. "It's Rosy," she said. "She'll know something is wrong, but I can't talk to her right now."

"Do you want me to do it?" he asked, already dreading it if she said yes.

But Shelby shook her head. "She doesn't need to hear this over the phone. Once we get to the diner, we'll bring Dad back here and have it out. I want him to look Rosy and me straight in the eyes and try to justify why he would keep this from us. And, no, he's not going to use the wedding as an excuse."

Despite the thick emotion, Callen welcomed the air clearing. Once Rosy knew the truth, she would demand that Buck get the treatment he needed. Of course, she'd almost certainly be furious not just with Buck. Callen knew there'd be plenty enough anger to go around for him, too.

Anger that he damn well deserved.

When they reached the diner, Callen spotted Buck's truck, but he instantly knew something was wrong. Both of the truck doors were open, and several people had huddled around and were looking inside.

What the hell was going on?

Shelby must have picked up on the bad vibe, too, because as soon as he'd come to a stop, she barreled out and rushed toward Buck's truck. Callen was right behind her.

"What happened?" Shelby shouted as she ran.

Will Myers, who owned the grocery store, was one of the people by the driver's side, and he looked up at Shelby. And even though Callen didn't know Will that well, he could tell from the man's face that something had indeed happened.

"I'm not sure," Will said, his face pale and his eyes wide with concern. "Buck had some kind of dizzy spell or something."

With Callen right next to her, Shelby pushed by Will and two others, and she made a sharp gasp when she saw the problem.

Buck was unconscious.

CHAPTER FOURTEEN

"I WANT TO kick or punch something," Shelby snarled, and she knew no one in the hospital waiting room would accuse her of sounding like a cranky toddler.

Well, no one who didn't want to risk her yelling at them—which would be her version of actually kicking and punching, but she was looking at a couple of chair legs that might catch the brunt of a kick or two.

And Callen was looking at her as if he might offer himself up as a punching bag.

He felt bad about keeping her dad's secret. She knew that. He was pacing across the waiting room just as she was, and his expression was worried with a spattering of "I'm screwed."

But mostly it was worried.

It not only mirrored what she was feeling, but Shelby also knew it wasn't going to ease up anytime soon—not until they heard from the doctor and nurses who'd whisked her father into an examining room. Whenever that would be. Even though it seemed like a millennium or two, it had only been about ten minutes since they'd done that whisking away.

"He was too pale," she muttered when the urge for her to kick or punch lessened some.

Callen didn't go for sugarcoating, something that only would have riled her more. He made a sound of agreement, groaned and scrubbed his hand over his face. Maybe he was getting the kicking and punching urge. Of course, he'd likely want to aim that at himself. No way could he be pleased with himself for agreeing to her dad's dumb-head plan of keeping something like this quiet.

The ER doors swished open, and she immediately heard the sounds of hurried footsteps and distress. Lots of "oh dears" and what appeared to be a whimper. A few seconds later, Rosy came rushing in. She was swishing, too, because she was still in her wedding dress that swept through like a big pink plow, leaving a trail of sequins and seamstress pins in its wake.

Judd was right behind Rosy, and behind him were Lucy, Mateo and Alice, who still had pins clamped in her mouth. Obviously, they'd been in alteration mode, though Lucy had changed out of the bridesmaid dress and was back to her usual jeans.

"Oh dear," Rosy repeated.

Judd wasn't oh dearing, though. His gaze zoomed straight to Shelby. She suspected Judd was plenty worried, too, but he had a slightly different way of showing it. Intensity that was well past the kicking and punching mode.

"Where's Buck, and what the hell happened?" Judd demanded.

To answer the first part of the question, Shelby motioned toward the corridor with the examining rooms. The second part wasn't quite so easy to answer. It probably would have helped had her throat not clamped as tight as a miser's fist, and she found herself motioning to Callen to do the explaining.

"Buck passed out at the diner," Callen said. "He regained consciousness and wanted to go home, but Shelby and I brought him here."

"Oh dear," Rosy said. There was a whole lot of shakiness in those two muttered words.

Shakiness that Shelby saw in Lucy and Mateo. They were holding hands and generally looking terrified. Lucy won the prize on that, though, maybe because she'd been the one who'd spilled a secret that never should have been a secret in the first place. Shelby didn't blame the girl, though. If her father could convince Callen to do this, convincing Lucy would have been a snap.

"Oh dear," Rosy said again. It had all four adults and Mateo reaching out for her. Judd was closest, and he gathered her into his arms while keeping his attention on his brother.

Clearly, Judd was going to want a whole lot more info than Callen had just given him, and it seemed to Shelby that Judd's cop instincts had zoomed in on Callen as being the primary source of that whole lot more.

Callen looked at her, silently asking if she wanted to be the one who spilled all of this, but Shelby gave him the go-ahead gesture with the lift of her hand. She knew the basics—well, now she did—but she suspected Callen knew more. And besides, no way was she going to attempt to justify to Rosy and Judd why her father had kept this to himself or why Callen had agreed to keep quiet right along with Buck.

However, before Callen could speak, Shelby heard yet another swish of the ER doors and more hurried footsteps. This time it was Kace, Nico and Havana. Shelby had texted Kace right after she'd called Judd to bring Rosy to the hospital, but she hadn't noticed Callen texting Havana. However, since the inn was just up the street from both the diner and the hospital, it was likely Havana had got the news from someone who had seen or heard what was going on.

"What happened?" Kace asked, and he hurried to Rosy's other side.

Shelby gave Callen another hand motion to let him know he was going to be the mouthpiece here, and she went to Lucy. She slid her arm around the girl, drawing her close.

Callen gave each of them a glance, then nodded the way a person would when mustering up whatever courage was needed to face a firing squad or a pack of rabid wolves. "Buck has a tumor on one of his lungs. He found out a couple of weeks ago."

He paused, no doubt giving them a chance to absorb that. Shelby saw the shock first. Easy to recognize because she'd experienced the same thing when Callen had told her. She wondered if they would also experience the need to kick or punch something when Callen spelled out the rest.

"Weeks?" Rosy questioned.

Callen nodded. "Buck told me, but he asked me to keep it to myself. He didn't want anyone to know until after the wedding." Again, Callen paused for some absorption, followed by reaction.

And he got it.

"What?" Pretty much all of them except Mateo and Lucy said that. They stayed quiet, but the others sure didn't.

"Dumbass," Judd ground out, and she thought he meant that for both Buck and Callen.

Judd likely would have added a lot more profanity if Rosy hadn't given him a parental whack on the arm. Rosy was visibly upset, but apparently that hadn't stopped her from remembering that there were kids in earshot.

"Idiot," Kace contributed, obviously going for nonprofanity.

"Good grief." From Nico.

"Have you lost your flippin' mind?" That from Havana, and it was aimed at Callen.

Alice mumbled something, finally took out the pins and said, "You don't put off something like a tumor." Which was the most logical of the scoldings.

Scoldings that continued when the blame shifted from Callen to her father.

"What the heck was Buck thinking?" That from Nico, and Kace grumbled something similar.

"Did you both lose your flippin' minds?" Havana again.

"Sweet baby Jesus," Nico contributed.

"Dumbass," Judd said, even though he knew it'd get him another swat from Rosy—which it did.

They groaned, threw up hands, and a few glanced up as if seeking some kind of divine answer. Shelby was reasonably sure the only one who was going to give them answers about this was Buck, and it wasn't an answer that any of them were going to accept. Well, other than Callen, and he'd already accepted.

She huffed and amended that when she looked at him. They were all deep in some ditch of emotion that was scummed with uncertainty and fear, but Callen was probably deeper in that ditch than any of the rest of them.

"Sometimes people screw up, even when they're trying to do what they think is right," Mateo said, causing them to turn in his direction. He definitely didn't seem comfortable with that attention, either, and some of them—specifically Judd—didn't seem especially receptive to the opinion.

"Just saying," Mateo added.

Shelby let go of Lucy so she could punch Judd on the arm and give the boy what she thought might be a much-needed hug. Then she stepped away when she realized that Lucy appeared to need a hug from her brother.

"This is my fault," Rosy said. That caused another shift in their attention, and this time all of them shifted in her direction. "Buck did this for me, you see." And with that, she burst into tears.

They all swarmed around her, each of them trying to get in a hug or a comforting pat. It wasn't easy to get close to her, though, in that dress. It might as well have been body armor.

There were some murmured denials about this being her fault, but none of them denied the second part. Because they knew that Buck had indeed put off telling them so that it wouldn't put a cloud over the wedding. And now, instead of a cloud, they had a blasted tornado looming overhead.

Rosy cried and was comforted while sequins fell around them. Shelby got her share of hugs and soft whispers, too. Family, friends and a seamstress, all coming together to try to help. Shelby noticed, though, that some were closer—proximity-wise—than others. Lucy, Mateo and, yes, even Callen were holding back some, so Shelby remedied that. She latched on to whatever part of them she could and hauled them closer into the comfort mix.

She heard Callen's sigh of relief.

Shelby looked up at him, to let him know that while she was more than willing to dole out some comfort, she wasn't ready to forgive him for keeping quiet.

But she was ready.

Nothing good could come from her holding a

grudge against him for that. Well, nothing good
other than she might like to wallow in some misery
for a little while longer. Still, she couldn't mentally
kick or punch him more than the job he was doing
on himself.

The sound of yet more footsteps had them all
moving back. Not easily. Since the netting and sequins had adhered to some of their clothes, it was
a little like pulling apart a pan of sticky cinnamon
rolls. They managed to untangle themselves as
Dr. Breland, Buck's doctor, came toward them. Of
course, he got peppered with a bunch of questions
that centered around "How is he?" but the doctor just
waited until they'd settled before he spoke.

"Buck's still in the examining room, and his condition is stable. No injuries. From what I can tell, he
simply passed out, and since he was seated in his
truck, he didn't hit his head or anything."

That settled the tornado a little for Shelby, and
she refused to think of just how badly he could have
been injured had he been driving at the time. Refus-
ing didn't stop the thought from coming, though, and
she found herself muttering one of Judd's *dumbass*es.

"Buck figures by now you all know about his
tumor," the doctor went on. "And he knows you're
probably all a little upset."

"A lot upset," Judd snapped. *"A lot,"* he emphasized with a glare at Callen.

The doctor nodded in a calm, unruffled way.
"Buck will talk to all of you." He stopped, frowned.

"Most of you," he amended when he looked at Alice and Havana. "He didn't mention you two. But for now he wants to see Rosy, Shelby and Callen. Then Kace, Nico and Judd. Judd, he gave specific instructions that he'd box your ears if you came in cussing."

As if in defiance, Judd cursed under his breath, something that Shelby was betting he wouldn't do when he got into the room with Buck.

"This way," the doctor said, motioning toward Rosy, Callen and her.

They followed Dr. Breland down the shiny tiled corridor that Shelby imagined would be shinier if the sequins on Rosy's dress continued to shed. She started to blurt out something about it being bad luck for the groom to see the bride in her dress, but Shelby figured they'd already met their quota of the bad.

When they went into the examining room, it surprised her to see her father sitting up, and he certainly wasn't as pale as he had been when he'd been passed out behind the steering wheel. There was actually plenty of color in his cheeks, but she doubted it was from a sudden onset of good health. No. He was embarrassed layered with a hefty dose of dread.

Rosy ran to him. Well, as much as she could run while dragging all those yards of fabric, and she showered Buck's cheeks with kisses. Buck caught her in midcheek smooch to shift her mouth to his. The kiss he gave her was soft, long and incredibly intimate. So much so that Shelby looked away, her gaze colliding with Callen's.

"I'm sorry," Callen said to her, and while Shelby knew he meant it, she didn't get the chance to respond because her father said those exact words.

"I'm sorry." Buck glanced at each one of them as he repeated it, and then he held up his hand before they could start bombarding him with protests, whys and more hugs.

God, it was good to see him sitting up like that. Good to see the color in his face. But Shelby still wanted to throttle him.

Her father's attention settled on Rosy. "You look so beautiful. My beautiful bride in her beautiful dress."

Rosy managed a smile. "You really think so? You don't think the dress has too much sparkle?"

It was enough to trigger seizures, but Shelby had to hand it to her father when he said, "It's perfect, just like you." He gave both the dress and Rosy an approving look. "I love you, and I didn't want anything to get in the way of me marrying you. That's on me, not you. I kept this secret for me. Remember that."

It was a kind thing to say, especially since Rosy was still crying, but she was also shaking her head as if she was going to continue to take some of the blame.

Her father turned to Callen next. "I was wrong to ask you to keep this quiet. Wrong to put this on your shoulders. I just wanted…needed your help, and I knew you would do it. I knew there'd be a price to pay, that Rosy and Shelby would be upset, but I didn't figure you'd stay around long after the wedding to deal with their aftermath."

In other words, he would cut and run. Which Callen wouldn't have done.

No, Shelby mentally amended.

He would have stayed and faced their anger just as he'd done in the hospital waiting room. Because at the core of it, Callen loved Buck and would walk through hell and fire for him. Or in this case, he'd deal with a crying bride and a pissed-off daughter.

Her dad finally looked at her. "I'm sorry I didn't tell you, but I'm even sorrier that I mucked up things between Callen and you."

"Wh-what?" Shelby managed. The first "I'm sorry" she got just fine. She deserved that apology, but the second one led her to believe that her father thought there was something to muck up with Callen.

Something like a relationship.

Callen and she did have one of those. Sort of. After all, they'd had sex and she had almost forgiven him for keeping the truth from her. Maybe she had anyway. But *relationship* seemed to be something, well, more than sex. More than even onetime forgiveness. It seemed like another step toward that broken heart that was looming like a second tornado.

Shelby didn't have the heart to argue with her dad. With Callen. Or with anyone else. She felt spent, raw and afraid.

Very afraid.

"What will happen now?" she asked, almost too scared to hear the answer.

But Buck wasn't the one who responded anyway. Dr. Breland came back in. "I'll need a word with Buck," he said. "I have to go over some things."

"I'd like for them to stay," her father insisted, and he caught onto Rosy's hand. Then Shelby's.

The doctor nodded. "Your blood pressure's low, and you're anemic. I think that's why you fainted. We'll find a way to fix that, but the tumor is the big fix." He looked Buck straight in the eyes. "No more delays. I want to keep you overnight and get you scheduled for surgery."

The room went so quiet that Shelby heard one of the pins from Rosy's hem ping to the floor.

Dr. Breland shifted to Rosy then. "I'm sorry, but you're going to need to postpone the wedding."

CHAPTER FIFTEEN

CALLEN COULD SAY with absolute certainty that he got no sense of accomplishment from lifting hay bales and hauling them onto a flatbed and driving those hay bales out to the pasture, where he had to lift them yet again.

Yes, he could physically do it, but it got old fast when he had to do it repeatedly while he worried about Buck. Still, he knew this was what Buck needed from him now.

Rosy and Shelby, too.

Since Buck's hospital stay was now in its third day, they should be with Buck, and Callen could lighten their burden a little by helping out at the ranch. Of course, that meant working deep into the night at the inn to run his own business, but burning the candle at both ends had a way of numbing some of the fear over Buck's health.

There'd be surgery; Callen had learned that much, and that would happen in five days, a week from when the wedding was supposed to have taken place. Now, instead of Buck finalizing whatever plans a groom made, he'd be under the knife and then hopefully recovering. Callen wasn't exactly sure yet what a recovery would entail, but he'd heard the terms *chemo* and *radiation* thrown around.

There had also been some discussion about moving Buck to a large hospital in San Antonio. And that still might happen if things didn't go well during the operation. There were some concerns about Buck's blood pressure and how his age would affect his recovery. For now, though, Dr. Breland and one of the other local doctors would be doing the surgery.

Callen drove the tractor in from the pasture and made a check on the horses. Mateo and Lucy had volunteered to do a lot of that particular chore, but the kids were also in the middle of midterms at school. No way did Callen want them to back off on their studying to tend horses or cook meals. Thankfully, pizza had fixed the meal problem.

If only the rest of his problems could be fixed so easily.

In addition to Buck, Callen was worried about Rosy and Shelby. And all the hay hauling and chores weren't going to make that better. Only the surgery and a clean bill of health could do that.

Callen checked the time. It was almost one o'clock, which meant he'd have time to visit Buck at the hospital before heading to his office at the inn. Shelby and Rosy would almost certainly be with Buck since they'd hardly left his side, but perhaps they'd get good news and Buck could come home while he waited for surgery. That would all depend on his blood pressure and the results from the lab work that had been done on him.

Maybe when Buck got home, Callen could finally sit down and talk to Shelby. He hadn't done nearly enough groveling for the secret-keeping.

But he'd bought condoms.

Callen wasn't sure if that made him optimistic, stupid or if it just gave him something to focus on besides worrying and hauling hay. He was leaning toward the stupid.

He grabbed a quick shower, changed into the spare shirt he'd brought with him and was headed down the stairs when there was a knock at the door. A heavy-handed one. Followed by a shout.

"Callen, I know you're here, and we need to talk."

Gavin.

Shelby's ex wasn't the last person on earth Callen wanted to see, but he wasn't high on the welcome list, either. Callen went to the door so he could tell Gavin that this "need to talk" would be very short so he could get to the hospital.

That didn't happen.

The moment Callen opened the door, a fist came flying at him. Quick reflexes had him ducking the full brunt of the punch, but Gavin still managed to get a glancing blow off Callen's cheek.

"That's for Shelby," Gavin declared, and with that handful of words, he doled out a different kind of punch.

Oh man. That was a lot of alcohol on his breath,

enough to have Callen needing to take a step back. Gavin must have seen that as some kind of retreat because he swung again, his fist going wide and smacking into the door. He howled in pain. A drunk, slurry howl punctuated with what Callen guessed was attempted profanity. All Gavin actually managed, though, was a few syllables.

"You bastard," Gavin finally got out. "I love her."

Callen didn't have to guess about this part. Gavin was talking about Shelby, and apparently he had decided that he should declare his love to a man who he then wanted to beat up.

"Uh, you broke up with Shelby," Callen reminded him.

"That was a mistake." One that he apparently wasn't going to own up to because he just kept going. "You don't love her," Gavin went on. "You just came here to have sex with her and break her heart."

Callen could have pointed out that according to popular opinion in Coldwater, Gavin was the heartbreaker, but Callen knew differently. Shelby had been fine with the end of the engagement. And while Callen hadn't come back to have sex with her or do any heartbreaking, he had indeed done the first. Might end up doing the second before this was over.

And yet he'd bought those condoms.

That stupid label was getting harder and harder to ignore.

"You're not even going to stay around," Gavin

went on, his slurred voice a shout now. "You'll high-tail it out of here as soon as Buck's better."

That was the plan, had been the plan all along, but Callen didn't care to share that with Shelby's drunk ex with a bad aim. Gavin's next punch slammed into the jamb, and his howl of pain was even louder than the first.

It wasn't the only howl, though. Another came from outside, and when Callen looked in the drive-way, he saw Silla behind the wheel of her car. So she'd driven her drunk brother to confront him. Either Gavin had been very persuasive in getting her to bring him or else Silla was still holding a grudge. Either way, she was here, and that meant Callen didn't have to come up with another way to get Gavin out of there.

"Go home, Gavin," Callen advised him. "Sleep it off. While you're at it, get your knuckles cleaned and bandaged. You're bleeding."

Gavin didn't take that advice well because another punch came Callen's way. Enough was enough. Callen came out on the porch so he could shut the door and lock it before he caught onto the back of Gavin's belt and the collar of his coat. He marched him toward Silla. Well, as much as you could march a drunk man. There was some staggering and weaving going on.

Silla got out, making sounds of outrage and protest, but Callen just gave Gavin a final push so that he landed in his sister's arms. "Why the heck would you drive him here to do this?" Callen demanded.

Callen thought maybe she would have some clever answer—something about believing Shelby and Gavin were soul mates or such crap. But as she stuffed Gavin into the car, she shook her head and gave Callen a blank look.

"Because he's my brother," she said. "He asked me to do it, so I did."

So, not a clever answer after all, and it wasn't as if Callen could huff and declare it dumb reasoning since it was uncomfortably similar to what he'd done for Buck. Buck had asked, and Callen had done it.

"Gavin wants Shelby back," Silla added. "And once you're out of the picture, it'll happen. You'll see. She'll be so upset when you leave, and she'll go running back to Gavin. Of course, I'll talk him out of taking her back because my brother shouldn't have to settle for Callen Laramie's leftovers."

The anger just zoomed right into Callen. Leftovers! He stopped, trying to figure out how to aim all this dangerous energy zooming and bubbling inside him. He couldn't beat up a drunk idiot or his equally idiot bitch of a sister. Well, maybe he could beat up the drunk, but that would only delay him even more, and he doubted there'd be much satisfaction in it.

Much.

Reining in his fury, Callen just turned and headed to his truck. When he drove away, he couldn't resist calling out to them. "Dookie Heads!"

Obviously, he could have come up with a new insult or at least one that was age appropriate, but judging from Silla's stunned expression, it'd worked.

Callen didn't speed away. In fact, he took his time, trying to steady himself before he saw Buck. The fight—or rather the attempted fight—with Gavin hadn't exactly put him in a soothing mood, and he didn't need to go into Buck's hospital room like that.

There were already too many other things un-soothed there.

However, it did make Callen wonder if he should talk to Shelby about it. Not to tattle but to give her a heads-up in case... Well, he wasn't sure what stunt Gavin could pull, but he didn't want Shelby blind-sided. He especially didn't want her running back to Gavin when he left. Silla was wrong about that.

He hoped.

Shelby deserved a heck of a lot better.

The slow drive worked, some, because by the time he'd parked at the hospital, his steaming anger had mentally moved to the lukewarm burner. Another burner got going, though, as he walked into the hospital and saw Shelby. She was coming out of the hall that led to the patient floor where Buck was staying.

She stopped when she spotted Callen. Clearly hesitating, and while he knew why she had that reaction, he despised it. Just days earlier they'd had sex—great sex!—and now it felt as if there were miles between them. Miles he had put there, so he had no one but himself to blame.

"Good—you're here," she murmured. "Dad's been asking for you."

"Yeah, I got a little hung up."

"Ranch stuff," Shelby supplied. "Thanks for doing that."

This sounded like small talk to him, and he hated it. Hated not being able to touch her. "I can lift hay bales all by myself," he said, hoping it would make her smile.

It did, but then she must have remembered there wasn't a whole lot to smile about because it quickly faded. "Thanks," she repeated.

Since that was civil and because she was still standing there, Callen nudged the conversation out of small-talk zone. "You know I'm sorry, right?" he asked.

Shelby nodded. Paused. Nodded again. Then she tipped her head in the direction of the cafeteria. "I'm going to grab some coffee while you visit with Dad. See you in a bit."

Well, along with the double nod she'd given him after his apology, that was better than "don't let the door hit you in the ass," and Callen would keep the picture of her smiling in his head for a while. Not a bad start to what would almost certainly be a bad visit.

Or not.

When he stepped into Buck's room, he saw things he shouldn't see. Not bad things, just unsuitable for his eyes. Rosy was on the bed, and Buck and she were making out. Callen truly hoped he could rid his memory of Buck's hand up Rosy's shirt. He turned to do an about-face so he could leave, then knock. Knock hard and loud so they'd have some warning.

"Callen," Rosy greeted him with a giggle and a flushed face. "Come in. We've been expecting you."

Obviously not, since he doubted they'd wanted him to witness what he had any more than he did. Except maybe it was a sort of good thing for him to see. Rosy and Buck clearly weren't in a doom and gloom sinkhole of despair. Buck was blushing some, too, but it was the blush of a man who'd got as sexually lucky as he could get while in the hospital.

"Buck and I were just working out some wedding details," Rosy announced.

No, they'd been making out, but Callen didn't call them on that. "Oh?" he settled for saying.

Rosy nodded, beamed. "We've decided we'll go through with the wedding on the planned date. If Buck's still in the hospital, then we'll have it here." Still beaming, she kissed Buck again and picked up her purse. "I'll go find out if we could use the cafeteria and the chapel."

Callen didn't get into questioning whether or not that was a good idea. He just smiled when Rosy gave him a hug and hurried out.

He glanced around, not actually surprised that there was more stuff crammed into the room than there had been the day before. A stack of books and magazines. Flowers—everywhere, including one with a now-sagging Mylar balloon.

And in the center of the flowers sat Billy the stuffed armadillo.

Creepy as ever. Today, he was wearing green surgical scrubs and had a toy stethoscope draped around his neck. Someone—Rosy, no doubt—had put a tiny sign in his hands that said, "Get Well Soon, Buck."

"Is Rosy handling this as well as she seems to be?" Callen asked.

Buck sighed. "Not really, but the new wedding plans will help and give her something to do. What would help even more is for me to be out of here by then and get married at the inn."

So, the wedding was on no matter what. And in a perfect scenario, it could happen. Buck's surgery was a week before the wedding, and he could have recovered enough by then. If it wasn't cancer, that was.

"Anything on a possible family for Mateo and Lucy?" Buck asked.

"I'm working on it."

"Good. Good," he repeated, and he patted Callen's hand when Callen sat in the chair next to the bed. "Because here's how this could play out. With my bad health, CPS will remove them, and Rosy will claim she can handle them. She can't. Not by herself."

Callen silently agreed. Rosy's heart was in the right place, but her head often wasn't. Plus, she would be sick with worry over Buck, and that would take her head out of it even more.

"I could convince Rosy to back off on fostering the kids," Buck went on, "but then Shelby would just step up to take them. She's a good daughter, but that's too much to put on her. It seems to me that it's something she should want to do rather than something shoved on her."

Buck had obviously given this a lot of thought. So had Callen. "Shelby would do it. And I would help her."

"I know that, too, but Shelby and you aren't a family. At best, you're just trying to figure out if you even like each other."

"I've figured out that I like her." Callen tried to keep it light. That didn't make it less true. He liked her and he wanted her. Normally, a good combination.

"Glad to hear that." Buck's smile returned, but it wasn't one of those that Rosy could genuinely dole out. "But I know I didn't help with that by creating this friction between you. Putting Mateo and Lucy in that mix is wrong. They need a family, a solid one that's been together through thick and thin and will continue to stay together."

Callen couldn't argue with that. Though Buck had done a decent enough job raising a horde of kids on his own, he might not be up to doing that again for a while. If ever. It was the "if ever" that was tightening Callen's stomach.

"I have a confession to make," Buck went on. He coughed and waited a moment to regain his breath.

"I asked you to come to the ranch to help me, but I also wanted you here for Shelby. I wanted you two to get together."

Callen's shoulders stiffened.

"Yes, I know," Buck continued before Callen could speak. "It was wrong, but she's been half in love with you for years. She moaned out your name."

Callen blinked and experienced nearly every other physical reaction a man could have from shock. "She what?"

"Moaned," Buck repeated. "Last night she slept here. In that." He motioned toward a chair. "And she moaned out your name."

Well, hell. That couldn't be good, not in front of her father, anyway. Callen definitely wasn't going to ask Buck to elaborate since it had a whole sex vibe about it, but he wanted to suggest that the moan was possibly because she'd had to sleep right next to the creepy dead stuffed thing named Billy. But since that would be a dis to Rosy, he could darn sure dispel the other part of Buck's comment.

"Shelby's not half in love with me," Callen assured him. "She's, uh…" He didn't draw a blank. Just the opposite. Callen could come up with several possible ways to fill that in.

She's on the rebound. Which wasn't as true as some thought it was.

It's lust. Which was absolutely true—and on both sides—but not something Callen would admit to Buck.

It's a leftover childhood crush.

Callen went with the last one, but when he said it aloud, it only caused Buck to smile and pat his hand. "She moaned out your name," Buck said as if that explained everything that needed explaining.

Thankfully, the uncomfortable conversation came to a halt when Rosy rushed back in. "It's a go," she announced. "We can use both the chapel and the cafeteria. They even offered to supply the food."

She made that last part sound like a good thing rather than something she should definitely turn down. Callen had eaten in the cafeteria, and it wasn't a wise choice for tasty celebration treats.

"That's great," Callen assured her, and Buck echoed the same.

"I hope Buck and you finished your chat," Rosy quickly added. She took Callen by the arm and led him to the door. "Because you should go check on Shelby."

Instant alarm. "Why? What's wrong?"

"I'm not sure. I saw her talking on the phone to someone while she paced across the waiting room. She seemed upset."

Rosy had barely got out that last word when Callen said a quick goodbye and headed out to find her. By the time he'd got to the waiting room, he'd worked up all sorts of bad scenarios, including but not limited to Shelby having some kind of meltdown about her father. But he was several steps beyond being merely confused when he finally saw her.

She smiled at him and quickly halved the distance between them, only to motion for him to follow her toward the corner. Not exactly private, but they wouldn't be standing in the middle of the room, either.

"Did you beat up Gavin?" she asked once they were there. "Silla just called and said you had."

Silla—of course. The woman hadn't wasted much time, but at least Shelby didn't seem upset but rather amused. Or proud.

"No, I can't take credit for that," Callen admitted. "Gavin sort of beat himself up. But I did call him a name." And he hoped she wouldn't ask exactly what name.

"Yes, Silla mentioned he was drunk." Her smile vanished, and she got an *Oh God* look in her eyes. "I'm sorry. That's what I should have said right off the bat. I'm sorry that Gavin went to you and tried to start something."

"So, why did you smile?" he asked.

Her chin came up, and she touched one of the buttons on his shirt. For a button touch, it seemed to be strangely intimate. And he was reasonably sure that it signaled something huge.

That Shelby had at least partly forgiven him.

"Because I thought you were defending my honor or something," she explained. "It's stupid and childish."

Yeah, it was, but Callen didn't say anything. He just stood there and let her fondle his button. Maybe this was like a gateway maneuver that would soon lead to her touching him.

"I knew you weren't hurt," she went on. "I mean, I could see that when you came in, so I just figured you'd managed to defend my honor without breaking a sweat."

"No sweat broken," he assured her, and because he couldn't stop himself, he moved a strand of hair off her cheek. Much better than button touching. But he needed to add a disclaimer here that had nothing to do with the subtle foreplay going on between them. "I don't want Gavin or Silla to cause you any trouble."

"They won't. When he sobers up, Gavin will be embarrassed enough by this to back off for good. The same for Silla. They'll avoid me like we all steer clear of Gopher when he's wearing a raincoat."

Now Callen smiled, and maybe it was that easy smile that lulled him into blurting something he probably shouldn't have blurted. "Did you really moan out my name last night?"

Shelby's eyes widened. "Why? Did Havana say something about that?"

"Havana?" What the hell would she have to do with this? He shook his head. "No, Buck mentioned it."

"Oh." Her forehead bunched up. "Did he say if I moaned out anything else?"

"No, that was it, but I think he knows the context of a moan."

She nodded, shrugged. Looked up at him. Her fondling finger slid off the button and bingo—onto his chest. "Want to hear me moan your name in person?"

"Yeah." But it took him several flustered seconds to get out that simple answer.

She brushed a quick kiss on his mouth, goosing him with a punch of lust. "Good. My place, tonight, around six." The goosing turned to an avalanche when she added, "This time, bring a box of condoms."

CHAPTER SIXTEEN

SEX PLANNING TOOK, well, planning. And energy.

Because of the fatigue, stress and worry over her dad, Shelby hadn't actually considered that. She'd gone all loosey-goosey, making herself believe that she could just go home after lunch and have the afternoon to get ready for what would almost certainly be great sex with Callen.

Stress-relieving, distracting, pleasurable, great sex.

After the past couple of days, she was certain they could both use it. What she hadn't considered in her loosey-goosey-ness was that she'd be this exhausted. All for a good cause, though.

Dr. Breland had finally released her dad from the hospital so he could go home and wait until his surgery. Wonderful news that had included not only getting her dad and Rosy back to the ranch but also moving the gazillion things that had accumulated in his hospital room. Bridal magazines, books, a whole florist shop of flowers and, yes, Billy. Shelby had transported the icky armadillo, too.

It had been for a worthy cause, Shelby reminded

herself. With her taking care of the moving duties—
which had involved multiple trips—Rosy had got to
spend some time alone with Buck. She'd managed
to get it all done, but now she was paying the price.
She was bone tired and feeling the effects of func-
tioning on only a handful of hours of sleep for the
past couple of nights.

Shelby checked the time when she got home. She
still had an hour before Callen got there, so she could
grab a shower and dress. It wouldn't be that slow
pace where the anticipation of the evening could
build, but Callen could do better things than anticipation anyway.

Thankfully, she'd already tended the horses. She'd
done that early in the morning after coming back
from the hospital. Having that chore out of the way
gave her a little extra time, so she called for a pizza
to be delivered in an hour. Then she dropped down
on the sofa just to put up her feet for a minute or two.

A minute came and went. Then two, and Shelby
forced her eyes open. Something was wrong. She
didn't need any extra minutes to figure that out. She
was no longer sitting but rather lying on the sofa,
and she had a blanket over her. Moonlight streamed
through the windows.

No. Wait.

Not moonlight. Sunlight.

She jackknifed to a sitting position, her startled
gaze trying to figure out what the heck was going on.
The pizza was there on the coffee table, the box open,

and Elvira was licking the cheese. Two pieces were missing, so either the cat had got very hungry, or…

It was the *or*.

Callen was there. He was standing by the sofa, and he was sipping some coffee. "I was about to leave you a note," he said. "I have a meeting this morning. An important one that I can't reschedule, and it starts in about ten minutes. Sorry."

Morning. That was why there was sunlight. And it forced all of her loosey-goosey/"put her feet up for a minute" memories to come crashing into her.

"I didn't get to have sex with you," she said.

He nodded, and the groaning rumble in his chest let her know that he wasn't any happier about that than she was. The kiss he gave her was the same as that rumble. It had so much need in it, and it stirred the sleep away. It could work miracles.

But apparently what it couldn't do was get Callen out of this meeting.

"Gotta go," he said, landing another kiss on her now-disappointed mouth. "Oh, by the way, it's true. You do moan out my name when you're asleep."

Heck, that wasn't an especially grand accomplishment, and to prove it, she moaned out his name just fine as he headed out the door.

CALLEN WAS PRETTY sure that time had crawled to a near stop. He was also certain that Shelby and he had paced ruts in the old linoleum floor. Kace was putting in some miles on it, too, but he sat occasionally to give Mateo or Judd a crack at what was turning out to be a premium pacing surface.

The nonpacers—Rosy, Nico, Havana and Lucy—had claimed a cluster of seats together near the back wall. Rosy had the dead stuffed armadillo on her lap, declaring it was her good-luck charm. Heck, maybe it was, but it was creeping out everyone who trickled in and out of the waiting room to check on Buck.

"Maybe I should switch from white roses to violets," Rosy blurted out. "A violet bouquet would look so pretty against my pink dress."

There were some sounds of agreement. Mild agreement. The mild wasn't because people weren't interested; it was just that it had been Rosy's umpteenth wedding suggestion made during the two hours Buck had been in surgery. Callen knew it was a way for the woman to keep her mind off Buck, but it was a reminder for the rest of them that the wedding might not even take place.

A week was a long time to make a quick enough recovery from major surgery, and then say I do.

But if anyone could pull it off, it'd be Rosy and Buck.

Judd grumbled something under his breath, and there'd been enough grumbles that Callen had decided that was Judd's preferred coping method. Havana had her method, as well. She was working on her laptop, her long tangerine-colored nails making pecking sounds on the keyboard. Then there was Lucy. She was chewing on her lip while she pretended to read a book. Nico was stretched out, his Stetson covering his face.

Callen supposed a nap could be considered a coping method.

Shelby and he had their own ways, as well. Their pacing pattern would intersect every couple of minutes or so, and they'd make eye contact. Things passed between them. Not sexual things or missed opportunities for sex. But the worry and the uncertainty. It was all there in that brief glimpse in her eyes, and Callen suspected she was seeing the same thing in his.

"Or maybe I should go with sunflowers," Rosy piped up. "They're so cheerful. I could even make a mini bouquet of them for Billy to hold."

There were a couple of *hmmm*s and a grumble from Judd.

"I killed him, you know," Rosy said.

No mild reactions that time. They all stopped their coping and turned to look at Rosy. Even Nico. He lifted his hat so he could peer out.

"Are you talking about Buck?" Shelby asked. "Because if so, you didn't delay his surgery—"

"No. Not Buck. Someone else. I didn't mean for it to happen. It just did, and I was so sorry afterward," Rosy added. She brushed at tears, which had Shelby, Callen and Kace moving toward her.

"Who did you kill?" Kace asked, and thankfully he didn't sound like the sheriff questioning a suspect.

Rosy sniffed some more. "Billy. I accidentally hit him with my truck."

Even though Callen was aware that was what she'd named the armadillo, it still took him a moment to shift from a murder confession to, well, roadkill.

"I just didn't see him," Rosy went on. "I'd spilled my Dr Pepper and was trying to wipe it up, and I took my eyes off the road for just a second. That's all it took, one short second, and I smacked right into him."

Judging from the silence, everyone was trying to figure out what to say. "I'm sorry," Lucy managed, which turned out to be a stellar answer because Rosy smiled at her.

"I felt so guilty that I wanted to bring him back," Rosy added. "I wanted him to be around forever."

While that was touching, he was glad Rosy wouldn't legally be able to do that to any of them.

The "coping" started up again, and while Callen paced, he looked around the hospital. There'd been lots of visits here over the years. ER visits because of sports injuries and fevers and such that just couldn't wait for a regular office appointment.

Some of those early visits had been follow-ups for the injuries that Avis Odell had given him. Nico had had plenty of checkups, too, but that was only after he'd got out of the hospital in San Antonio.

Bad memories.

No matter how fast you paced, they were always right there snapping and nipping at your heels.

Shelby and he crossed paths again, but this time she stopped and caught onto his arm. She studied his eyes as if trying to figure out what new thing she saw in them. Of course, it wasn't new, but it seemed to take her a moment to figure it out.

"Don't feel sorry for me," he warned her in a whisper. That had worked for Rosy with the Billy-murder, but Callen felt too raw for that from Shelby. He wouldn't break, but he might lose an edge that he needed to keep in order to get through this.

Shelby came up on her toes and put her mouth right against his ear. "You have a very nice ass," she whispered. Her expression didn't change, and she moved right back into the pace.

Well, it was just as effective as Lucy's "I'm sorry" had been to Rosy. Maybe more. Because Callen found himself smiling. That ended, though, when Dr. Breland came out of the corridor and started toward them. The doctor's somber look had Callen ditching the smile, and he went to Shelby so he could put his arm around her.

Suddenly everyone got to their feet, and they turned their complete attention to the doctor. Callen didn't like to think that so many things hinged on whatever the man said. He especially didn't like to think that Buck's life hinged on it.

"Buck came through the surgery, and we removed the tumor," the doctor explained. He held up his hands when the barrage of questions started. "We don't know yet if it's cancer. We won't have those results back for a couple of days."

Hell. More waiting. As much as that frustrated Callen, he tried not to show it. Shelby had burrowed against him. Rosy had done the same to Mateo, and Havana had hold of Lucy.

"Buck's in recovery, and he's heavily sedated," the doctor went on. "He wants to see you. All of you," he emphasized. His huff let them know that was an argument he'd had with Buck and lost. "According to Buck, you're to go in alphabetical order by first name. I guess that's his way of not showing favoritism."

Maybe because they were all in a mind haze of worry, they started working their way through the alphabet. Callen would be first. Well, unless Buck wanted to appease Rosy and ask to see Billy. Barring that, Callen would be first and Shelby last. A sort of sandwich for the others. Callen only hoped Buck didn't tire himself out so that he wouldn't have much energy to speak with Shelby. Rosy and she needed Buck the most right now.

"Since there are so many of you," the doctor went on, "you only get two minutes each, and I'll be timing it. Don't say anything, and I mean anything, that will upset him."

"Oh dear," Rosy whimpered. "I won't bring up the sunflowers, then, because I'm not sure how he feels about them."

As before, they gave her mild murmurs of agreement, and the doctor motioned for Callen to follow him. The hospital wasn't that big, so it didn't take them long to get down the hall and to the recovery room. He spotted Buck right away in the bed surrounded by machines.

God, he looked so pale, but then Callen hadn't expected better since the man had just had his chest cracked open.

"Two minutes," the doctor reminded Callen as he went in. "Not a second more."

Buck lifted his eyelids, not easily, and when he tried to speak, there was no sound. "*Bumfuzzle*…is a funny word…don't you think?" Buck finally said.

Callen glanced back at the doctor. "He's heavily medicated," Dr. Breland reminded him.

So it would be this kind of conversation. Callen was almost relieved. It would be an easier one than some heart-squeezing outpouring of possible bad outcomes and such.

"Yeah, it is," Callen agreed. "So is my personal favorite, *catawampus*."

Buck managed a slight nod and an equally slight smile before his eyelids fluttered back down. "Shelby's falling in love with you."

Callen went stiff. Said nothing.

"Go gentle with her, Callen." He paused, made a soft grunting sound. "You're my favorite kid." Buck made an air pat in the general direction of Callen's arm.

"You're going to say that to the rest of them, aren't you?" Callen asked.

"Absolutely. And it'll be true."

With that, Buck drifted off.

FOR THE FIRST time in her life Shelby wished that her name had been Anne or, heck, even aardvark. That way she wouldn't have had to wait so long to see her dad. But since she was at the bottom of this particular alphabet selection, she'd had to wait through Callen, Judd, Kace, Lucy, Mateo, Nico and Rosy.

Havana had given up her turn, so that had shaved a couple of minutes off her waiting time, but it still felt like an eternity. It didn't bode well that Callen, Judd and Kace had all come out of the recovery room with somber expressions that they'd tried to cover with fake optimism.

The general consensus from those first three was that "Buck looked great but he's a little out of it—which is to be expected." She doubted that *looking great* part, hence her diagnosis of fake optimism.

No sunny outlook for Lucy. She'd come out dabbing tears from her eyes and had then asked the meaning of *catawampus*, making Shelby wonder exactly what had gone on during their conversation. Mateo had asked the meaning of *bumfuzzle*, making Shelby wonder even more. The wonder continued when Nico came out grinning and announced that he was "Buck's favorite kid." He'd added a fist pump.

All right. So that stung a little, but then maybe her dad had categories of favorites. Such as favorite kid whose name started with an *N*.

Rosy had come out of recovery beaming and was pleased to let them know that Buck had approved her choice to get violets for the bouquet. Shelby wasn't sure that was a wise way to use her two minutes, but at least Rosy wasn't crying, asking about the meaning of odd words or spewing fake sunshine.

Shelby had already made her way to the recovery room door so that she'd be ready when Dr. Breland gave her the go-ahead. When he finally did, she rushed in, not wanting to eat up seconds with the trek from the door to the bed.

"Dad, I love you, and I want you to get better fast," she blurted out. She'd rehearsed it to make sure she got it all out. "Don't worry about a thing. Just heal."

Her dad looked at her, one of his eyes going in a different direction than the other. That confirmed the "heavily medicated" part. His sallow skin and hollow face confirmed that Kace, Callen and Judd had BS'ed her about his looking good. He looked like crud, but she suspected that was normal after surgery.

"Shelby," he said, his voice weak and rattled. He did an air pat of her hand, and she braced herself for possible comments about favorites, strange words or flowers. "You mustn't blame yourself."

Okay. She hadn't been expecting that. "Dad, it's me, Shelby," she clarified just in case.

"I know. Don't blame yourself," he repeated. "You're not the reason your mother died."

Everything inside her went still. "Uh, what?" she asked.

"Your mother," he said as if that explained everything. "Not your fault that she was leaving us."

"Uh, what?" Shelby repeated.

Nothing. Her father's eyelids lowered, and he went back to sleep.

"Sorry, but your time's up," the doctor told her.

She shook her head to clear it and started walking. That had been the fastest two minutes of her life. And in some ways, the longest. What the heck had he meant? She wanted to believe it was just some fragment of a dream that had fallen out of the drug haze, but it had felt like so much more.

Shelby still hadn't managed to shake off the haze when she made it back to the waiting room. Only Callen and Rosy were still there, though.

"Judd took the kids back to the ranch," Rosy explained. "He'll stay there tonight so you and I can get some rest."

That was good. She wouldn't have to worry about the kids. But she did have to worry about what her father had told her.

"Are you okay?" Callen asked.

"No." In hindsight, she should have gone for some of the fake "all is well," but Shelby didn't feel so well. "Dad said I shouldn't blame myself for my mother leaving. You two don't know anything about that, do you?"

Their silent stares weren't from surprise, she decided. No. That was more of a deer-in-the-headlights look. Looks that turned to glances that Callen and Rosy aimed at each other.

"You two don't know anything, do you?" Shelby repeated.

It was Callen who broke the silence, and he dragged in a long breath. "Come on, Shelby. Let me take you home so we can talk."

As they walked out, Shelby heard Rosy mutter, "Oh dear."

CHAPTER SEVENTEEN

CALLEN FIGURED HE was the worst person to deliver the kind of news that he was about to deliver to Shelby, and that was why he wanted to do everything he could to soften the blow.

He was going to use booze.

Perhaps sex.

Whatever it took to keep her from falling apart. She was already fragile and worn-out from Buck's surgery, and hearing something like this could send her right over the edge.

She didn't press him for information as he drove her home. Probably because she knew what was coming was yet another bombshell. Worse, it was another of Buck's secrets that Callen hadn't spilled to her. Realizing that had him rethinking sex. Sex probably wasn't going to happen, so the booze was going to have to do double duty.

When Callen reached her house, he got her inside and helped her out of her coat before taking off his own. Still no questions, and she sat obediently on the sofa after he led her there.

With her hands folded in her lap, her eyes tracked

him as he went to the kitchen and grabbed the bottle of Irish whiskey that he'd noticed the morning he had made coffee. The cat was there, sitting by a nearly empty food and water dish and glaring at Callen as if he were responsible for multiple crimes against felines and humanity. Since he was feeling guilty about withholding yet another secret, Callen located the cat food in the pantry and dumped some on top of the dish. He then filled the water bowl.

That didn't appease Elvira, and with an annoyed flick of her tail, she sauntered away. Perhaps plotting his demise.

He brought the bottle of whiskey and two shot glasses to the living room, and he filled both before setting the bottle on the table. He dragged over a chair so he could sit facing her.

"Don't baby me," she said, breaking the silence, and surprising him. "I know you have something heart-wrenching and possibly life destroying to tell me, but you don't have to baby me."

"Okay." Taking her at her word, Callen drank both shots. He doubted that actually qualified as anti-babying, but he could use the booze to steady his own nerves.

"Say it fast," she insisted.

He nodded and went with fast. "Your mother was leaving your dad the night she was killed in a car accident. She was going to divorce him. Buck didn't tell you because he was worried you'd blame yourself because you and your mom had apparently argued right before she left."

Shelby just kept staring at him, and he hoped she was trying to process that rather than going into shock. It was actually a relief when she finally moved. She poured herself a drink and took it in one gulp.

"Okay," she muttered. He thought her speaking was a good idea, but then she started repeating it. The first three times wasn't that alarming, but when it continued, Callen worried that "the edge" was right there, waiting for her to go over.

He got out of the chair, kneeling in front of her, and he took hold of her shoulders. "What happened wasn't your fault."

She finally stopped repeating "okay" and looked at him. "I was a pain in the ass during those days. Moody and bitchy. I argued with her at the drop of a hat."

Yes, he remembered some of those arguments. "You were a teenager," he reminded her. "Hat-dropping arguments come with the territory."

She shook her head, and he could tell she was about to launch into a guilt trip, so he cupped her chin and forced her to make eye contact. "Your mom and Buck argued, too. I'm guessing your mom left because she just wanted a different life."

"One without me," Shelby concluded.

"One without anything she had here," he amended. "Maybe she felt she didn't have a choice about that, that she had to go to keep her sanity or something."

"Like you. You had to leave."

Callen didn't even try to argue that. Because it was true.

"And you still need to leave," she added. "You still need that other life to keep you sane."

Callen frowned. He darn sure hadn't wanted the conversation to swing in this direction. "The old baggage made it hard for me to be here," he admitted.

"*Makes* it hard," she corrected him. "I saw you when you were looking around the hospital, and I knew you were thinking about when you'd first come to the ranch. About your injuries. About Nico's."

He had indeed been thinking that, and since Shelby was clearly so tuned in to his emotions, it seemed stupid to keep his memories about that under wraps.

"You left because everywhere you go, there are things to trigger the past for you," Shelby went on.

Again, he couldn't argue about that, but he could try to get this chat back on track. This wasn't about him, but it sure seemed as if Shelby was setting him up for something. Maybe she was about to tell him that it was okay for him to leave. Maybe she was going to push him away. For his own good, of course. But it wouldn't be good for her right now. Not with her stewing in this emotional bog.

"My situation was different from your mom's," he assured her. "I seriously doubt she would have given up seeing you. I figure she would have gotten the divorce, and then split custody. She would have still been your mother."

Shelby went quiet again, hopefully considering— and believing—that. "How long have you known?"

Actually, Callen had hoped she wouldn't consider *that*. "Not long. Buck told me after I came back."

"After he told you about the tumor, something he was keeping from everyone else," she summarized. Shelby's eyebrow lifted. "Are there any more of Dad's secrets you're keeping?"

"No." Thank God. Two had been plenty enough.

"You're sure?" she pressed, and he couldn't blame her for not trusting him. "What about when you were in the recovery room with him? No two-minute secret revelations in there?"

Callen shrugged and even managed a little smile. "Only that I'm his favorite kid." Best to add the other part in case Buck did a tell-all. "And that you were falling in love with me."

Her eyes widened, filled with surprise, and he didn't think it was because of the favorite-kid part. *Hell*.

"Buck was drugged," Callen added in reminder. "He didn't know what he was saying."

She stared at him. Nodded. "Yes, he did. I am falling in love with you."

Now it was Callen's turn for wide eyes—and a hefty side of skepticism. Considering the other part of the conversation they'd just had about baggage, leaving for sanity's sake, etc., this felt like a ploy to get him running. No way could he do that, not with Shelby's emotional state, but it confirmed to him that sex was indeed off the table.

Or not.

Shelby hooked her arm around his neck, yanked him to her, and she kissed him. Definitely not the reaction he'd been expecting, and while kissing her always felt right, it was wrong. And Callen needed to tell her that while his head was still clear. Or rather clear-ish since the kiss was already taking its toll.

He tore his mouth from hers and made eye contact again. "Shelby, you're upset. Rightfully so. You're tired, and you're not thinking straight."

She made a quick sound of agreement. Then tacked on a sound of disagreement, too. "I'm upset and tired. And I'm using you. Or at least I would if you'd hush and kiss me."

Oh man. This was not what he wanted. Well, a certain part of him did, but that part was stupid. "Sex might not be the way to go here." Though it pained him to say it.

"It'd be a distraction. One I need. One you probably need, too. There's no harm in that."

And she kissed him again.

The taste of her slammed through him, and the slamming continued when she moved off the sofa and into his arms. Body to body, in an off-balancing kind of way since he was still kneeling. He bobbled to keep them from tumbling over, but that turned out to be a mistake, too, because it caused her breasts to slide against his chest.

Now he was the one who was distracted, and his willpower was spiraling down in a nosedive. Definitely not good. Still, Callen managed to break the lip-lock again long enough to speak. He probably should have considered first, though, what stellar argument he could use to get Shelby to reconsider this.

"Uh" was what he managed.

Not exactly his fault, though, for the nonstellar response. There was a contributing circumstance when the sliding continued, and her lower body brushed against the front of his jeans. The next contributing circumstance, however, came from the nudge she gave him. A wicked, willpower-draining nudge that nearly caused his eyes to cross.

"I'd rather not talk if you don't mind," she said. Had her voice taken on a silky sex tone, or was that his imagination?

It was her actual voice.

Callen became sure of that when he realized there wasn't enough thought power left in his brain to have an imagination. His dick had got in on this, and common sense and such vanished with his erection.

"You'd better have a condom," Shelby added, obviously breaking her own *don't talk* rule.

Callen nodded but couldn't mention that he had two in his wallet because he kissed her. Yeah, he was weak, but her mouth was right there in front of him. Her hot, sultry mouth that urged him on when she deepened the kiss.

He did some deepening, too. And touching. Again, because she was right there, he slid his hand between them and ran his fingers over her nipples. They weren't hard to find because they were puckered and tight, straining against her bra and top. He helped with that by yanking off her top and shoving down her bra. He helped himself by lowering the kiss to her nipples.

Very sensitive nipples, he soon discovered.

She moaned, the same silky sex tone as her voice, and Shelby threw back her head, surrendering to the pleasure. But she didn't *just* surrender. Her now-bowed body smushed her zipper to his, which in turned pressed his erection in the one place it wanted to be. Minus their clothes, of course.

Callen would have been content to delay the clothing removal while he nibbled at her nipples, but the urgency kicked in for Shelby. The need for him to give her more than just his tongue and mouth. She gave him a clear signal by putting her hand on his dick and squeezing. She added some sliding moves in there, too, her hand working him hard enough that the urgency soared for him, too.

Callen shifted, putting his arms around her so he could drag them both to the floor. He considered the bed, briefly considered it, but he doubted Shelby was going to wait for that. She was already unzipping him and landing some damn effective if not manic kisses on his neck.

He had to pause what he was sure were some damn effective kisses of his own so that he could get her out of her clothes. He had a head start above the waist, but he went after her jeans. Not his finest finessing effort to undress a woman. That was because of her boots. They had to come off first before he could peel off her jeans and panties.

And he found exactly what he wanted.

Callen would have landed a few kisses there, too, but Shelby's string of profanity grabbed his attention. She'd got off his belt but was struggling with his boots. With a final curse word, she gave up, unzipped him and freed him from his boxers. Judging from the way she took hold of him, the rest of his clothes were going to stay on.

"Condom," she ground out, taking his wallet from his back pocket. And just in case he'd missed the urgency, she proceeded to kiss and suck his neck to let him know she wanted this to happen now.

Since that only whipped up an even-bigger fire inside him, Callen tried to give her *now* as fast as he could. He got on the condom. How, he didn't know. It wasn't easy doing such a complex task with a kissing, moaning, naked woman beneath him.

Especially this woman.

Shelby was his definition of urgency and whipped-up fire.

Because he was finally in the right position, he

kissed her when he plunged into her, and his mouth caught one of those incredible moans of pleasure. Man, he'd remember that for a long time. He'd remember the rest of it, too.

There was pleasure, of course. So much pleasure. That kick of a primal need so strong that it made everything else melt away. It pinpointed his focus to her, just her, and the maddening strokes that would feed the need, along with making this end all too soon.

He could slow it some by easing up on the thrusts, but Shelby didn't make that easy for him when he tried it. She lifted her hips, hooking her legs around him and pushing him in deeper. To give herself what she needed.

Her climax didn't come as a ripple but more like a flash fire. Instant, hot. Thorough. Her long moan of pleasure turned to one of relief. The pressure-cooker heat was sated, for the time being, anyway.

Callen had to fight to stop her climax from giving him his own flash fire. All those wet muscles tightening and pulsing around his erection. Hard to fight it when his body just wanted to surrender. Still, he held on a little longer so he could kiss her and taste the relief and pleasure she'd just taken from him.

He gathered her in his arms, dropped his face into the curve of her neck and finally let go.

NAKED, SHELBY LAY in bed and listened to the sound of the water as Callen took a shower. She'd considered joining him in there but had wanted a few moments to herself to work out the muddle going on in her head.

Way too much muddle.

But she knew it would have been a whole lot worse without the sex. Callen was likely feeling as if he'd taken advantage of her or some such nonsense. But it was just that—nonsense. She'd wanted to be with him, a sort of cleansing the mental palate, and it had worked like a charm. A good orgasm was priceless. A good orgasm from Callen was priceless and…

Complicated.

Not for her. Shelby had already worked out her feelings in that area. She wanted him, and he seemed willing to fulfill her want in a very incredible way.

However, Callen was a decent man, and he would no doubt go on a guilt trip. Not just for having sex with her when she was at a low point but also because he would know she was dealing with the fallout from her father's latest secret.

Sheez. Who knew Buck could be so sneaky? And enlist Callen in that sneakiness? Well, she certainly knew it now. Shelby also knew something else. Something that would add to that complicated set of feelings Callen was having right about now.

I am falling in love with you.

She winced. She probably could have come up with a different way of reacting to what her father had mumbled to Callen when they'd visited in the recovery room. A chuckle at the absurdity of it would have done it. Or maybe just a gaping, stunned silence. Instead, she had said those words. Words that struck fear into the hearts of men like Callen.

Obviously, though, sex had overcome that fear some, thank goodness. Now maybe the orgasm had helped soothe him as much as it had her. If not, she would go for a second round of sex. He'd left his wallet on the nightstand, and she could see another condom peeking out of it.

And she could also see Elvira peeking around the door as if checking to make sure it was all clear so she could hog her portion of the bed. Shelby could have sworn the cat rolled her feline eyes when Callen came out of the bathroom. Elvira meowed what could only be a protest and sauntered away.

Shelby certainly didn't protest. Callen smelled great. Looked great, too, with his hair all damp and tousled. But the best part was that he was wearing only a towel. One that was barely large enough to cover the parts of him he'd tried to cover. When he walked toward her, Shelby got an incredible peep show.

"You look...distracted," he said.

She just kept her focus on the peeping. "I am." She didn't meet his eyes until he sat on the bed next to her. "You're the best possible distraction."

Unlike her *I am falling in love with you*, that made

him smile. Of course it did. It smacked of lust rather than any kind of complication.

He leaned in, gave her a scorcher of a kiss and was still smiling when he pulled back. Smiling and studying her as if trying to figure out if the distraction sex had helped or hurt.

It had definitely helped.

"I used to fantasize about you when you were still at the ranch," she admitted. "But with my then-limited fantasy fodder, it only involved kisses and getting naked."

His eyebrow rose. "How old were you when you had these fantasies?"

"Age thirteen to sixteen. And then when you left the ranch, age sixteen to…now."

She caught his naughty chuckle with her mouth when she kissed him, and she made a naughty sound of her own when she flicked that towel off his hips and pulled him to her.

Specifically, on top of her.

If she'd planned it better, she would have tossed back the sheet covering her, but that could happen later. For now, she just kissed him and slid her hands and fingers along his bare back. Oh, the muscles. How they quivered and reacted to her touch. Especially the ones on his superior butt. She kept it slow and easy, but it was definitely rebuilding a fire.

Callen took over the kissing, giving her an amazing one before he lifted his head and looked down at her. "Are you okay?" he asked.

It didn't kill the mood. That would have been next to impossible. But Shelby felt the downer nudge that she was going to have to answer him rather than move the sheet and have her way with him.

"I'm fine," she said, but he was going to want details. "I don't blame myself for my mother leaving, but I wish my dad had told me."

He studied her a moment longer. "Are you mad at him? At me?"

She had to consider that. "Neither. I'm sure it'll cause me some low moments, but I think it's worse right now because it came on the heels of Dad's surgery."

Callen sighed, brushed a kiss on the corner of her mouth. "I'm sorry you had to find out this way."

If she could have shrugged she would have, but with Callen on top of her that would have been hard to do. "I suspect my dad will feel bad about the way he spilled it." And she paused. "Which is why I don't want you to say anything about it. I doubt he'll remember it, and we can maybe just keep it between us until he's recovered."

His eyebrow came up again. "Are you asking me to keep a secret?"

"I am," she admitted. "There's just something about you. A secret magnet." She paused. "You're sure you're not keeping any others?"

"Positive. No others."

"Not even secrets about Christmas presents?" she teased.

He got that startled look. An oh-shit. "I haven't really had time to shop yet. Or to tell Havana to shop for me."

"No worries. I haven't had time, either." Though she wouldn't mention she had ordered some things from the internet. Including a gift for Callen.

He continued to study her, brushing a strand of hair from her cheek while looking deep in her eyes.

Uh-oh.

She could feel it coming. And it came, all right.

"You told me you were falling in love with me," he said, his words slow and cautious. Shelby bet he'd practiced saying this in the shower. "You did that to push me away."

The relief that came was almost as good as an orgasm. Almost. "Yes!" she said with entirely too much enthusiasm. "But it clearly didn't work because here you are in my bed, wearing only your birthday suit and a smile."

And he was indeed smiling. Probably from relief, too, but it could have also had something to do with her hand sliding down between them to find him hard, huge and ready.

He gave a very manly grunt of approval and pleasure but still managed to ask, "So, we're okay?"

"Absolutely. Callen, don't worry. I'm not falling in love with you."

Not a lie. That was because she was *already* in love with him.

But thankfully Shelby had no chance to blurt that out because of Callen's well-timed, speech-robbing kiss.

CHAPTER EIGHTEEN

ONCE AGAIN SHELBY found herself pacing and waiting. This time for the results of her father's biopsy.

She could say with absolute certainty that pacing/
waiting wasn't nearly as stress relieving as sex with
Callen. Since sex couldn't happen, though, in her dad's
hospital room, pacing was her most suitable outlet.

Callen wasn't pacing with her this time. He was
standing behind a seated Rosy, who was going over
details of tables and floral arrangements for the reception. She'd done charts for both venues, the hospital cafeteria and the inn. Heck, Rosy had done charts
for pretty much everything, but the one thing not in
her plans was postponing this wedding. As far as
Rosy was concerned, this wedding and reception
were going full speed ahead.

Shelby was somewhat less convinced of that.

Her father's color was better, and he was sitting
up now, but he had just had surgery, and with the
wedding only four days away, she didn't believe
that would be enough recovery time. Neither did
Dr. Breland.

When Shelby and the doctor had voiced their

concerns—multiple times—Rosy had simply made another chart showing Shelby and anyone else who'd look suitable paths for Buck to be wheeled down the respective aisle. Buck had agreed with everything his bride had suggested even when the suggestion was a questionable one.

"Billy will go here," Rosy said, pointing out the armadillo's spot in the seating arrangement.

Both Callen and Buck looked at it as if it were riveting information, but Shelby suspected their minds were on what was occupying hers. The test results that would either have them limp with fear or limp with relief.

She was counting heavily on the latter.

It caused her stomach to jitter to think that in the next few minutes, their lives could turn on a dime. If it was cancer… But Shelby cut off that thought before it could fully form. Something she'd been doing for the past two days. Thankfully, Callen had cooperated with an adequate amount of sex to help keep her distracted.

And he'd also helped by not mentioning that whole *l*-word issue again.

Shelby didn't want that to change. She didn't want that to play into anything that was happening here or that would happen in four days. When the wedding was over, Callen needed to feel that she wasn't going to lapse into a puddle of tears when he packed up and went back to Dallas. And she wouldn't do that.

Well, not until after he'd left, anyway.

Then all bets were off.

Callen still had some favors to do for her dad. One favor, anyway. Finding a good home for Lucy and Mateo. So far, he seemed to have a big goose egg when it came to that, but she knew he was trying. Havana had mentioned it, too, when she'd said Callen had been making daily calls to his social-worker friend.

Shelby didn't know what Callen would do if a home for the kids didn't pan out, but he wouldn't just ditch the duty. That meant she'd need to get involved. She'd have to agree to take Lucy and Mateo so that Callen could get on with his life in Dallas.

That jittered her stomach, too. Sometimes, love sucked.

"We're up to forty-one bridesmaids now," Rosy said, beaming. "I bought them all little Santa earrings and necklaces, and they'll each be carrying a poinsettia instead of a bouquet."

Apparently, size mattered to Rosy when it came to bridal parties, though Shelby wondered if anyone would be able to see the bride with all those maids cluttered around. Still, if this wedding went off according to either one of the plans, it would be sort of a family reunion/wedding/Christmas Eve celebration.

Shelby was still in the pacing mode when the door opened and Dr. Breland walked in. Even though they'd all been expecting the doctor, there was sort of a stunned silence that fell over the room, and all of them combed their gazes over the doc's face as if trying to get a preview of what he was about to tell them.

Dr. Breland shut the door and stepped in the center of the room. "It's cancer," he said.

For two little words, they sure packed a nasty wallop, and Shelby was wishing she'd been sitting for it.

Cancer.

Her father had cancer.

She caught onto the bed rail and tried not to look scared out of her mind. That wouldn't help her father or anyone else.

"I'm sorry," Dr. Breland added, his attention on Buck now.

Rosy muttered her usual "Oh dear," while Callen pressed his hand on her shoulder. Callen was obviously trying to stave off a "scared out of his mind" look, too, but the muscles tightened and flexed in his jaw.

"We believe we got all the cancer during the surgery," the doctor went on. "That's the good news, but there's an asterisk. Buck will need treatment, both radiation and chemo. And, no, it shouldn't wait until after the wedding," he said when Buck opened his mouth.

The good news was, well, beyond good even with the asterisk. They'd got the cancer. They'd got it. The relief of that weakened her knees even more, but Shelby managed to go to her father so she could be closer to him.

"I'm not going to die from this," Buck murmured.

So much relief there, too, and it made her realize just how well he'd been covering his worry. She wanted to both kiss him and throttle him for that.

Shelby went with the kiss, and she held on to him, hugging him and whispering a prayer of thanks. It went along with all those other prayers she'd already sent up for him.

Rosy also went in for a hug and kiss, spreading that to Callen and her, and they spent a couple of moments just gathering their breaths.

"What are the symptoms of the treatments?" Callen asked the doctor after he'd gathered his.

"It varies from patient to patient. Fatigue and nausea are the most common. It could compromise Buck's immune system, so it wouldn't be a good idea for him to be around a lot of people."

"Well," Rosy said. "Well," she repeated, and there wasn't so much of her usual rosiness now.

Her dad's deeply sorrowed expression mirrored that, and he muttered soft words of apology to Rosy. Giving her comfort. Comfort that he extended to Callen and her with long looks.

Great. Shelby had thought the worst would be just hearing and dealing with the diagnosis, but this was smearing bad news with grief.

"Maybe you two could get married here in the hospital room," Shelby heard herself say. Yep, it was her idea, all right, and this after she'd tried to talk her dad and Rosy into postponing. Apparently now, she was going to offer a solution that was the opposite of a postponement.

All of them turned to Shelby, clearly waiting for more, and she saw something in her dad's and Rosy's faces. Hope. So she kept trying to dole out more.

"We could bring in cameras," Shelby explained, "and fix them so the wedding guests can watch the service from the inn. Sort of a virtual wedding."

Rosy slowly bobbed her head, and the bobbing got faster and more enthusiastic. "I could wear my dress and a pink mask so that I don't get my germs on Buck."

Her father brightened a little, too. "And the reception could still go on at the inn. Maybe someone could rig a camera so we could watch from here."

"We could bring over cake and food from the reception," Callen suggested.

Rosy beamed now, and Shelby could tell her head was filling with adjustments and such. "Callen, you could throw my garter for Buck, and Shelby could throw the bouquet for me. That'd work better than Buck and me tossing them around to each other in a hospital room."

Callen didn't look especially thrilled at garter throwing duties, but he probably would have agreed to anything at that point.

Her father wasn't going to die. This cancer wasn't going to kill him.

Yes, that was worth celebrating.

Callen's phone buzzed, and his forehead bunched

up when he looked at the screen. "Excuse me for a second. I need to take this," he said, and he stepped out into the hall.

Rosy continued the plans without him. "The minister would have to wear a mask, too, and maybe I can sanitize Billy so he could be our little ring bearer."

Buck didn't seem so jazzed about that, but he was still smiling. So was the doctor. "I'll be back later to go over the treatments," Dr. Breland told them, and he headed out just as Callen was coming back in.

"I've got more good news," Callen said, putting his phone away. The words were right, but there was something in his expression that let Shelby know that this was maybe going to be another round of good news with an asterisk. "CPS thinks they might have found a great home for Lucy and Mateo."

Rosy made a gasp of happiness, pressed her hands to her heart and then gave Callen a hug. "You did it," Rosy said. "You did exactly what Buck asked you to do."

He had indeed. It would be wonderful for the kids. The start of what could be a normal, safe and happy future. There was no way Shelby could feel any sadness about that. Even if she did for the most selfish of reasons.

Because this meant that once the wedding was over, there'd be no reason for Callen to stay.

That was one heck of an asterisk.

THREE DAYS. THAT deadline kept repeating like a broken record in Callen's head. In three days Buck and Rosy would be married, and in less than that, Lucy and Mateo could be in their permanent home.

Could be, Callen silently emphasized.

He had practically memorized the copy of the report that Lizbeth had sent him on the family who wanted Buck's kids. Sarah and Dan Millhouse. They were in their late thirties and were financially stable with Dan being a lawyer and Sarah a music teacher. They had one other child, an eight-year-old girl, Katie, who they'd adopted when she was two.

There wasn't a single red flag in the report, and Callen had looked hard for one. So had CPS and Lizbeth, who had already vetted the couple. The only thing left was a meeting so that both the family and the kids could see if the fit on paper was the right fit in reality.

Callen added the date and time of that meeting in bold letters on his agenda. Tomorrow at 1:00 pm. He wouldn't miss it, and neither would Shelby, Nico or Rosy. No Buck, though, since he'd be starting his first treatment right about then. But they would stand in for him.

If things went well with the first visit, there'd be a second meeting the following day at the Millhouse home in San Antonio. After that, Lucy and Mateo would move in for a trial period with the couple and their daughter. Callen suspected that could happen as soon as the wedding was over. Maybe even on

Christmas Day. CPS was pushing for sooner rather than later because of Buck's health problems. It would prevent them from moving the kids into a temporary home—which CPS would legally be required to do.

So much uncertainty.

Along with some certainty, too. Nico had stepped up to the proverbial plate and was going to put the rodeo on hold so he could take care of the ranch until Buck got back on his feet. Judd would pitch in there, as well. And Kace. In fact, they'd worked out a schedule.

One that hadn't included Callen after Christmas Eve.

Callen dragged in a deep breath at that thought and went back to tackle the mountain of paperwork on his desk. However, he didn't get far before Havana appeared in the doorway. Her hair was red today with a scattering of green bows, and she was carrying what appeared to be a miniature Christmas tree under her arm.

"Before you say no," she greeted him, "just give it a chance. You really need some merriment in this office."

Havana's idea of merriment wasn't the same as his. She plopped the tree on his desk, waved her hands in front of it, and a pair of big mechanical eyes opened in the branches. A mechanical mouth opening followed, though it was actually just a horizonal slit on the lower part of the tree. It began to jiggle, sway and sing "We Wish You a Merry Christmas."

"It's more traditional than the stuffed Santa you kicked," Havana explained. "And it plays a variety of songs."

There was nothing traditional about a singing/dancing Christmas tree, but Callen had complained so much since they'd been here that he choked back the words that would cause Havana to call him Scrooge or Ebenezer again.

However, he did have to add, "There'd better be a way to turn it off."

"Oh, there is. It's motion-activated." She waved her hand in front of it, and the music stopped. The slit mouth closed, and the eyeballs disappeared back into the branches. "So, you won't kick this one?" she asked cautiously.

"The jury's still out on that, but it can stay for now."

She smiled, and then bobbled her eyes in a way that made him think of the tree. "If you're this agreeable, you must be getting lucky with Shelby."

Lucky was a complex label for it. Yes, he was having sex with her, and it had indeed improved his mood. Callen was pretty sure it was doing the same for her, along with taking her mind off Buck's treatments. So all was well.

Except that it wasn't.

Three days went through his head again. It was entirely possible that everything he needed to do here would be done by then. He'd pack up, leaving the singing Christmas tree behind, and go back to Dallas. As planned.

"As planned," he repeated in a mumble under his breath.

Havana gave him a questioning glance and was probably about to grill him on it, but he waved his hand in front of the tree to get it singing.

"Sneaky," she concluded, doing the hand wave to get it to stop. "But I was only going to mention that you haven't done any Christmas shopping yet. It's December 21."

He figured she'd said that to stir some urgency in him. It didn't. "That means I have four more days." Or rather three since he could be leaving on Christmas Day.

"Less," Havana corrected. "With the wedding on Christmas Eve, you'll be too busy to shop that day. Plus, all the stores here will close early. Some won't be open at all."

"Then I'll shop at the ones that will be open." And Callen went back to work. Or rather tried to do that.

Havana, however, didn't take his work cue. "You'll need gifts for your brothers, for Lucy and Mateo. For Rosy and Buck. And Shelby, of course. If you wait much longer, the selection around here won't be much of a selection at all. You might get stuck giving Pringles, Tic Tacs and beer from the Quik Mart."

True. But his brothers might appreciate Pringles and beer.

"I can help if you want," Havana offered. "I can

use the sites I normally use to order gifts you give, and I can have them sent express mail."

Callen was somewhat embarrassed that he didn't even know what gifts had been sent "from him" over the years. In Buck's case, it had probably been something expensive.

And impersonal.

"I'll take care of it," he told her, though he wasn't sure how. This might require one of those Christmas miracles. Or settling for Pringles, Tic Tacs and beer.

"Wow. I might have to give you a different nickname. Of course, Scrooge changed, so I guess it still applies." She headed for the door, then paused. "Your two o'clock appointment's running late, but he should be here soon. I'll send him up when he gets in."

Callen made a sound to indicate he'd heard her, and he closed Lizbeth's report on his computer so he could get back to work reading the financials that his CFO had sent him. Normally, the numbers pleased him—because money meant security and comfort— but he put that aside and moved on to a contract for a land lease he needed for an especially large lot of cattle he'd arranged to buy.

Head 'em up, move 'em out.

He continued reading through the contract even after he heard the footsteps on the stairs. His two o'clock, Gus Hernandez, who obviously hadn't run late as Havana had said. Callen looked up when the footsteps reached his doorway. And he did a double take.

Not Gus.

But someone else Callen instantly recognized. Someone he damn sure didn't want to see.

Avis Odell walked through the doorway of Callen's office.

"Sonofabitch," Callen spit out, and because he suddenly found himself short of words, he grumbled it again.

It'd been seventeen years since he'd seen this snake, but time dissolved. Not the memories, though. Not the pain. Those two things came back with a vengeance.

Avis stood there, taking up most of the doorway with his wide shoulders and six-six height. The years had not been kind to Avis even though he was only about a decade older than Callen. Hard to believe Avis had only been in his early twenties when he'd nearly killed Nico, but the man had been a thug even then.

He hadn't thought it possible, but the slime coming off the man had gone up some notches. Greasy blond hair and wrinkled clothes straining over his beer gut and the huge bulky muscles that had gone partly to flab. The smile he flashed Callen let him know that Avis wasn't fond of brushing and flossing.

Callen tamped down the bile that churned in his stomach. And the flashbacks. He tried to tamp those down, too, but part of him—a part he hated—would always be that kid who Avis had stomped into the ground. Callen wanted to punch him, but he considered if he'd be able to stop at just one punch.

No.

With this rage eating away at him, he could end up doing to Avis what the man had nearly done to Nico and him.

"What the fuck do you want?" Callen snarled as he got to his feet, and the snarl would have been much more effective if the movement hadn't set off the singing tree. It launched into a jaunty rendition of "Jingle Bells."

Avis grinned as if amused. Entertained, even. But Callen put a stop to that. Even though he'd indicated to Havana that he wouldn't punch this particular part of the Christmas decor, that was exactly what Callen did. The tree shut up.

"I just wanted to pay you a friendly visit," Avis said. "I read something in the newspaper about Buck McCall's wedding. Some interview his bride-to-be had given, and she mentioned that you'd come back here to Podunk."

Avis would have taken the seat next to Callen's desk, but Callen kicked it out of the way, too, and it crashed against the wall. "The next thing I go after is you," Callen warned him. "Get out. There'll be no friendly visits between us."

"Now, now. You might want to reconsider that. Might want to consider a lot of things—like why I came to you and not one of your brothers. If Judd sees me, he'll likely take a swing at me and lose his badge. He never lived under my roof, but from what I've heard, he's got a hot head. Kace might try to run me out of town and end up having to give up his badge, too. And Nico. Poor Nico. Think of all the bad memories he'll have of our time together."

Hell. Sonofabitch. And shit.

The rage came harder, hot and raw, and he wanted nothing more than to beat this snake to a pulp. He couldn't, of course.

Well, not unless Avis threw the first punch, that was.

Then it wouldn't put Kace and Judd in a legal bind of having to arrest their brother for taking care of the trash. Callen moved out from behind his desk to give Avis a shot at doing just that.

Avis kept his hands in the pockets of his ratty jeans. "I want money," he calmly announced. "Fifty grand should do it. That's chump change for a guy like you. In exchange I won't disrupt Buck's wedding, your brothers' lives or mess with any of your Christmas plans. I'll be on my merry way."

It took a couple of seconds for Callen to get his jaw unclenched. "Blackmail?"

Avis made a sound as if Callen had totally misinterpreted. "No. Payment for you and your brother living under my roof."

"It wasn't your roof," Callen snapped. "You were just fucking the woman who was supposed to be taking care of us. She didn't. She allowed you to use your fists on us."

Avis readily nodded. "My old, wicked ways. But I did my time in jail and paid for what I did."

He could never pay enough. *Never*.

Callen looked him straight in the eyes. "I'm not giving you a cent."

Avis shrugged, smiled. "You might want to re-think that. I'll give you some time. A couple of days. See you Christmas Eve, Callen."

And with that, Avis walked out.

CHAPTER NINETEEN

CALLEN STOOD THERE, trying to rein in the rage. All that old shit came flying at him until he knew there'd be no reining today. He headed for the door, triggering the soon-to-be-dead tree to start singing "Rudolph the Red-Nosed Reindeer."

"Cancel my two o'clock," he called out to Havana, and it sent his assistant running to the doorway of her own office. "And get rid of the damn tree."

Along with some sounds of extreme disappointment—for the tree—she also added, "Are you, uh, okay?" That question was for the canceled appointment and his storming down the stairs.

Callen didn't answer her because, no, he wasn't okay. He was too pissed off to see straight. But he seriously doubted that was going to affect the fist that he wanted to shove in Avis Odell's face.

He threw open the inn door, the cold air giving him a jolt while he braced himself to face Avis. But the man was nowhere in sight. Callen hurried to the inn parking lot. Not there. He shifted his gaze from one side of the street to the other. He saw plenty of people, most calling out some kind of holiday greeting, but no Avis.

Shit.

Callen stood there, trying to figure out where a snake would crawl. Maybe he'd just driven off. And was waiting to come back tomorrow. Callen would give him the same answer. No way in hell was he going to pay up. But in the meantime, Avis might make trouble.

He took out his phone to call Kace but reconsidered that. His brother had a full plate right now between his job as sheriff, running his own small ranch and helping out Buck. Besides, Kace or Judd might indeed take a swing at the man, and if they did, they could lose their badges.

That left Nico, and there was no way Callen would call him. Nico was the least likely of them to punch somebody, but Avis was right. Just the jolt of seeing him could be hell for Nico.

Since he wasn't ready to go back in, Callen walked up the street to see if Avis had stepped into one of the shops. And he practically ran into someone else he didn't want to see today.

Gavin.

"Get the hell out of my way," Callen snapped. And if Gavin didn't listen, he would catch the brunt of Callen's temper.

"Sorry." Gavin held up his hands. Strange hands. Or rather strange gloves. There were snowmen stitched on each of the fingertips. Girlie snowmen with puffy scarves and stuff. It took some of the fight out of Callen because he knew there was no way he could slug Gavin when he was wearing shit like that.

"Oh. A gift from my grandmother," Gavin said when he followed Callen's gaze. He lowered his hands. "I was just coming by to see you. I want to apologize."

"Save it because I don't want to hear it." Callen might not have the option to slug Gavin, but that didn't mean he had to be nice to him.

Gavin stepped in front of him when Callen started to walk away, and it had Callen rethinking his notion about slugging him. There was a lot of dangerous energy bubbling up inside him, and bashing in Gavin's face might help with that.

"Accept the apology," Gavin said. "Please."

Callen hadn't wanted the *please* to play into this. And it wouldn't have, had it not been for Gavin's sincere look that went along with it.

"I was wrong about a lot of things," Gavin added. "I know what I say won't have much weight with you right now, but it won't happen again." He held out his snowman hand for Callen to shake.

Callen debated whether to shake his hand or break it. But the cold had drained some of the hot temper. Besides, he didn't want to continue having a pissing contest with Gavin because it might come back on Shelby.

And that was the reason Callen went for the shake,

but he made it a hard one so that Gavin winced a little.

"Say, I know it's none of my business, but it's cold out here," Gavin said, pulling back his hand and giving it a little wiggle. No doubt to get rid of some of the numbness. "Shouldn't you be wearing a coat?"

Yeah. He should. But his temper hadn't chilled nearly as much as his body, and Callen wasn't ready to go back inside the inn just yet.

So, he started walking with no particular destination in mind. Then he stopped outside the window of Ted's and glanced in at the display necklace and creepy Russian nesting dolls. The same ones that'd been there for at least seventeen years. It was probably his rotten mood, but it riled Callen that nothing had changed. Of course, pretty much anything was going to rile him at the moment, so he jerked open the door and went inside.

"I'll buy the necklace and the dolls," Callen snapped. His tone definitely wasn't one of Christmas shopping merriment.

Ted Barlow was sitting behind the counter of a glass display case, and he blinked in surprise when he looked up from the book he was reading. His mouth fell open.

"I want to buy them," Callen repeated. "Now, take them out of the window and put something else in there."

A therapist would have had a field day with that,

but with his mood, Callen might have punched the therapist, too.

Still wide-eyed with surprise, which might have been bordering on shock, Ted hurried to the window. Well, as much as a man in his eighties could hurry, and reaching into the display, he started scooping up the items to bring them to the counter next to the old-fashioned cash register.

"If you want these wrapped, it'll cost extra," Ted said.

Callen hadn't actually considered what to do with them now that he was about to be the owner, but wrapping was a good option. "Yes, wrap them and have them taken over to my room at the inn."

With the shock/surprise wearing off some, Ted smiled, and Callen could practically see the dollar signs in the man's eyes. "Who's this for so I know what name to put on the gift card?" Ted asked.

Another good question, but it didn't take Callen long to come up with "Rosy." She would appreciate the gold necklace, and he doubted the dolls would creep her out since she was a taxidermist.

Ted nodded with even more enthusiasm when he started ringing up the items. While he did that, Callen looked around, and his attention landed on a pocketknife in the display case. It wasn't flashy, but it had a horse carved into the wood handle.

"That's an antique," Ted explained when he saw what Callen was studying. "It's nice."

Despite Ted's weak sales pitch, Callen was sold. "I want that, too. Wrap it up for Buck."

If Ted's smile got any wider, he might risk dislocating his jaw. Callen figured he was taking the same risk with his scowl, but it was easing up a bit. Plus, he was actually doing some Christmas shopping, something that would please Havana.

And speaking of Havana, Callen spotted some silver and purple stone dangling earrings that looked as if they'd be gaudy and expensive enough for her taste.

"Those, too." Callen motioned toward the earrings.

"Uh, those are a little pricey. Six hundred."

Callen had no idea if that was a reasonable price to pay. Nor did he care. "Ring them up and wrap them," he instructed Ted.

"You want Shelby's name on the card for this one?" Ted asked. "Seems like a nice gift for your girl."

Callen huffed, though he didn't know why. Of course Ted knew about Shelby and him. Everyone did. "No, they're for my assistant, Havana. Double wrap the box, though, because Havana will try to peek when the gifts are delivered."

Of course, the earrings wouldn't replace Havana's usual Christmas bonus, but she might be surprised and pleased that he'd given her an actual present.

Since he was here and apparently on a roll, Callen went to another display case that was crammed full of jewelry, knickknacks and just plain weird stuff. Like pipes carved to look like snakes and a mechanical monkey holding a tambourine. Since the monkey had a switch that would likely turn on that clanging tambourine, Callen nixed buying it. No way did he want to have to listen to that.

However, he did spot something by the cash register.

Shelby's business card. Horse Services: Training, Boarding and Sales.

Sales.

Callen recalled seeing a bay mare and a paint gelding at her place, and he could buy them for Mateo and Lucy. Of course, he'd need to arrange to keep them boarded at Shelby's. But if the home worked out and the kids moved, it would give their new parents a reason to bring them back to Coldwater. That way, they could see Shelby, Rosy and Buck.

With those two names ticked off his list, Callen went to the next display case. Three bronze figures of cowboys. One on a horse, one slinging a lasso and the other hauling a saddle on his shoulder.

"You looking at those for your brothers?" Ted asked. "'Cause they're kind of pricey since they're signed by the artist and all. I can give you a good deal, though. Fifteen hundred for the lot."

"I'll take them," Callen decided, and that left one person on his list. "Shelby," he mumbled under his breath.

Ted beamed again. "I've got a few engagement rings."

Callen scowled. "It's not that kind of..." *Relationship* was the first word that came to Callen's mind with the mental addition of *"It's just sex."* Since Ted was likely to repeat anything he said, Callen settled for saying, "Christmas."

Of course, Ted would just assume that next Christmas would be the right timing for an engagement ring, and he would pass on his assumption as gospel to anyone who'd listen.

"Shelby's not exactly the jewelry-wearing type," Ted concluded. "Not much for antiques, either. You see anything else in here you could get her?"

Good question, and Callen was mindful that anything he picked for her in this shop would also make the gossip rounds, though Ted would likely hold off on that until after Christmas so as to not blow the surprise.

Callen looked at the mishmash of items on the shelf behind the cash register. "I'll take all of those," he said.

This time when Ted's eyes widened, there was some concern in them. Probably because it was a strange mix. A pair of silver nunchucks, a body piercing kit complete with a navel ring, a gumball machine and two stuffed buck-toothed beavers poking their heads out from a stainless-steel barrel.

"For Shelby?" Ted asked. Clearly, the man was perplexed at the possibility.

But Callen just nodded. He'd donate them if he thought of something more suitable to give her. Which shouldn't be hard. Anything else would be more suitable. Still, he was pressed for time, so this might be as good as it got.

"With all this stuff sold, this might be the tipping point for me," Ted said as he rang up the items. "Might just go ahead and close the place." He motioned toward the For Sale sign.

"You'd really sell?" Callen didn't bother to take out the skepticism.

"Sure would. The wife's nagging me to retire. So is my back. It'd be easier to just sit at home in my recliner, reading a good book."

Yes, it would be, but it made Callen wonder if anyone would ever buy the place, and if they did, what kind of business would it become? Probably one that didn't have Russian nesting dolls, bronze statues, knives and Shelby's business card. Other than the dolls, Callen wasn't sure if that would actually be progress or not.

Ted's eyes lit up brighter than a Christmas tree when he saw the total. And with good reason. Those sales for Callen's ten-minute shopping trip probably exceeded what Ted usually made all year.

"Just have everything wrapped and delivered to the inn," Callen reminded him as he swiped his credit card, signed and headed for the door.

"If you change your mind about those engagement rings, just pop back over," Ted called out to him.

Of course, the people passing by the shop heard him. And one of those people was Shelby.

Callen figured it was both bad and good luck that she happened to be walking by at that exact second. His mood still sucked, and he hadn't wanted her to be embarrassed, hopeful, disappointed or whatever the hell else she might feel at the possibility of getting an engagement ring—especially one from Ted's.

However, there wasn't a trace of embarrassment or anything close to it in her eyes or in the smile she gave him. "Ted's doing some matchmaking, huh?" she remarked. "Be strong. Resist. That's what I'm doing." She added a chuckle, but the humor faded when she looked at his shirt. "Where's your coat?"

"At the inn. I forgot it."

Definitely no humor now. Concern. She hooked her arm through his and started leading him back toward the inn. "What's wrong? Why were you in Ted's, anyway?"

Callen didn't welcome either question. He didn't want to talk about Avis and didn't especially want to get into the details of his attempt at retail therapy. But he was cold, and while it was nice to steal a little of Shelby's body heat, he didn't mind returning to the inn. Maybe if Shelby was with him, Havana wouldn't pepper him with questions.

While he was hoping, Callen added that maybe he wouldn't catch pneumonia.

"How's Buck?" he asked.

She frowned a little because she knew he was

dodging, but Shelby nodded. "He's doing well. Minimal pain, and he's sitting up and talking. I didn't bring up what he'd said when he was in recovery."

He knew all of that, of course, because he'd gone to see Buck earlier.

"I want to buy two of your horses," Callen blurted out before Shelby could do some question peppering of her own. "As Christmas presents for Lucy and Mateo."

Clearly still suspicious, she went inside when Callen opened the inn door and he followed. It didn't seem manly to sigh with such relief, but the heat felt darn good.

The same good feeling didn't apply to Shelby's expression. Raised eyebrows and lips pressed flat.

"I'd pay to have them boarded at your place," he added as they headed up the stairs. "That way, they can, well, have some ties here no matter where they end up living."

She made a sound to indicate she was considering that, and while there was still a boatload of skepticism, she nodded. "It's an expensive gift. I'm sure they'd be happy with something other than a large living creature."

"I want to get the horses for them," Callen insisted. "Just send me a bill, and, no, don't give me a discount or anything. Charge me what you would anyone else."

"A discount for sex." Her smile returned for a moment. "Well, you are pretty amazing, so you probably do deserve a really deep discount."

It felt so good to see that smile and hear that slight smoky hitch in her voice. Hell, it felt good just to see her, period, and Callen hadn't realized how much he needed it until she touched her smiling mouth to his.

He spotted Havana peering out the doorway of her office, but Callen waved her off, pulled Shelby into his own office so he could give her more than a mouth touch. He kissed her, really kissed her, and the cold simply melted from his body, replaced by a nice buzz of heat.

The kiss lingered on until she eased back, met his gaze. "Now, will you tell me what's wrong?"

Callen debated it. He hated to ruin this moment by even mentioning his prior visitor's name.

"I have my ways of getting to the truth," Shelby added. She shut the door and slid her hand over the front of his jeans.

He smiled in spite of that fierce debate going on in his head. And he grimaced a little, too, at the jolt of pleasure from that slick move of her hands. He wanted to let that jolt turn to full-blown sex against the wall, but there was something in Shelby's eyes that told him they weren't going to get that far—not until he'd told her what had put rocks in his belly.

"Avis Odell showed up," he said.

With her gaze still nailed to his, she pulled back her hand, and for a moment he wondered if she even remembered who that was.

She did.

"What did that sonofabitch want?" she snapped, and that "something" in her eyes was now a hot ball of temper.

Callen didn't especially want to feed that temper since he was still working on reining in his own, but he didn't want to keep this from her. Especially since Avis could go to Shelby next. The thought of Avis doing that gave Callen another layer of temper that he didn't need.

"He wanted money," Callen said. "He said if I paid him he wouldn't disrupt the wedding."

She whipped away from him, throwing her hands in the air. "That shithead sonofabitch. I hope you told him you weren't going to pay him a cent."

"Yep, I did."

"Good," she spit out, her tone still tight and mean with anger. But then she stopped, swallowed hard. "Did you beat him up? I hope you didn't beat him up," she quickly added. "Because if you did, he'll have you arrested."

Callen shook his head. "I didn't beat him up." But he knew he likely wouldn't be able to say that if Avis came back. "I'll need to tell Kace and the others. I just wanted to calm down some first."

She made a sound of agreement and glanced around as if trying to figure out what to do. What she did was lock the door. And in the same motion, she pulled him to her for a hard kiss.

CHAPTER TWENTY

SHELBY WASN'T SURE if she was doing this more for Callen or herself. Maybe it was a tie. But she needed to do something to cool down this powder keg of anger and what faster way to do it than replacing it with a powder keg of lust.

Callen seemed to have some hesitation about that, though, and he pulled back from what she was certain was a darn good kiss to look at her.

"You don't have to do soother sex for me," he said.

She gave that a few seconds of thought. "Then we have to have soother sex for me. Because I need it."

That rid him of the hesitation, but she might have helped that along with another kiss and by sliding her hand over his erection. Shelby had figured that was the fastest way to end this conversation, and she was right.

Callen made a manly sound of hunger and went after her. A full, long, deep kiss, complete with some quick grappling. This wouldn't be finesse sex—which she knew he was really good at, too. No, this was fast, rough and completely satisfying. Along with an orgasm, it would exhaust them enough that they would be able to discuss Avis Odell without her using every word of profanity in her vocabulary.

"This feels like I'm using you," Callen grumbled with his mouth against hers.

"No. I'm using you. Big difference." She considered getting him out of his shirt, but no-finesse meant the removal of only the necessary clothing. Instead, she unzipped her own jeans. "And just to cover all the emotional bases, there are no strings attached to this. It's just sex."

Sex with the man she loved, but Shelby wisely omitted that part.

Good thing, too, because Callen accepted what she'd said and got right back into the swing of foreplay. He kissed her neck while he got her out of her boots and jeans. It felt strange since she was still wearing her coat and shirt, but the thought of "strange" went away when his hand got busy between their bodies. Shelby knew he was just getting unzipped and freed from his shorts, but his knuckles did some interesting bumps and brushes along the way.

That orgasm nearly happened right then, right there.

She was hot, ready, and she wanted him in her now.

However, the urges of fast, furious, grappling sex had to pause for a sec to consider the logistics of an office orgasm. The first obstacle came when Callen lifted her, wrapping her legs around him and trying to put her back against the door. That didn't work because there were hooks and shelves there. She cursed the idiot who'd designed those obstacles.

Callen cursed, too, when he glanced around all the wall space. Again, idiot design because there was no space. Ditto for the floor, though Shelby didn't figure that out until she had already started dragging Callen in that direction. He stopped her, glanced around again, his attention landing on the adjoining bathroom.

Also postage-stamp size.

He must have discarded that notion because Callen raked what appeared to be well-organized files, pens and such off the left side of his massive desk. The stuff tumbled onto the meager floor space.

Then, thanks to Callen, Shelby tumbled onto the desk.

If it was uncomfortable, she didn't notice. That was because Callen tumbled onto her, and one of the most interesting parts of his body was aligned with the neediest one of hers.

"Condom," he growled.

More profanity. More nudging and bumping while he grabbed one from his wallet. Thank goodness he'd replenished his stash, and this time she saw three of them in there.

His eyes were wild and stormy when he looked at her, and he had on his warrior face. She hadn't needed anything else to get her to the flashpoint heat stage, but that alone would have done it.

He kissed her when he plunged into her, and she

quickly realized that was to muffle the rather loud sound of pleasure that she made. He already knew her and probably didn't want to alert Havana as to what they were doing.

Mercy, he was so good at this. Moving at just the right pace and hitting just the right spot. It was enough to make her crazy. Even better, it was enough to make her come.

Callen kissed her for that, too, covering her mouth with his when the orgasm roared through her. He didn't stop kissing, either, until he probably thought it was safe. But he didn't stop moving. He continued those deep thrusts, giving her every last bit of pleasure that she could get from the climax.

And because she knew him now, she could tell he was close to finding his release. So Shelby lifted her hips and helped him along with that. It worked. One last big push. He pulled her into his arms. His mouth pressed against her neck.

Only then did Shelby moan out his name.

He lifted his head, grinned, and he made the moment even more incredible by kissing her. Slow and gentle this time. Tender. With way more emotion than he'd probably intended.

It was perfect.

But it didn't last.

All Shelby did was move to her left, and she felt the "thing" spring to life. Some kind of lopsided blob of pine needles. With a rattle of rolling eyes and a slitting mouth, it began to sing "Holly Jolly Christmas."

CALLEN TRIED TO stand back and just watch the activity going on in the living room at Buck's house. Something that Rosy and Shelby were doing, too, as Lucy and Mateo chatted with Sarah and Dan Millhouse and their daughter, Katie.

Chatted was a loose interpretation of what was going on, though.

Sarah and Dan were talking with regular input from Katie, and the conversation ranged from Santa to hobbies to their favorite subjects in school. But Lucy and Mateo were in their quiet, eyes-down mode that some might mistake for sullen. As opposed to just guarded.

Callen had to give it to the Millhouses, though. They didn't give up. Sarah, who led the chatting charge, just continued on about how excited she was that Lucy and Mateo might come live with them. Katie piped in about wanting a brother and sister. Dan talked about them having their own rooms and their pet golden retriever named Jelly Beans.

Mateo and Lucy remained guarded.

"And here are some more cookies," Rosy announced, coming to the rescue.

She breezed into the living room with a fresh plate of sugar cookies. All of them were in the shape of armadillos. Heaven knew where Rosy had found that particular cookie cutter, but anyone who'd ever seen the sweet treats probably wished that it would disappear.

It was the second round of cookies that Rosy had served. Along with hot chocolate, cider, homemade fudge, gingerbread men and green Rice Krispies treats in the shape of Christmas trees. It was enough food to give the entire town a sugar high along with extreme weight gain, and Callen was afraid there'd be even more if the guardedness continued. That was why he reluctantly decided to try to help.

He glanced at Shelby, a "go for it" look passing between them, and Callen strolled from the back of the room over to the sofas and chair where they all sat. He'd already introduced himself, of course, had already mentioned that he'd once been one of Buck's foster kids, but now it was time for a deeper conversation.

And he could think of nothing.

He didn't want to bring up Buck's chemo or the hell that Mateo and Lucy had been through before they'd come here. Definitely no mention or thoughts of Avis Odell—though that was on his mind. Avis had threatened a Christmas Eve return, and that was only two days away. Still, he wouldn't let the gut-twisting anger of that interfere with this.

"Did Lucy tell you she's going to be a bridesmaid in Rosy and Buck's wedding?" Callen threw out there. "It's on Christmas Eve."

Sarah and Dan smiled. "How wonderful," Sarah

gushed, turning to the girl. "What color is your dress?"

"Red," Lucy answered, and for some reason she gave Shelby an uneasy glance. Something passed between them, too.

"I'm sure that color will look beautiful on you." More gushing from Sarah.

Then silence.

"The three of you should come to the wedding, too," Rosy insisted, and she hurried into the dining room and came back with an invitation. Sarah wasn't so gushy when she saw the picture of Billy on the front, but she still smiled.

"I think we can manage that," the woman said after getting the nod from her husband.

The gushing returned, all from Rosy now, who was thrilled they'd be coming, though Rosy did feel the need to tell them that they'd all be seeing the ceremony through video feed. That brought on a more detailed than necessary explanation about Buck.

Then the silence came again.

And lingered.

"Shelby can lift a hay bale all by herself," Lucy said, her voice hardly louder than a whisper.

Callen barely bit off a laugh, but the comment got the attention off the kids and onto Shelby, who joined them in the living room. "I'm a woman of many talents," Shelby joked.

Yes, she was. And Callen wasn't joking about that. Nor was he just thinking about sex, either. She had a knack for lifting dark moods, and she even had Mateo and Lucy smiling a little.

"Lucy's a wonderful cook," Shelby offered. "And Mateo's great with the horses."

"Except for Sweet Caroline," Mateo muttered.

Callen was about to say that nobody was good with that she-witch, but he thought of something else that might brighten the mood and stir some conversation. "I wanted to give Mateo and Lucy horses for Christmas."

"For real?" Mateo asked.

"For real," Callen assured him. "It's the two horses that Shelby trained. A bay mare and a paint gelding."

"And their temperaments are much different from Sweet Caroline," Shelby added. "I'll chip in my own gift of boarding them for as long as you need."

"For real?" Lucy that time.

Callen expected questions or concerns about the logistics of horse ownership from the Millhouses, maybe even a couple more "for real?" questions. But he got more than concerns and questions. Lucy actually squealed, like a girl. Of course, considering she was a girl, that wasn't a huge surprise. But the hug she gave him surprised the heck out of him. Ditto for the one that Mateo gave him after his sister had finished. Then the pair rushed to Shelby to hug her, too.

Apparently, his first attempt at Christmas shopping had been a success and an even-better one with Shelby's offer of the boarding.

"That's a wonderful gift," Sarah exclaimed, and

she went to Callen and Shelby and hugged them, as
well. Dan shook their hands, pumping enthusiastically, and Katie wanted to know if she'd be able
to ride them, too, and was assured that she could
do that. And more. That maybe Shelby could sell a
horse to Katie, too.

"Maybe we can get Lucy and Mateo saddles and
tack for Christmas?" Sarah asked and got another
nod from Dan.

Well, this just kept on rolling in the right direction, and there was suddenly no more silence to fill.
The talk turned to a very happy conversation about
horses, names, riding times and such. Callen got another hug from Mateo.

And then it happened.

Lucy and Mateo were on the couch, not hugging
the Millhouses, but actually chatting. The ice had
been broken, and Callen could see the beginnings
of what might be a perfect fit.

For a moment, just a moment, it was bittersweet.
The thought that the kids wouldn't be here with Buck
and Rosy. However, any trace of bitterness faded,
leaving just the sweet. They'd still have Buck and
Rosy. Shelby, too. But they'd also have a family. And
Callen would be fulfilling the promise he'd made
to Buck.

There couldn't be anything bittersweet about that.
Couldn't be.

The sound pulled Callen from his thoughts. A vehicle coming to a stop in front of the house. They'd

had many visitors over the past couple of days, so it wasn't a surprise that there'd be more. But the surprise came when Callen went to the door.

And saw Avis.

The man stepped out of an old pickup truck, and smiling, he started toward Callen. The rage came, the very stuff that Callen had been trying to punch deep down into his gut. He seriously doubted that he'd have much success punching it down right now.

"What the heck is he doing here?" Shelby mumbled, coming up behind Callen.

"Stay put," Callen told her, and shutting the front door, he charged out toward Avis. "Get right back in your truck," Callen warned him. "You're not welcome here."

"Now, is that any way to be?" His tone was smug. "I'm just here for a friendly reminder about that money you owe me."

Callen heard the door open and close behind him, then the running footsteps. He didn't even need to look back because he knew it was Shelby. Obviously, one of her many talents wasn't listening when he told her to stay put. He expected her to try to pull him back so that he wouldn't start a fight with this piece of shit.

But no. That didn't happen.

It was Shelby who charged forward, and she balled her hand into a fist. A fist that she then rammed right into Avis's jaw.

The man's head snapped back, and the rage flared

hot and red in his eyes. For a couple of seconds, anyway. Then he must have remembered that getting punched by a woman half his size wasn't something a macho moron like him should be whining about. Plus, there was a better way for Avis to get Callen's goat.

"You're gonna just stand there and let your girlie punch me," Avis asked. "Because she hits like a powder puff."

Callen groaned. That was so the wrong thing to say, and he reached for Shelby, a little too late. Shelby slugged Avis again, and this time blood flew from the man's nose. She followed it up with a kick to his balls.

Nothing tamped down the rage that time. It was there, in Avis's suddenly watering eyes, but so were the weak whimpering moans he made while he cupped his nuts and dropped to his knees. Shelby would have gone after the man again, but this time Callen managed to snag her around her waist.

"I will not let that sack of turds come here and say anything," she snarled. "And I don't punch like a sonofabitching powder puff."

Well, the "say anything" wasn't going to happen in the next couple of minutes because Avis was still mute from the pain that Callen imagined was searing through him. He looked pale, clammy and ready to puke.

He puked.

Callen moved Shelby back even farther so it wouldn't get on her boots.

As temper searing—and disgusting—as this encounter was, the puke and the pain actually helped Callen rein in his own rage.

The same could not be said of Shelby.

She was cursing and still trying to get at Avis, kicking and punching at him. Callen and she ended up spinning around a couple of times while he fought to keep a grip on her.

"You get out of here, you sonofabitch," Shelby growled. And, yes, it was a growl.

The threat and accompanying growl must have put the fear of God—or in this case, the fear of Shelby—into Avis because the man managed to get to his feet. While still cupping his balls and hunched over in pain, he hobbled back to his truck and got in. The man gulped in some deep breaths, started the engine and then lowered his window.

"You're gonna pay for this," Avis snapped, the warning aimed at Callen. "You're gonna pay big."

The words and expression were mean enough, but when Shelby broke loose from Callen's grip, the man's mean expression turned to panic. Avis hit the accelerator and sped away.

CHAPTER TWENTY-ONE

CALLEN HAD TO make his way through the maze of Christmas decorations, carolers, shoppers and well-wishers who were clogging the sidewalk that led to the police station. All that cheer and merriment didn't improve his attitude one bit, and he knew what was waiting for him inside wouldn't help.

Or rather *who* was waiting inside.

Kace, Judd and Nico.

Callen had called each of them, saying he needed a family meeting, and they'd agreed—eventually. Though Judd had got in a dig about Callen not having any family. Or something along those lines. Callen deserved the dig, but he'd also known it wouldn't stop Judd from coming.

"Callen," someone called out in greeting. It was Ginger Monroe, who'd been the dispatcher for multiple decades now. "Well, you're a sight for sore eyes."

Ginger winked at him with what genuinely looked like "sore eyes." They were red and puffy, and she was dabbing at the corner of her left one with a Kleenex. "Bad reaction to some new mascara," she added when he stared at her.

He could see why a reaction had been possible. There was perhaps a pound of that mascara on what might not have even been lashes. Perhaps just gobs of the black goo.

"It's good to see you, too," Callen told her, and he tipped his head to what was now his brother's office. "Are they here?"

"Yep. All of them," Ginger verified. "Kace didn't say what the meeting was about, but if y'all need anything, just let me know."

Since Ginger might try to listen at the door, Callen decided to get her off their scent. "We're just discussing some bull sperm I want to talk them into buying. I've got a couple of gallons that are about to go bad if it doesn't get used soon."

It had the intended effect, complete with Ginger's mouth squeezing up like a prune and her saying "ewww." With that task done, Callen headed to Kace's office, stepped inside and shut the door.

Scowling, Kace was seated behind his desk, and his expression certainly wasn't one that even remotely conveyed he was interested in buying bull sperm. Or anything else for that matter. Judd was pacing like a jungle cat. No sperm-buying interest there, either. Nico was lounging, his Stetson covering his face, his legs stretched out as if he didn't have a care in the world.

Since there was no easy way to say this, Callen just went with fast. "Yesterday, Avis Odell came to the inn and demanded money. He said if I didn't give it to him, that he would disrupt Buck and Rosy's wedding."

Judd cursed.

Kace cursed.

Nico lifted his hat from his face and eased to a sitting position.

Callen didn't have to guess what was going on in their heads. The shock, the flashbacks, the anger. Well, except for Nico.

"Why didn't you just tell him to piss off?" Nico asked.

Callen nodded. "I did, more or less. Then about an hour ago he showed up at Buck's."

Kace and Judd cursed again, and a mean jungle-cat look went through Judd's eyes. "Is he still there?" Judd snapped, and it didn't sound as if he was simply asking a question but also setting up a potential ass-whipping for Avis.

"No, he left," Callen explained. "But he came when the Millhouse family was visiting with Lucy and Mateo. Let's just say the family was more than a little alarmed, and I'm not sure how it'll affect their decision to take the kids."

That hurt. A cut to the bone. Avis had already dicked around with so many lives, and now he might have ruined a solid chance for Lucy and Mateo. Of course, if that ruckus had sent the Millhouse couple running, then they likely wouldn't be the parents the kids deserved.

"I'm not paying Avis a penny," Callen insisted, "and neither will any of you."

"No arguments there," Judd agreed. "I want to kick his ass."

"Shelby already did. It didn't help. Much." Though it had given Callen some satisfaction to see Avis on his knees and puking.

They looked at Callen as if he'd sprouted an extra ear. "Shelby?" Nico questioned.

"Yeah, she punched him twice and kicked him in the balls before I could stop her."

Kace studied him a moment. "How hard did you try to stop her?"

"Hard," Callen verified. "Because I wanted to kick his ass myself." He paused. "Avis made a threat, telling me I was going to pay for that. He might try to press charges against Shelby."

A burst of air left Judd's mouth, but it wasn't a laugh of humor. "You really think Avis is going to admit he got his balls busted by a woman Shelby's size?"

"I believe he will if he thinks he can gain something from it. I won't let Shelby be arrested for this," Callen added, and made sure that wasn't up for debate.

Thankfully, no one argued about it. Callen doubted the lack of debate would hold once he told them his plan.

"I made some calls and found out that Avis is staying at the motel just off the interstate exit for

Coldwater," Callen explained. "I plan to go there and *clarify* that there will be no payment and that I want him to leave."

"Clarify," Kace repeated on a huff. He scrubbed his hand over his face. "You mean threaten."

Callen nodded, causing Judd to grumble some profanity. "I'd be better at a threat than you," Judd insisted.

No one debated that, either. Judd could be downright scary.

"But I don't want you to get caught up in this," Callen said.

"Bullshit," Judd spit out. "That dickhead nearly killed Nico and you when you two were just kids. I'm involved. I'll get my coat and go with you." He headed out the office door.

Kace sighed, got up, taking his coat off the back of his chair to put it on. "I'll drive. And I'll do the talking."

Callen frowned now. "I really didn't want to involve any of you. I just came here to let you know what was going on. But you don't have to do this," he added when Nico stood. "Avis came after me, and this is my fight. You don't owe me anything."

Nico just patted his back. "We're brothers" was all he said as he headed out.

We're brothers? That didn't seem like much of an argument, but when Callen walked out with them, he thought maybe it was the only argument that mattered.

Yes, brothers.

"If punches are thrown, they need to come from one of us," Nico added under his breath to Callen as they made their way to a cruiser in the parking lot.

"Any punches will come from me," Callen assured him. That would protect the badges and keep Nico out of it. It didn't matter that Nico was actually taller and probably stronger than any of them. He was still the kid brother.

Kace took the wheel with Judd in the front seat. Callen and Nico took the back. It was only about five miles to the motel, which wouldn't give them too much time to think. But Callen figured they were all dealing with the bad memories and flashbacks right now. Especially Nico.

"Say, did you really buy that body piercing kit from Ted's?" Nico asked.

Well, maybe Nico's mind wasn't where Callen had thought it would be.

It took Callen a moment to realize that Nico had meant that question for him and another moment to realize what he was talking about. "Yeah." And because both Kace and Judd looked back at him, Callen felt the need to explain, "It was part of a group of things I bought. I didn't specifically buy a body piercing kit."

"Does that mean you don't have plans for it?" Nico pressed.

"That would be a no. I don't have plans," Callen assured him. "Why?"

"Because I wanted to buy it as a Christmas gift for Havana. I thought she'd get a kick out of it and we could try it out on each other."

There were so many things wrong with that answer that Callen wasn't sure where to start.

Nico laughed before Callen could say anything. "Just kidding about the trying-out part, but she would get a kick out of it."

She probably would, and while Callen didn't especially like having the image in his head of his brother and trusted assistant, it was better that than making a mental list of all the things that could go wrong with this meeting.

"Ted sent the gifts to my room at the inn," Callen said. "Drop by and I'll give you the kit." While Nico was there, he could also give him the Christmas gift he'd bought for him.

"Thanks. Ted said you nearly cleaned out his inventory," Nico added.

"There's still plenty of junk in that store," Judd grumbled.

Nico made a sound of agreement. "Yeah, but he was boxing stuff up when I was over there about an hour ago. He said he was closing up shop for good and was going to sell the rest of his inventory to some vendor in San Antonio."

It made Callen actually feel a little guilty for being part of making that happen. Ted's was a fixture on Main Street. Still, Ted was getting on in years and couldn't run the business forever. But it made Callen wonder again what would happen to the place. He didn't dwell on it for long, though, because Kace pulled into the parking lot of the motel.

"Avis is here," Callen said, tipping his head to the man's truck. "He's in room 116. I keep a PI on retainer," he added when his brothers glanced at him. "He made some calls along with running a background check on Avis. He's forty-two with an address on the south side of San Antonio. No arrests since he got out of prison. Twice divorced, no kids. Currently unemployed."

Which probably explained why he was trying to hit Callen up for money.

"You should have gotten the size of his asshole because that's where my boot's going," Judd grumbled.

And that was why Callen had wanted to do this alone.

"Keep your boots on the ground," Kace said, sounding not like a big brother but Judd's boss. "You, too. And you," he said to Nico when he shifted his glance to him.

"He didn't say anything about fists," Callen muttered, causing Nico to chuckle and give him an elbow jab. That, in turn, caused Kace to shoot them a glare.

They all got out, and Kace took his phone from the dash and slipped it into his coat pocket. Probably to have it ready in case something went wrong. Of course, Kace wouldn't need to call the cops since he was one and had a very pissed-off deputy by his side.

Together, they went to the door, but Kace moved

ahead of them, and he was the one who knocked. Judd and he automatically moved to the side. Cops' stances in case someone shot at them through the door. But no shots. Avis opened the door.

And he smiled.

"Whew," Nico said, waving his hand in front of his own face. "Two words of advice. Breath mints."

Avis quit smiling, and confused, he looked at Nico as if that had been the last thing he'd been expecting. On this one point, they were on the same page. Callen hadn't expected it, either. Nico's "advice" was a little too lighthearted considering there was nothing light about this.

The confusion on Avis's bruised face didn't last long, and he shifted his attention to Callen. "I see you brought your get-out-of-jail-free cards with you. Two of them with their shiny badges. But that don't matter none. Your girlfriend's still gonna answer for what she done to me."

Nico groaned, tsked. "More words of advice. Grammar lessons. Good grammar matters when you're trying to make a point."

Avis's teeth came together. "You wiseass brat."

"Now see, that's much better. No double negative that time." Nico grinned the way a teacher would at a prize student.

It was effective at getting Avis to take a quick step toward Nico. A step that got interrupted when Judd slapped his hand on Avis's chest.

"Two words of advice," Judd warned him, the words sharp as razors and as mean as a snake. "Don't."

No one pointed out that Judd had only used one word instead of two. And probably because Judd looked ready to tear off multiple body parts, Avis took that "don't" to heart and didn't take another step.

Hell in a handbasket, Callen hadn't needed any proof that Judd was a badass, but that was a prime example of it.

"I understand you paid Callen two visits," Kace said to Avis. While Kace's voice was lacking that whole snake-meanness, there was an edge, simmering and hot just beneath the surface.

"Yeah, I went to see him," Avis admitted. "And on the second visit, his batshit crazy girlfriend assaulted me."

Kace slid his gaze over Avis. "A woman a foot shorter and a hundred and fifty pounds lighter assaulted you?" Kace asked. "With what?"

As expected, Avis seemed uncomfortable. "She got the jump on me when I wasn't looking."

"You mean when you were trespassing on her family's land," Kace amended. "Did she tell you to leave first?"

Avis's forehead bunched up. "Well, yeah. But that don't matter none."

"Yes, it does," Kace argued. "A big guy like you comes onto her property. A convicted felon at that, and she has a right to defend what belongs to her family. If there was no weapon involved, she didn't use excessive force. She asked you to leave, and you didn't. In fact, she could file charges against you for trespassing. I'd be happy to make that arrest. In fact, I'm going to read you your rights in anticipation of those charges she'll file."

As Kace did indeed recite the Miranda warning, the anger flared in Avis's eyes and his face went red. It wasn't a flattering combination with the purple bruises on his face and his swollen nose.

"I see what you're doing," Avis snarled. "You're throwing your weight around."

"You know a lot about that, don't you?" Callen snapped. He was feeling a new dose of anger, too.

"Yeah, I do." Still red, still flaring anger right and left, Avis's attention settled on Callen. "My business is with you, not your brothers. There's no law against showing up at the inn day after tomorrow. It's a public place."

"And what will you do at the inn?" Kace calmly asked.

Now Avis smiled. "Just look around, talk to people. Visit. And Callen here knows what he needs to do to make me change those plans."

Callen opened his mouth, but Kace spoke before he could. "How much money did you want my brother to pay you to back off?"

Avis's smile widened. "It's up to seventy-five grand now 'cause I'm a mite pissed at what his girlfriend did."

"Seventy-five grand?" Kace, again, and again he spoke before Callen could. "And if he pays it, you go away?"

"That's right."

Kace took out his phone, showed it to Judd. "Did you record that confession, too?" he asked Judd.

Judd tapped his pocket, nodded. Nico did a pocket tap as well, indicating that he also had a recording. Callen didn't huff, but he felt stupid. He refrained, however, from telling Kace to send out a memo the next time they confronted an asshole and needed recordings.

Avis made a feral sound, and he lunged. Not at Kace, Judd and Callen. But at Nico—his favorite target.

Judd reached for the man. Kace, too. But it was Callen who got to him first. He waited a split second until Avis took the first swing, which Callen dodged. Then Callen unleashed hell on the man. He put all the anger, all the pain into the fist that he slammed into Avis's face.

Avis staggered back, and Callen went after him again. He landed the next blow in his gut, and Callen would have just kept punching and punching if he hadn't felt the hand on his arm.

"It's enough, Cal."

It was hard for Callen to hear over the thundering rush of blood in his ears. Everything inside him was primed to beat this snake into dust. But the "it's enough" had come from Nico.

Callen reined it in, barely, just enough to let Nico pull him back.

"You're better than he is," Nico added. "A whole lot better. But I figured you needed to do that."

He had needed it, and Callen hated that it still hadn't tamped down the anger and the pain. It still hadn't erased the past.

Once Nico had Callen outside, Judd stepped into the room. "You dickhead asshole," he snarled right in Avis's face.

Even though Avis was still woozy, he took a swing at Judd. Judd didn't dodge it. He let it connect with his jaw. Then he smiled through the blood that was now on his teeth. "Assaulting a police officer. You really are a dickhead."

And then, as if he didn't have that rattlesnake temper and a bloody mouth, Judd calmly strolled out.

"So many charges," Kace said, still in the doorway. He showed Avis the video he'd just taken of Avis punching Judd. "Trespassing. Attempted extortion. Attempted assault on the person you were trying to extort. Assault on a police officer. That all adds up to lots and lots of jail time for someone like you. And I'll file these charges if and when you're stupid enough to come after me, my family or anyone connected to my family or my town. Understand?"

Avis glared at him.

"Understand?" Kace repeated, and this time the badass came out.

"Yeah, I understand." Avis tried to sound badass,

too, but it wasn't effective because he whimpered in pain when he rubbed the spot on his gut where Callen had punched him.

The four of them walked away, and Callen purposely didn't look back. It might spur him to go after the man again. That couldn't happen because it would only make things worse. Now he needed to convince himself of that.

"I want to see Shelby. Now."

Callen hadn't even known he'd said it aloud until Nico flicked a glance back at him. "I'm sensing a lot of unresolved anger in you. With the mood you're in, you think that's wise?" Nico asked.

No. It wasn't wise. But Callen was going to pay her a visit anyway.

CHAPTER TWENTY-TWO

SHELBY RAN OUT the door the moment she spotted Callen's truck pull up in front of her house. As she ran, she looked for any bruises she was certain would be there.

There wasn't a mark on him.

Well, no injuries, anyway. But she could see the dark emotion in his eyes. Emotion that didn't mesh with the perky pink wrapped presents he had tucked under his arm.

"Ginger called and said you and your brothers had all left the police station together," she blurted out. "Are you okay? Are your brothers okay?"

"We're fine." He looped his free arm around her shoulders, snuggling her against him, and he brushed a kiss on the top of her head. "Ginger told you, huh?"

"Well, Ginger and three others who called to say they'd seen all of the Laramie brothers driving eastbound in a cruiser."

The corner of his mouth lifted, but she couldn't tell if that was from the dry humor of the fast-speeding gossip train or if there truly was something to smile about.

"According to reports, departure times varied," she added, hoping to test the reason for the smile. "But the general consensus was that somebody was about to be on the receiving end of a butt-whipping. Was there a butt-whipping?" she asked when he didn't say anything.

He still didn't answer until they were inside. "I punched Avis a couple of times." Without looking at her, he closed the door, set the packages on the coffee table and took off his coat.

"You wanted to punch him more than just a couple of times." Shelby sighed. "You wanted to hurt him, bad. And he would have deserved it, too, but you held back because hurting him wouldn't have changed the past."

Callen pulled her back into the crook of his arm and gave her another kiss on the head. "And that's why I wanted to come and see you."

Like his half smile, that was a little bit cryptic, but just the fact he was here was enough for now. "Are your brothers okay?"

"Yeah." While he stood there holding her, he stayed quiet a moment. "Judd's scary as shit—you know that?"

Now she smiled because there was some humor in his tone. "Yes, indeed. Judd puts the *hard* in *hard-ass*. But he's a good cop, so I'm guessing he didn't throw any punches."

"No. But he took one…for the Laramie team, I guess you could say. He baited Avis, and Avis slugged him. That and the attempted extortion will be enough to make Avis go back to his rat hole."

Good. None of them needed a thug like that around. "I figured he'd try to press charges against me."

Another long pause. "No." He lifted her hand, softly cursed at the bruised knuckles and gently kissed them. "I'm so sorry, Shelby."

"Hey, you shouldn't be apologizing. It's not your fault that a-hole showed up." She caught onto his face, turned his head to make eye contact. "And just know if you need another a-hole beaten up, then I'm your woman."

Oh, there it was. The real-deal smile. But it didn't last. He groaned. "What about the Millhouse family? Are they running for the hills after what they must have seen and heard from the Avis mess?"

"Not running," she assured him. And she was about 95 percent sure that was true. They had looked a little shaken, though, but that could have been because of the sugar overload from Rosy's cookies. "Lucy and Mateo are going to visit them tomorrow, and then the Millhouses will be at the wedding. I think it'd be nice if all sides made a decision about the placement by Christmas."

Nice but it would also be somewhat of a miracle since that was only three days away. And that was a reminder that the wedding was only the day after tomorrow.

She tipped her head to the presents he'd brought in. "Gifts for Rosy and Buck?" she asked.

"Uh, no. They're actually Christmas presents for you. I didn't know the person who wrapped them would use pink paper."

Well, now. That lifted away any trace of a dark mood. "You didn't have to get me anything." But what fun that he had. "Can I open them now, or should I wait until Christmas?"

The moment she included that "wait until Christmas" part, Shelby knew she'd screwed up. Because it was a reminder that Callen might not even be around on Christmas Day.

"Whenever you want," he said. "They're nothing big. Just tokens."

"Even so, there are two, so two tokens make a near gift. Not bad for December 22. I'll open them now." Shelby sank down on the sofa, picked up one of the boxes and shook it. "You probably don't know this about me, but I'm somewhat of an expert when it comes to gift rattling. This sounds like a book to me. Or maybe a small life raft."

She tore into the paper as he sat next to her and took out the gift. It was indeed a book. *Cooking for Dummies*.

"Say, isn't that the cookbook that's been in Ted's for the past twenty years?" she asked. "The one that sat next to the nunchucks and the body piercing kit?"

"Yes," he admitted. "I bought the contents of the entire shelf." He held up his index finger. "But before you get your hopes up, I gave the body piercing kit to Nico. He had his heart set on it." He handed her the other gift. "But here are the nunchucks."

"Awww." She stretched that out a bit, opened the package and yep—nunchucks. "You are so good to me."

"Anything for the woman who kicks ass as well as you do." He kissed her, not on the head this time but on the mouth. It was a lingering one that Shelby knew could lead to other things.

Like straight to the bed.

First, though, she wanted to do something. "I have a gift for you, too." She leaped off the sofa and hurried to the still-to-be-fully-decorated tree, and she took out his present that she'd put underneath.

She'd surprised him. Shelby saw that right away. Maybe made him a little uneasy, too, that this might be something more than just a token.

"Don't worry," she said. "I didn't get you an engagement ring or anything else that comes with strings attached." She put the gift on his lap. "And note that I used real Christmas paper."

"Nice." He ran his hand over the green sparkly wrap and the gold bow. Unlike her, he took his time opening it, and then gave her a puzzled look when he took the gift from the box. "It's a rearview mirror."

She made a dinging sound as if he'd got a question right on a game show, but she caught onto his hand when he reached to pull back the strip of green paper she'd used to cover the actual mirror.

"I know I'm always bringing up that mirror-gate incident where you didn't look back at me," Shelby explained. "So, I thought you'd want to know what you missed seeing."

She let go of his hand so he could peel back the paper, and she got the exact reaction she wanted.

He laughed when he saw the picture of herself that she had inserted there. It was one she'd got Lucy to take of Shelby grinning and waving.

"There's another layer," she instructed.

Callen peeled off the smiling shot to reveal one of Shelby in an exaggerated sob. She had even fisted her hands as if rubbing them against her eyes. Copious amounts of mascara ran down her cheeks.

"I wanted to give you a sense of the full range of my emotions," she said. "And that's why there's a third and final layer. But to see that one, you first have to close your eyes. *Really* close them," she emphasized.

Just in case he cheated, Shelby took the rearview mirror from him and hurried to the back of the sofa. She stripped down, tossing her clothing aside as quietly as she could until she was wearing only her birthday suit.

"Keep your eyes closed," she reminded him, and she put the mirror back in his hand, positioning it so that she and her nakedness would be the reflection he'd see. "Okay, eyes open," she said when she had the pose right.

She immediately saw a problem with what she'd

thought would be a laugh-out-loud, sexy gift. She couldn't see his expression. Only his eyes as they met hers in the mirror and then his gaze as it tracked down her body. He had to shift the mirror some to take her in.

"Very nice," he concluded.

Callen turned, lightning fast, and he caught onto her, pulling her across the back of the sofa and onto him. There was laughter, all right, followed by a scorcher of a kiss.

"This is much better than the gifts I gave you," he drawled.

"Then you'll have to make up for it." And she scorched him with a kiss of her own.

MAYBE IT WAS because of the raw energy and emotion he'd brought to her doorstep, but Callen decided to try to smooth some of that away.

Of course, Shelby had already smoothed a whole bunch with that incredible gift. One that'd made him laugh while it also reminded him that he'd just plain sucked with that old goodbye—or rather the lack of a goodbye. That meant he needed to do better next time— He pushed the notion of "next time" aside. That wasn't going to help what he had in mind here.

And what he had in mind was making love to her.

Yes, they'd had sex, and it'd been better than great, but there had always been that need gnawing away to make everything feel so urgent. So life and death. So now. He wanted to take that down a notch and build a slow but steady fire that would soothe them both.

Since she was already naked, Callen scooped her up, tossing her over his shoulder caveman style, and because slow and steady could still be fun, he gave her a light smack on the butt. Then gave it a little kiss because, after all, it was right there next to his mouth. She giggled, reached down and gave him a swat, too.

He eased her onto the bed and nearly lost his breath when he got a good look at her. "So much better than the view in the mirror," he let her know.

Callen went to her, putting his knee on the bed between her legs, and he lowered himself to kiss her. Yes. Much better because now he could touch her. He took her mouth as slowly as he could manage, tasting and teasing while he slid his hand down her body.

No way was he going to just skip over her breasts since they were one of his favorite parts. Her breasts were small, almost delicate, which didn't exactly mesh with her personality, so it was like finding an extra special hidden treasure. He kissed her there, too, and enjoyed the way her body bucked beneath him when he took her nipple into his mouth. He sampled and tasted there until she hit him on the back.

"Get naked," she demanded.

Obviously, Shelby was starting to feel some of their usual urgency.

Callen did pull off his boots, and he unbuttoned his shirt, but he didn't stop kissing her. Undressing just gave him different angles of her that he could reach with his mouth.

Her stomach. He kissed her there while he undid his belt.

Her hip. That was a nice spot for his tongue while he unzipped his jeans.

He went for the inside of her thigh when he shucked off his shirt. Since Shelby was making some sounds of pleasure, he lingered there while removing his jeans.

Getting out of his shorts required something special. He kept his mouth in the general area of her thigh. Then moved in. And in. Until he hoped he made the kiss very special. Judging from the way Shelby groaned out his name and pulled his hair, he had succeeded.

Callen would have kept on succeeding, if she hadn't used the grip on his hair to pull him back up to her. "In me now," she demanded.

So, even more urgency. It was there for Callen now, too. He was hard as stone and starting to throb. It didn't help that she had hooked her legs around him and was trying to pull him into her.

"Condom," he reminded her, and it was possibly the only thing he could have said to her that got her to release his hair and the leg grip she had on him.

He grabbed a condom from his wallet, and the second he got it on, Shelby latched on to him. Not on to his hair this time. But his dick.

It got his attention, and his own urgency went through the roof.

Thankfully, there was a fix for it. Him inside her. Just as she'd demanded. And she was clearly ready because he'd barely managed a couple of thrusts when her climax came. There was nothing delicate about it. She closed around him like a greedy fist, and all those muscles went to work. Squeezing and pulsing. Drawing right in.

Callen wasn't sure how he managed to hang on, but he did. Still moving inside her, he waited until her eyes had cleared. Until their gazes were locked. Until he saw the pleasure glow around her, and only then did he let himself go.

CHAPTER TWENTY-THREE

SHELBY AND LUCY stood side by side as they looked at themselves in the mirror. It was a full-length mirror, one at the Lightning Bug Inn in what had been designated as one of the dressing rooms for the bridal party. Because it was full-length, Lucy and she had no trouble seeing that something had gone horribly wrong.

"Don't you just love the embellishments I made to the dresses?" Rosy asked them.

No. Shelby didn't love them, and she suspected from Lucy's grim reaction that she didn't, either. Rosy's embellishments were what appeared to be tiny cloth armadillos that had been haphazardly glued to the red dresses. Well, haphazard except for the row of them that lined the side pockets. There were at least two dozen on each of the dresses, and it looked as if someone had sneezed the ashy gray critters all over them.

"I got a whole box of little Billy replicas," Rosy added. There was plenty of glee in her voice and expression, and since Shelby would have rather sat on a cactus than dim that glee, she just smiled. Lucy managed to do the same.

"Very touching," Shelby settled for saying. "It's like Billy will be right here with us instead of only being at the hospital with Dad and you."

"Yes!" Judging from her enthusiasm, that was exactly what Rosy had been going for.

"It's…special," Lucy piped in.

Such a clever—and kind—girl. Both a lie and the truth, and it caused Rosy to give another "yes!"

"I didn't have time to put them on all the dresses," Rosy went on, "but I've left the box and some glue out at the reception table for the other bridesmaids so they can help themselves."

She hoped Rosy wouldn't be too disappointed if there weren't any takers for the armadillos, but she doubted Rosy would even notice. Soon, Rosy would be whisked away in a limo that Callen had arranged, and she'd be taken to the hospital where Buck would be waiting for her so they could finally say their *I do*s.

Shelby had considered being there with them, but she'd nixed the idea. Her dad and Rosy had had so few times when it'd been just them as a couple, and she thought that maybe this was the way to start their marriage. But to start it, they first had to get Rosy into her dress.

And there were time and space constraints.

Time because Rosy needed to leave for the hospital in less than a half hour. Plus, there were thirty-something other bridesmaids, and while most would arrive in their dresses, they might still need to freshen up, and there was only one bridesmaid's room. A room that was the same tiny size as Callen's office—which was now being used as a groomsman's dressing room. They were no doubt bumping elbows in there right now, but that would be small potatoes compared to the bumping that was about to go on in here.

Shelby went to the pink bridal gown that was draped over several chairs. It had been pressed like a frozen fish filet in a plastic bag. Not a regular garment bag, either, but one of those space-saver deals that had required a vacuum cleaner to suck out the excess air and flatten it enough to be transported. The moment Shelby released the seal on the bag, Lucy, Rosy and she might be knocked unconscious or get trapped under the expanding fabric.

"Take cover behind the mirror," Shelby told Lucy and Rosy, and she waited until they were in place before she gulped in some air and went for it.

The dress expanded like a self-inflating pink bus. The fabric swooshed out, flinging sequins in every direction. Some landed on Shelby's eyelashes. Probably in her nose, too. But when the fabric had finally finished swooshing, she was relieved that she still had about six inches of space to move around. Heaven knew how Rosy was going to fit in the limo, but that wasn't Shelby's problem.

"Oh, it's so beautiful," Rosy gushed, and she managed to sidestep and maneuver to make her way to

Shelby. Lucy was right behind her. "And I was wrong to worry about it looking wrinkled. It doesn't."

Yes, it did, but that was because it was crinkled satin. Hard to tell which wrinkles were supposed to be there and which were a result of the pressurized bag.

"Go in and find the zipper," Shelby instructed Lucy. They'd already worked this out on paper, complete with a diagram and dimensions of the dress. Too bad Rosy couldn't just wear the paper because getting her into the garment looked a lot more hazardous in person.

Lucy dragged in the kind of breath that a diver might take before jumping into deep water, and she trudged forward, shoving aside the wads of satin, toile and lace until she reached the back of the dress. She slid down the zipper and motioned for Shelby to go on to the next step. Shelby took hold of a giddy, giggling Rosy and moved her toward the open zipper.

It took more than a little effort, but they finally got the woman into the dress. It took even more of an effort to zip her up. Then even more for Lucy and Shelby to back away without stepping on any of the fabric.

Rosy turned toward the mirror. "Oh, it's so beautiful," she repeated, and added "happy tears" when she started to cry. "I've been fighting them all day."

So had Shelby, but she wouldn't cry. Would. Not. Cry. This was a day for happy stuff, and red eyes and a clogged nose weren't on her happy list. Rosy, though, had lost that particular fight now, and her mascara was running. Since Havana was in charge of makeup, that would be a fix she'd need to make.

For now, Shelby gave Rosy another once-over to make sure everything was covered that was supposed to be. It was. Of course, with that much fabric, it would have been impossible to screw that up.

And Shelby saw it then.

When she looked at Rosy, she looked past the yards of pink and at the woman's face. Dazzling. Just dazzling.

"You're such a beautiful bride," Shelby said. She hadn't tamped down the emotion in her voice, so it set Rosy to crying again. But since they were more happy tears, it only added to the dazzling.

"Okay, let's get out of here before I start blubbering," Shelby told Lucy. "You and I go first, and then Havana can get in here for the makeup touch-up."

The six-inch walk space wasn't easy, especially when the armadillos on Lucy's dress tangled with some of the ones on hers. The little Billys now had spatterings of pink sequins on them. But they finally made it out into the hall.

Where there wasn't much more room.

Bridesmaids were literally lined up on both sides of the wall. They were primping, adjusting dresses and bobbling around while they put on heels. There was plenty of elbow bopping going on out here, and it would have felt like some kind of walk of torture had it not been for the friendly, familiar faces and the warm welcomes.

It was one blast from the past after another.

Rosy had made name tags for everyone and on them she'd had printed the dates when the girls—who were now women—had lived at the ranch.

Buck's kids.

Shelby remembered many of them. Zinnia Carter, the blonde beauty who had introduced Shelby to beer—which Shelby had promptly thrown up. Elie Monroe, the genius who'd helped Shelby through algebra. Lupe Sanchez, the busty brunette who had almost certainly been Callen's first lover.

Shelby smiled at Lupe in spite of that.

It didn't matter to Shelby that she hadn't been his first. She was his current lover, and that was better than being first. However, there weren't enough rose-colored glasses to make herself believe that her "current" status would last much longer.

No.

Now that his promises to her dad were nearly fulfilled, Callen would be going, and he would unknowingly take a sizable piece of her heart right along with him.

Shelby felt someone squeeze her hand and looked up. *Lucy.* "You look like you're about to cry, and I don't think they'll be happy tears."

Clever indeed. Shelby smiled at her, kissed her cheek and then studied her. "Are all of yours of the happy variety?" she asked when she spotted the girl blinking back some of her own.

"Mostly," Lucy answered after a hesitation. "But

I'm worried about Mr. Buck. Mateo and I went to see him, and he said he was okay, but he had to wear a mask, and he looked really pale."

Of course this had been bothering Lucy. Probably Mateo, too, and Shelby silently cursed herself for not talking to them more about it.

"Yes, he's pale, but he'll get better," Shelby assured her. "The doctors believe they got all the cancer, but he's getting the treatments to make sure of that."

"You're sure?" Lucy asked. "Because sometimes grown-ups try to keep things from kids. Don't keep anything bad from me."

"I'm not, and I won't."

Despite the crowd, Lucy stopped, studied her expression and then nodded. "Good. Because I, uh, love Mr. Buck. I, uh, love you." The relief came, and she gave Shelby a long, hard hug.

"I love you, too, Lucy."

Well, crud. Shelby had to go another round with fighting the blasted tears. Somehow, she managed to keep her eyes dry. Well, dry-ish. But it was hard to do because it was an incredible moment. Lucy—her newest sister—was going to be okay. Even if things didn't work out with the Millhouse family, the girl was still on her way to recovery.

By the time Lucy and she made it to the end of the hall, Shelby had fought her way through the latest tear threat, and she'd got through the wall of kids with minimal damage. She had also lost some of the sequins but now had what she was certain was lipstick kisses on various parts of her face. Maybe Havana could fix her up, too.

And speaking of Havana, Shelby spotted the woman at the reception table. She was gluing armadillos on her already-armadillo-covered dress.

"Aren't these just the coolest things?" Havana asked.

"They're special," Lucy said when Shelby was at a loss for words.

"Exactly!" Havana agreed. "They're so Rosy. Say, is Rosy ready for me to do her makeup?" Havana picked up a hamper-sized bag that would take up at least 75 percent of the free space in the dressing room. "Got my primp stuff."

"Yes, she's ready, but you should probably hurry," Shelby explained. "Rosy needs to leave soon."

"I'll get right on it." Havana added a kiss to both Lucy's and Shelby's cheeks before she started her trek down the hall. "In the meantime, you should take a final look at the party room. The guests are starting to arrive," she said from over her shoulder.

Shelby and Lucy headed that way, but they stopped when the front door of the inn opened and snow blew in. Nico came in right along with it.

"It's snowing?" Lucy blurted out.

"Sort of. I rented one of those machines. It'll follow Rosy to the hospital and spew some of the white stuff there, too. I thought she'd like that."

"She will," Shelby assured him. "What about the cameras? Are they working?"

"They are. Just doing the final test on them right now."

He led them into the party room, where there were indeed already guests milling around and seated at the tables. The room was not only where the guests would watch the ceremony, but it was also where the reception was being held.

Rosy had gone for all the flowers that she'd considered. *All of them.* Sunflowers, poinsettias, violets and roses. The explosion of colors worked surprisingly well with the pink tablecloths.

Nico motioned to an open laptop that was sitting on a small corner table. "This image will be projected there." He pointed toward a large screen mounted on the wall. "We have audio, too."

Nico pressed a new button, and not only did Shelby see her father sitting in his hospital bed, she heard him say, "There's my girl." He smiled, but there was some alarm on his face. "Are you okay? Are those bruises?"

It took Shelby a moment to realize what he meant. "Oh no. Lipstick kisses from your other girls. There are a lot of them here, Dad. Here, because of you."

Buck's alarm morphed to a reaction that Shelby knew all too well—misty eyes. There was a lot of that going around, but once again she fought the tears and won. No stuffed-up nose and red eyes for her on one of the most important days of her father's life.

"I love you, Dad." She touched her fingers to her

lips and then pressed them in the direction of the screen. Later, she'd give him a kiss in person, and she didn't mind that she'd have to do that through a mask.

"Love you right back," he said.

Since Nico was waiting to adjust something on the laptop, Shelby waved goodbye to her father and took a look around the party room. It was perfect—despite the prominent placement of the rearing stallion as a centerpiece and the zombie bunnies that Rosy had apparently ordered in bulk. It got even more perfect when Callen walked in.

Oh my.

Callen in a sleek black suit was even hotter than cowboy Callen. Long, lean and hers—for today, anyway. Smiling that smile that stirred sins and heat, he walked toward her.

"Hey," Shelby greeted him.

"Hey, yourself. Interesting dress," he said when he skimmed his gaze down her body.

"They're special," Lucy repeated, with more humor in her voice this time. Humor aside, it was a reminder for Shelby that this silent lust exchange between Callen and her wasn't private.

"Special indeed," Callen agreed. "They've got Rosy written all over them."

"More like Billy glued all over them," Lucy muttered, making Shelby beam. It probably wasn't good to encourage smart-assery or sarcasm, but it was healthier than the gloom that Lucy had carried around with her.

"Rosy's responsible for this, too." Callen lifted his tie. Yes, it was the shape of an armadillo. "She got them for all the groomsmen."

Better than the zombie bunnies or the generously endowed rearing stallions, so that was something at least.

"You've been crying," Callen said to Lucy. His forehead bunched up, and he led them to a small alcove and out of the earshot of the other guests.

"Some," Lucy admitted. "The good kind of crying. Not Shelby, though." There was some admiration in Lucy's voice.

"Another of my vast skills," Shelby joked. "Just call me 'dry-eyed McCall.'"

Lucy eked out a smile, took in a deep breath and looked at Callen. "Thank you for everything you've done for Mateo and me. Thank you for working to find the Millhouses."

Callen winced a little, and Shelby knew why. Yes, Callen had found them by pressing his social-worker friend, but he was no doubt blaming himself for Avis showing up and maybe ruining things.

"I'm sorry about what happened," Callen told Lucy.

Yep, Shelby had been right. He was blaming himself.

Lucy shrugged. "It's okay." She paused, chewed for a moment on her bottom lip. "I feel a little bad, though, about Mr. Buck. I mean, if Mateo and I do leave, he'll be okay, right? I mean, he won't be mad at us or anything, will he?"

"No, he won't be mad," Callen assured her just as Shelby said, "Of course not." Shelby was the one who continued. "It's the way things work. Kids come to my dad until they find a home, and then they go and live happily ever after."

That last part wasn't exactly an exaggeration. Shelby had seen proof of that as she'd walked down the hall. Saw proof of it, too, with Kace and Nico. Callen and Judd, though, were still works in progress.

"I'll make sure everything is in place," Lucy volunteered. "Maybe I can put napkin capes on the bunnies at the tables where children will be sitting."

"Great idea," Shelby assured her.

The girl hurried away so fast that Shelby knew Lucy must have realized that she wanted a moment alone with Callen. Actually, what she wanted to do was kiss him, and she sneaked in a quick one. And again had to push away any thoughts about their kissing days being numbered.

Since she wanted something to lighten her own thoughts and cool down the heat simmering between them, Shelby took out the nunchucks from her dress pocket and wrapped them over her wrist. "I wanted to wear them to show you how much I appreciate the gift you gave me."

Callen smiled, put his mouth against her ear and flicked his tongue over her lobe. "I appreciated the one you gave me."

Good grief. That didn't cool down anything. Just the opposite. If Callen was soon going into the retreat mode because he'd be leaving, he was showing no signs of it now.

Shelby decided just to go with it. If it lasted only minutes more, then she'd take each and every one of those minutes. Except she didn't even get a single minute before there was an interruption.

"Callen, Shelby," someone called out.

Shelby didn't mind this particular interruption when Sarah, Dan and Katie Millhouse came walking into the room. Shelby was relieved. Even after partially witnessing the incident with Avis, they'd come. That was a good sign. And while it wasn't a bad sign, both Sarah and Katie were wearing red dresses spotted with the armadillo patches.

"Miss Rosy asked us to be bridesmaids," Katie happily announced. "This is just the coolest dress."

So, a good sign after all, and even Sarah didn't seem to mind. Shelby couldn't say the same for Dan, though. Definitely no "coolest" vibe from him as he looked down at his tie.

Shelby reached out to shake their hands and only then remembered she still had the nunchucks wrapped around her wrists. Sarah's eyes widened. "You're not expecting trouble today, are you?"

"No," Shelby quickly assured her. "They're good-luck charms." She got them off fast and shoved them back in the pocket of her bridesmaid dress.

Great. Now both Dan and Sarah had uncertain looks on their faces.

Callen didn't groan, but Shelby suspected that was what he wanted to do. "I'm glad you came," Callen told the Millhouses. "Maybe we can talk—"

But that was all Callen managed to say before Havana came rushing in. "Rosy's in the limo. Let's not get into how we managed that," she added. "Anyway, she said she wanted us to start as soon as she got to Buck's room."

Which wouldn't be long at all. Only minutes.

"I've already started lining up the bridesmaids." Havana shifted her attention to Callen. "Judd's doing the same for the groomsmen, but I think you should get involved in that."

"Definitely," Callen grumbled as he headed out. Wise call since Judd lacked the finesse and patience for a chore like that.

Shelby motioned for Lucy, and she waited until the girl joined them before she went back to help. Havana had it under control, though. The bridesmaids were now lined up on one side, the groomsmen on the other.

The line seemed to go on for infinity, coiling not just in the hall but also in and out of the rooms. Despite all the excited chatter, Judd and Havana were in the middle giving orders. As expected, Judd's orders were a little less friendly than Havana's, so Callen stepped in to take over a duty that Judd seemed very happy to relinquish. He moved to the back of the line.

So did Shelby, but first she made sure Lucy was with Sarah and Katie. Thanks to Callen, Mateo was positioned with Dan.

Chatter continued. So did the attempts to adhere the cloth Billys onto some of the dresses. There were tie adjustments and talk about the "old days" when they'd lived at the ranch. Shelby smiled when she realized that Nico was filming everything with camera feed that was no doubt being sent directly to Rosy and Buck. Rosy would be dabbing at tears, and her dad would be the happiest man on earth.

The music started in the party room. "The Wedding March." An unexpected touch of tradition, but it only lasted until about half of them were in the party room, and then it switched to "Boot Scootin' Boogie." Like the flower explosion, that felt right, too.

It took a little shifting and letting people go ahead of her, but Shelby managed to be next to Callen as they reached the party room door, and they walked in together. Like the kisses, she wanted to hang on to moments next to him, as well. Even if they were surrounded by one hundred and fifty friends and family.

Everyone cheered when Rosy and Buck appeared on the large screen on the wall. As expected, Rosy was smiling and, yes—still crying. Her dad even had some color in his cheeks, though Shelby had to admit that might be a reflection from all that pink.

Reverend Jimmy Joe Daughtry stepped onto the small stage in the corner of the room. As he held his Bible, he positioned himself facing the screen.

"Dearly Beloved," he said.

With just those two words, Shelby burst into the loudest ever of happy tears.

CHAPTER TWENTY-FOUR

SHELBY'S CRYING SPELL hadn't surprised Callen as much as it obviously had her. He'd seen her emotions so close to the surface, and it didn't matter that they were mostly good emotions. It had still brought on the tears.

Then it had set off half the room crying along with her.

The inn had run out of tissues, but as soon as the vows had been spoken, the staff had brought in toilet paper, setting several rolls on each of the tables.

"Sorry," Shelby shouted to a crying woman who wandered past them with a roll of toilet paper in her hand. If she hadn't shouted, she wouldn't have been heard. Apparently, the DJ thought he needed to crank up the volume to make sure Rosy and Buck heard it all the way from the hospital.

"What?" the woman said.

"Sorry," Shelby repeated in an even-louder shout.

It took Callen a moment to realize that the shouter was Lupe Sanchez, who had taught him a thing or two in the hayloft when he'd been fifteen. Lupe gave him a flirty smile, no doubt remembering that *thing or two*, but she also must have recalled that she had eye makeup running down her face. Since she obviously didn't want that to mar his memory of her, she scurried away.

"Sorry," Shelby continued to shout as the criers came by to add their well wishes.

Callen thought they were gaining some positive ground, though, because those just doing the well-wishing seemed now to outnumber the criers. The staff might appreciate that, too, to cut down on the run on toilet paper.

"Sorry," Shelby said again, but this time Callen realized the apology was aimed at him. She blew her nose, and with her eyes red and puffy, it was not her best look. But he had a nice image of just how amazing her face, and body, could be.

"No apology needed," he assured her, and because he thought she could use it, Callen pulled her into his arms for a dance. There still wasn't a lot of room on the floor, but other dancers were weaving around the tables and in any space available.

"I made a fool out of myself," she went on.

"Nope, you didn't. Everybody knows how much you love Buck and Rosy, so it was expected. Not the nunchucks, though. You did raise some eyebrows when you took them out."

"I thought I had a Kleenex in my pocket." She frowned. "They made a lot of noise when I dropped them on the floor."

"Very few people noticed."

Not a lie, either. That was about the time the crying began, and that sound had muffled the falling nunchucks. What hadn't been muffled was when they landed on Havana's toes, but she had assured Shelby that nothing was broken and that she was certain the limp would soon go away.

Shelby looked up at him. Finally, no more tears, and some of the redness was easing up. "You're being nice to me," she shouted.

Since that sounded like some kind of accusation, Callen tried to follow her thought process. Nope, couldn't follow it. "Shouldn't I be nice?"

"No. You're doing it because you're leaving soon, and you're feeling sorry for me. Maybe a little guilty."

Callen wasn't sure how to respond to that, but it turned out he didn't get a chance to say anything because Shelby continued.

"I don't want you to talk about leaving," she went on. "Yes, I know it's going to happen in the next day or two, but I don't want you to mention it. I want these…moments."

Callen was touched, and, yes, he felt guilty. But he nodded.

"Good. One more thing," she continued. "I want you to spend the night with me at my place." Her gaze drifted toward Lupe. "Unless you have other plans."

"No other plans," he assured her. Especially not plans with Lupe. "I want to go see Buck and Rosy soon, but that shouldn't take long."

"I want to see them, too, but I'll wait until the reception starts to wind down. Whenever that'll be," she added. The crowd was still pretty thick. "I should be home around six or so."

He nearly said "then it's a date," but that made it seem too casual. It wasn't. Because it very well could be the last night they spent together.

No, it wouldn't be.

What they had was still going strong, and he could make trips down from Dallas. She could come up and see him. But it might be the last night he spent at her place before he left town.

"Uh-oh," she grumbled. "I know that expression. You're feeling guilty."

Yeah, he was.

"Well, don't," Shelby snapped as if he'd verified it aloud. "No strings, remember? If you need to leave, just do it. But you'd darn sure better look in the mirror. Not the one I gave you, either, but the real one in your truck."

Since that gave him another hit of guilt and because she managed a smile, Callen asked, "Will you be naked?"

Her smile widened. "You'll have to look and see."

Okay. That made him feel better, and he might have gone in for a kiss if someone hadn't tapped him on his shoulder. He turned to see the Millhouses squeezed into the dancing crowd.

"You think we can find a quiet place to talk?" Dan yelled.

Instant concern, and Callen hoped like the devil that this wasn't going to turn into a "sorry, but we can't take the kids" talk. He glanced around and saw no space that could remotely qualify as quiet or less crowded.

"Let's go upstairs," Callen suggested. He wound them through the other guests, and when they reached the stairs, he saw Mateo and Lucy.

"We asked them to wait here while we found you," Sarah explained. She, too, shouted, of course, which didn't make her sound very friendly.

Callen studied the kids' faces, but their expressions were as somber as he suspected his was. "You two okay?" Callen asked.

He only got nods from them.

"Oh, I can't keep it secret any longer," Sarah blurted out. "We want Lucy and Mateo. We want them to be part of our family." She threw her arms around the kids, then reached out and pulled Dan and Katie into the group hug.

Since Lucy and Mateo weren't exactly jumping for joy, Callen motioned for all of them to follow him up the stairs. It would have been a lot easier for them to do that if Sarah hadn't tried to hold on to the huggees. She had to finally give up just so they could fit up the narrow staircase.

The noise faded with each step, and while it wasn't exactly silent in his office, they would be able to drop the shouts. Not the concern, though. Yes, it was still there in spades.

"What's wrong?" Callen came out and asked them.

Lucy and Mateo exchanged glances. "We both want to go live with Mr. Dan and Miss Sarah. And with Katie," Mateo said. "But it feels a little bad, too. Because Mr. Buck and Miss Rosy have been so nice to us. You've been nice to us," Mateo added in a mumble.

"We don't want you to think we didn't like you," Lucy went on. She looked at Shelby. "Because we do. And we'll miss you."

Callen released the breath he didn't even know he'd been holding. Hearing them say that was a gift better than gold, and it sent a blanket of warmth all through him. "I'll miss you, too. But hey, you'll always be one of Buck's kids, and since Shelby and me are, too, it'll always make us your big brother and sister."

Lucy nodded, and Mateo gave a sound of approval just seconds later.

That brought on relieved breaths from Sarah and Dan. But Katie looked confused. "So, does this mean Lucy and Mateo will be my big brother and sister, too?"

Callen looked to the kids for that answer and again they nodded.

Sarah squealed with delight and dragged them into her arms again. Dan and Katie joined in. Callen would have been content to stand back and watch this happy scene, but Sarah's arm snaked out, and he was pulled into the huddle. Mateo did the same for Shelby.

It was a perfect moment, and Callen didn't think it spoiled the mood too much when someone bumped into the singing Christmas tree, and they hugged to "Grandma Got Run Over by a Reindeer."

CALLEN BRUSHED AWAY the fake snow that was flurrying outside the hospital. Someone had turned off the machine, but there was enough of the white stuff on the ground and caught in the winter wind that it was going to take one hell of a cleanup.

When he stepped inside the hospital, he noticed that everyone in the entry and waiting room looked as if they had severe cases of dandruff, but there was also a giddy happiness, too. Maybe a fake white Christmas created from a machine called Sno Blow was just as appealing as the real deal.

He wasn't especially surprised to see Judd sitting in the waiting room. Callen had seen him leave earlier, and word had got back that Judd was on his way to see Buck. Callen suspected Kace and Nico would come, too. But for now, Judd was texting or doing something on his phone.

"You've already seen him?" Callen asked, tipping his head in the direction of Buck's room.

Judd nodded. "I didn't stay long."

With the vague description, it was hard to tell if that was Judd's way of telling him to get lost or if he had something on his mind. Callen decided to test and see if it was the latter. He went closer and sank down in the chair next to him.

"You'll have to give me some clues here," Callen said. "I can't tell if the short visit was because Buck isn't doing well or—"

"Buck's fine. Never seen him happier."

All right. That eased some of the tightness in his chest. "So?" He didn't expect Judd to spill anything and was surprised when he did.

"Avis Odell is in jail," Judd threw out there. "Last night, I went to San Antonio and baited him into a fight in a bar."

"Jesus." Callen added a groan to that. "What the hell were you thinking?"

Judd shrugged, winced a little. "I was thinking I wanted him arrested. It didn't take much. Really, I just showed up and announced in a loud voice that I was a cop. I let him punch me in the gut a few times. He cracked one of my ribs—in front of witnesses."

"Jesus," Callen repeated. But this time he skipped the "what the hell were you thinking?" and moved on to a big concern. "You could have lost your badge."

Judd gave him a *not a chance* deadpan look. "I never laid a hand on him. The local cops that I'd called before I even went in showed up just about the time of Avis's third punch. He got charged with assaulting a police officer, and since he's on probation, that'll be revoked. And it's his third strike. He'll be behind bars for a long time. I'll make sure it's as long as it can be."

Callen wasn't going to cry any tears over that, but Judd didn't seem to be celebrating, either. "You're thinking Kace won't like you doing something like this?"

"He won't," Judd readily admitted. "In fact, he'll rip me a new one when I tell him."

"I won't rip you a new one," Callen assured him. "Heck, I'd thought about doing it myself."

"Figured you had. Figured it'd be better coming from me. I'm older than you and I've got a badge." He paused. "I thought it would put an end to this mess with Avis. Maybe even put an end to the past."

Everything inside Callen went still. "Did it?"

"No." Another pause. "But it felt good."

Callen suspected that was about the best they could hope for. He moved to stand up, but Judd stopped him with a question. "What are you going to do about Shelby?"

Now it was Callen's time to shrug. "To be determined. My life's not here," he added. "Hers is."

"Well, you know what they say," Judd commented, looking back down at his phone. "You can't go home again."

Yeah, but sometimes you couldn't get away from it, either. "Merry Christmas, Judd." And Callen went down the hall to Buck's room.

As they'd been instructed, Callen used the hand sanitizer from the dispenser mounted on the wall. A precaution they'd have to take for a while. When he peeked in, he saw Buck sitting in the bed as if he'd been waiting for him. No Rosy because the limo had taken her to the inn, where she could spend some time with the guests who were still at the reception.

Even though Buck was wearing a mask, it was easy to tell he was smiling because it made it all the way to his eyes. "I was hoping you'd come by for a visit," Buck greeted him.

"Wouldn't want to miss the chance to give best wishes to the groom. It was a nice wedding."

Buck nodded. "Won't hear me complaining despite being in this hospital bed." He lifted his left hand to show off his new wedding band. "Married to the love of my life."

And soon Buck would be able to start that life. Things were definitely heading in a good direction, and that didn't just apply to Buck's health.

"The Millhouses want Lucy and Mateo," Callen explained. "They're a great family, and the kids seem happy about it."

Buck's whole face lit up. "Good. That's very good." He patted Callen's hand. "I knew you could do it."

"I wasn't nearly as sure," Callen admitted, "but it's going to work out. Plus, the kids will be back to ride their horses, so you'll get to see them often."

"Rosy told me about the present you gave them. Generous, but then you always were."

Callen shook his head. "You're mixing me up with Nico. I'm the hard-nosed, hardheaded Scrooge."

But Buck only smiled. "Generous," he insisted.

The smile faded, though. "Judd told me about the trouble you had with Avis."

Of course he had. As a minimum Judd would have done that just so Buck wouldn't be blindsided if Avis showed up at the hospital. "I don't want you to be troubled by any of that."

"I'm not. I knew you'd work through it in your own way. I wish dealing with Avis was something I could have fought for you, but it wasn't my fight."

"No," Callen agreed. "And it all worked out."

They sat there, comfortable with the moments of silence that followed before Buck motioned toward a pink gift bag on the table next to his bed. "That's for you. I had Rosy bring it over. Not exactly a Christmas gift, but she wanted to put it in a nice bag anyway."

The moment Callen glanced inside, he knew what it was. The wooden memory box Buck had made for him when he was fourteen and had first come to Coldwater. The very one that Callen had never actually used.

"Figured you'd finally have some good memories to put in there." Buck patted his hand again. "I know you didn't want to come back here, but you did it for me. Thank you. You made a lot of things right, Callen. You fixed things."

Talk about an unexpected compliment, and Callen was pretty darn sure it wasn't even warranted. But that was when he realized something. Why Buck had really asked him to come back. It wasn't to fix *things* but to fix Callen himself.

And by damn, it had worked.

CHAPTER TWENTY-FIVE

SHELBY RAN HER hand down Callen's body and smiled when she reached his erection. "I think I found my Christmas present."

He smiled, too, all sleepy and slow, and he kissed her as he woke up. She figured the "morning wood" wasn't especially for her but more of just a man thing. But since Callen was naked in her bed—and it was Christmas morning—then she was going to claim it all as her own.

Callen accommodated her.

Perhaps because she was stroking him, he became fully awake. Fully aroused, too, and it wasn't just because of the man thing. No, that look was for her. And what a look it was. Even first thing in the morning, Callen was hot, and the stubble and heavily lidded eyes only added to that.

What would it be like to wake up every morning just like this? She supposed it would be like having a Christmas every single day. Both romantic and a little depressing, but neither had time to take root because Callen flooded her with foreplay.

He dipped his head under the cover and kissed her

breasts, and the pleasure shot through her. It shoved aside the playfulness. Shoved aside her breath and coherent thoughts, too. And he feasted on her.

Yeah, this was an awesome Christmas present.

As usual, his kisses, no matter where they landed, ended up driving her crazy enough that she started pulling at him. A condom wouldn't be a problem because he'd put some on the nightstand, and she grabbed one of the foil wrappers and thrust it under the cover at him.

He chuckled, took it, but continued more of those now-maddening kisses. The man certainly knew how to use his tongue. And his hands. She got a reminder of that as well when he trailed his fingers up her body. Still teasing. Still not putting on that condom.

"Just giving you more of that Christmas present," he drawled.

The teasing was incredible. No doubt about it. A body-soaring delight. But the only "more" she wanted right now was his sheathed inches inside her. Perhaps her urgent whimpers and moans let Callen know that because he finally made his way back up to her mouth.

He passed the condom back to her. "Put it on me," he said.

She'd never done that before, but Shelby soon figured out why he'd asked. It freed up his hands to touch her. Specifically, to slide his fingers into her.

Shelby cursed in two languages. Possibly three if you counted pig latin. And she got a different kind of proof. That he knew how to use his hands as well as his clever tongue.

No way could she manage the condom with her body writhing and seeking an orgasm that she didn't want to have yet. So she used one hand to clamp around his erection and tore open the wrapper with her teeth as she'd seen him do.

And the fun began.

Oh yes. This was payback. She just wasn't very good at getting the condom on him, of course. That meant lots and lots of touching. Some sliding, too, and she wondered why this didn't result in more hand jobs. Callen must have realized that could happen without his assistance because he took over the task. He had it on and plunged inside her in under two seconds.

She stopped writhing, and even he didn't move for several moments. Despite the burning need and insane urgency, he went still and just looked at her. The muscles in his face were tight, gearing up for the primal mating deal. His eyes, hot. But there was something else in there, too.

And while she didn't want to think about it, Shelby thought he was realizing this could be their last time together.

Thankfully, there was no dwelling on that, and her brain went back to its now-now-now mindless quest to get the orgasm that was already right there, chasing her down. It was impossible not to let it catch her, what with Callen at the steering wheel. It chased, caught and hurled her right over the edge of pleasure and relief.

Callen looked at her again. She could see him do that even though the climax had blurred her vision. And he was still looking at her when he let his own orgasm catch him.

"Shelby," Callen said, and even his postorgasm mutterings were still a sexy drawl.

He kissed the little spot just below her ear, and she thought maybe he had something important to say. Maybe something to add to this whole Christmas morning experience. And he did.

"I like the way you got that condom on."

Okay, so maybe it wasn't a romantic spouting, but it wasn't a sad, sloppy goodbye, either. He chuckled, nipped her earlobe with his teeth and got out of bed. She kept her eyes on his amazing butt until he disappeared into the bathroom.

Shelby checked the time—already 10:00 a.m., which meant she had to get up. In just two hours she'd be expected at the ranch to help Rosy pack the lunch they'd be taking to the hospital for Buck. His doctors had already approved the menu, and Rosy and she would be taking gifts, too. It wouldn't be their usual Christmas around the tree and fireplace, but this was the year for different things. After all, Callen had just given her a top-notch orgasm and was now in her shower.

She would need a shower as well, but for now she pulled on a robe. This way, she could keep his scent on her a little longer. And, yes, that made her somewhat pathetic, but like the man himself, his scent was pretty incredible.

By the time she made coffee and poured herself a cup, Callen had finished in the bathroom, and much to her disappointment, he was dressed. No more looking at his butt. Well, not naked. She realized the view of that particular part of him was almost as good in his snug jeans.

He went to her, kissing her and then stealing her coffee. She didn't mind since the kiss had been adequate payment, so she poured herself another cup.

"I need to leave soon," he said. "I'll stop by and see Rosy first, and then pop by Buck's room before I go see my brothers." His smile wasn't so easy now. "Kace is fixing lunch, and we're, uh, exchanging gifts."

Her eyebrow lifted, both surprised and pleased about that. There had been some great things that had come from Callen's trip back here, and mending fences with his brothers was one of them.

Another of those great things was, of course, Lucy and Mateo. After the reception, Callen had put red bows on the horses he'd bought for them and had made the kids very happy when he'd brought them over to do the official gifting. Callen had also said his official goodbye to the kids, since they'd be moving in with the Millhouse family today. Shelby would do her goodbyes this morning. And she wouldn't cry.

Well, probably not.

"I have the rest of your gifts," Callen said. He gulped down more coffee, grabbed his truck keys and headed out while adding, "Be right back."

That was her cue to get the ones for him from beneath the Christmas tree. All six of them. And judging from the shocked look on his face when he came back in, Callen definitely hadn't been expecting so many.

"I bought the entire shelf to the right of the door at Ted's," she explained. "So, you might not exactly have a use for some of the gifts. In fact, you might wonder why some of these gifts even exist."

That eased up his expression a bit, and the playfulness was back when he kissed her and then put three wrapped boxes on the end table.

"And don't worry—Ted wouldn't tell me what you'd bought, so I'll still be surprised. Open yours first," she insisted, and she topped off their coffee while he settled onto the sofa in front of his stash.

He didn't disappoint her when he enthusiastically tore into the paper and took out the Plexiglas cube with the puzzling object inside. It definitely fell into the "shouldn't exist" category.

"It's a burnt piece of ciabatta that looks like Elvis," she explained.

He turned it, studying the burn pattern that looked like a dirty panda to her, but there was a sort of smoldering look in the panda's eyes that could possibly be mistaken for Elvis by a poorly sighted person.

"You are so good to me," he said, repeating what she'd said after receiving the nunchucks.

"And the goodness continues." She handed him the next gift. A pornographic snuffbox amateurishly etched with a doggy-style copulating couple.

"Ted had that one tucked way out of sight," she added when Callen gave her a questioning look. "This one, too." She handed him the next gift. "Who knew that Ted had a little bit of perv in him, though he claims he thought it was an odd-shaped nun-chuck."

It was a cock ring.

Callen smiled a naughty little grin. "You bought a more interesting shelf than I did."

"Perhaps, but withhold judgment on that until you open this one." Shelby handed him package number four. "It's a first-edition copy of a *Dick and Jane*. Apparently, they once used books like these to teach kids to read, but since it, too, was hidden on the shelf, I believe Ted thought it went along with the cock ring, copulating couple theme."

He laughed, and Shelby had to admit that it was just as hot as the rest of him. In fact, it made her want him all over again, and, no, that didn't have anything to do with the gift. Well, mostly it didn't.

"And now we're moving on to a different theme. These were in front of the other things on the shelf and are therefore not sexual." She handed him the last two gifts.

"Too bad. You were on a roll there." He opened

the next one. A woman in a grass skirt who shook her hips in an approximation of a hula dance when you pressed the button where her navel should be. It was too stupid looking to be sexual.

The last gift also had a button, but it was no hula dancer. Be My Valentine was printed in a flowery font across the palm-sized plastic red heart that thumped, pulsed and beat when that button was pushed.

When she'd first seen it, it had made her smile, but it didn't do that to her now. It made her a little sad. And that made her mad. She was having her dream Christmas, and no downer thoughts were allowed.

Callen helped with that when he had her sit so she could open her three gifts—the remainder of the shelf behind Ted's cash register.

A hand-sized gumball machine.

"You know, back when I was ten, I would have killed for this," she told him. "I used to look at it with covetous thoughts whenever we'd pass by the shop. All that gum."

"The gum is still there," he pointed out, but they both frowned at the scabby white powder on what was now a congealed glob of time-ravaged gumballs. "I'll get you a fresh bag of those."

"Thanks." Though she would keep these. As disgusting as they looked, they were still from Callen. Still the fulfillment of a childhood wish.

"Open these two together," he instructed.

Since she was somewhat familiar with the con-

tents of the shelf he'd purchased, she wasn't surprised
to see the two stuffed beavers with serious overbites.
They had sat front and center behind the register for
as long as Shelby could remember. A very long time,
considering the thick dust coating on their bushy
heads and teeth.

"Where's their barrel?" she asked. "They were
always peeking out of one."

Callen nodded. "I couldn't see a single good reason for beavers to need a stainless-steel barrel."

She could have pointed out there was no reason
for a person to have stuffed beavers, but she opened
the last gift. Yep, it was the beaver barrel, but now
the lid was closed.

"I made it a memory box like the one Buck gave
me," Callen explained. "And I put a memory in it
to get you started. Open it when you want to think
of me."

She thought of him without opening it when he
gave her a scalding kiss and got to his feet. He gathered up his stash of gifts. "Thanks. See you later,"
he said, and he headed toward the door.

"See you later," she repeated. Simple words, the
kind of thing that people said all the time. But she
had to wonder if she'd get to say it to him again.
Maybe the next time, it would be just goodbye.

Since she was already thinking about Callen,

Shelby opened the door on the beaver barrel. And she laughed.

Inside, there was a picture. A selfie. Of a shirt-less, grinning Callen.

CHAPTER TWENTY-SIX

CALLEN LOOKED AT the assortment of presents he'd got. Definitely a different kind of Christmas for him. There were some contenders for the strangest gifts he'd ever received.

There was the scarf Rosy had knit for him that replicated a fuzzy armadillo when coiled around the neck. Since it was from Rosy, he'd wear it proudly.

Well, maybe not proudly, but he'd put it on.

It might go well with the group picture and snake hatband from Nico. Not snake*skin* but a silver grinning snake more suited for a circus costume than a cowboy. There'd be no such proud wearing of it because a kid brother—while loved—didn't get the same reverence that came with Rosy's gift. The snake, however, could become a conversation piece on his desk.

Judd had gone with giving Pringles and beer to all of them. And Callen doubted that Judd had got those gift suggestions from Havana. Nope. It was likely he'd chosen the first thing he'd seen in the Quik Mart, something Callen would have done had he not stepped into Ted's.

Kace was the only brother who'd gone with conventional gifts. New cowboy boots for all of them. A nice gift rather than strange.

The one Havana had given him had fallen into that nice category, as well. It was a digital picture frame with dozens of rotating photos. She'd put in shots from the wedding. Not the professional ones the photographer had taken. These were somewhat out of focus and somewhat lopsided, ones that she'd taken herself on her phone. A handful were of the screen of the wedding ceremony in the hospital, but most were of Shelby and him. Until he'd seen those pictures, Callen hadn't realized he looked so...

It took him a few seconds to come up with a word, any word, to fill in, but what finally came to mind was:

Needy.

The hunger in his eyes. The almost-possessive way he'd held Shelby in his arms. Hell, when they'd danced he'd had her pressed against him as if they'd been at a high school prom—only a millimeter away from foreplay or groping.

Probably not the casual but happy look he'd been aiming for.

He put the frame in the packing box along with some of the other gifts just as Havana came in holding her own packed box. Thankfully, she'd put the singing tree in there and had taken out the batteries so it couldn't launch into some merriment that would make Callen want to kick it.

Apparently, a needy man didn't want to hear such nonsense.

"This is the last one," Havana said. "I'm all packed up." But she set her box on his nearly empty desk when she looked down at his gift stash. "Sheez Louise. Who gave you those?"

And, yes, her attention was on the sex objects.

"Shelby. She bought a whole shelf at Ted's. And, no, you can't have them," he added when he saw the glimmer in her eyes. "I refuse to hand over any object that you might use on my brother."

She dismissed that with a flick of her hand, but the glimmer stayed. "Nico was just my Christmas plaything. Nothing serious at all about it. I doubt our paths will intersect much with me in Dallas and him on the rodeo circuit. Still, there will be other playthings in my future..."

Without a doubt there would be, but Callen closed the lid on the box to let her know that her plaything wouldn't get the penis adornment or the screwing couple snuffbox. They were from Shelby, so he would keep them. Probably from time to time, he'd look at them, in a nonsexual kind of way.

Now that she no longer had the sex gifts to distract her, Havana picked up her box and glanced around at his office. Or at least what would be his office for another couple of hours or so. There were a few things to be packed up.

"Let me put this box in my car, and I'll come back

up and help you finish," Havana offered. "When will the movers be here to deal with the furniture?"

"In the morning. Unlike us, they don't work on Christmas Day."

She made a soft sound of agreement but then stopped after taking only a step. "Are you sure you want to do this?" she asked.

"Yes." Callen didn't hesitate, but Havana certainly did. She opened her mouth as if she might argue, but then she headed for the door. Again, though, she didn't get far because Shelby came in.

He felt his stomach do a flip thing, as if it'd rolled over in its sleep, and Callen was reasonably sure his reaction wasn't because of what she was wearing. An armadillo scarf identical to the one Rosy had given him and a silver snake hatband—identical to the one Nico had given him—that sat on her head like a weird tiara. Her boots were new, too. Ditto for the identical department to Kace's gift.

It made Callen wonder if she also had got the Pringles and beer from Judd.

"Hi," Shelby greeted him.

"Hi back," Callen said. No stomach antics this time, but there was need. No doubt about it.

Her face was pink from the cold, telling him that maybe she'd walked farther than just the inn's parking lot. Maybe one of those head-clearing walks like the one he'd taken just a couple of hours earlier. Since the temps were only in the low thirties, he hoped the snake hadn't frozen to her head.

Shelby smiled. A tentative one that got even more tentative when she noticed the box Havana was holding and the other packed boxes in his office.

"I'm soooo glad you came by," Havana gushed. "It saves me a trip out to your place." The box landed on Callen's desk again while Havana hugged her.

"I wanted to bring you your Christmas gifts," Shelby said. She had the handle of a large gift bag draped over her arm, and she took out a small box to hand to Havana. "It didn't come from Ted's."

"Awww." Havana made a mock pout. "I wouldn't have minded the snuffbox." But she beamed when she took out the copper and leather braid bracelet from the box. Then she squealed. "Love, love it."

"Well, hang on to that love because this is from Rosy." Shelby pulled out an armadillo scarf. She touched her own. "We all got one."

Havana squealed again, bobbling on her toes in excitement. She put on both the scarf and the bracelet and hurried into the bathroom to admire them in the mirror.

Callen took a moment to admire Shelby. Or rather to examine her to see what she was thinking. Definitely no signs of a woman falling apart. That was good, he assured himself.

That was good.

"I'll call Rosy and tell her how much I love it," Havana announced when she came back in the room. She waved her bracelet for Shelby to see how it looked on her wrist. Somehow, it all worked despite Havana's now-green hair.

"One last gift." Shelby took the small wooden box from the bag. "From Buck. It's a memory box, and that means he now considers you one of his kids."

No squeal or toe bobbling this time. Tears sprang to Havana's eyes. "God, I wasn't expecting this." She fanned her face as if to stave off some full-fledged crying. "You think I could pay him a short visit just to tell him how special this is to me?"

"I think he'd like that a lot," Shelby assured her and got another hug from his assistant.

"Okay," Havana said as if to steady herself, and she fanned away more tears. "Now I have something for you."

Havana dug through her purse that was bigger than a suitcase and came out with a tiny box. She flipped it open with the flick of a thumb to reveal a ring.

Then Havana went down on one knee.

A classic pose for someone proposing marriage.

Callen couldn't say who was more stunned by that—Shelby or him—but he thought Shelby might be the winner.

"Shelby McCall, I'm asking you to be…" Havana paused and paused and paused. "…my best friend."

Havana giggled like a loon, stood and hauled Shelby into a hug. "Say yes," Havana prompted.

Shelby was looking at everything but him. Probably because she was afraid he might think she'd put

Havana up to this to prompt him into a proposal of his own. But Callen knew Shelby had had nothing to do with this. Nope. This was all Havana.

"Yes," Shelby answered, causing more foot bobbling and excitement from Havana. She took Shelby's hand and slipped the ring on her finger.

Callen went closer for a better look. Not a gag gift, which would have been Havana's usual. This was a small diamond, about the size that would have been in a teenager's promise ring.

Shelby smiled when she studied it, and this time she was the one who launched into a hug. "Best friends," Shelby whispered to her.

That set off Havana fanning more tears, and she quickly picked up the box from his desk. "All right, let me go see Buck and get out of your hair so you two can talk." She kissed Shelby's cheek, and as she'd done before, Havana stopped after taking only a step, and her gaze zoomed in on him.

"You're sure?" Havana asked.

Well, he had been, but this time there was some hesitation. Still, he nodded, causing Havana to shrug, and she finally walked out.

"It's been an unexpected Christmas," she said, looking at the ring.

She was still dodging his gaze, and that was why Callen went to her and lifted her chin, forcing the eye contact. No trace of tears. Good. He needed to tell her some things, important things, and he hadn't wanted to start that with tears close to the surface.

He started to speak, but Shelby put her hand over his mouth before he could even get a word out.

"I'm in love with you," she said, her words a little angry. "I know that isn't what you want to hear, that you preferred a clean goodbye, but you're not going to get one. You're going to get me telling you that I love you and that I'll move to Dallas to be closer to you."

He tried to speak but she just clamped her hand tighter.

"I won't move there in a stalker kind of way," she added. "But I just don't think I want to go through a day without seeing you." She shrugged. "Again, nothing stalker-ish. If you don't want to see me, then...I'll deal with it."

Well. Callen hadn't seen this coming, and he didn't know whether to feel incredibly flattered by her offer or to tell her that she'd lost her mind to give up the good life she had here.

He opted not to mention the lost mind.

However, he did opt to speak, and that meant moving her hand from his mouth. "You breezed right over the part about being in love with me and moved right on to seeing me daily and dealing with it."

She winced. "You noticed that, huh? I swear, I meant for that to sound better. Smoother. I even practiced it. Then I got here, and my stomach started flipping when I saw you. My heart went crazy, and I forgot how to breathe."

Interesting that those were similar reactions to

his, and it made him wonder if he could cause her
to lose her breath again by kissing her. So he tested
that. He slid his hand around the back of her neck.
As much of it as he could reach, anyway, what with
the armadillo scarf in the way.

And he kissed her.

He made it slow, warm and with the promise of so
much more. Callen was certain he'd succeeded when
he pulled back from her and saw her. Shelby's eyes
were still partly closed, her mouth partly open, and
she had a dreamy look on her face.

"I love you, too," he said.

The dreamy look vanished. Her eyes popped
wide-open. Her mouth snapped shut, and with her
forehead bunched up, she stared at him.

"I love you," he repeated, and because she looked
ready to launch into many, many questions, Callen
pressed his fingers to her mouth so he could tell her
the rest. "There's no reason for you to move from
the home and people you love. I bought Ted's and
will set up a regional office here. Havana will run
the Dallas office."

She blinked, shoved his fingers from her mouth
and launched herself into his arms. The kiss she gave
him was the very definition of needy. Maybe with
some greedy thrown in. And some fire. Lots of fire.

Shelby had been the cause of nearly every unplanned hard-on that Callen had had from age fourteen to age eighteen, and she was the cause of the
one he got now.

One he planned to use in the next couple of minutes.

First, though, he wanted to get some verbal confirmation to go along with the kissing and the touching—which she started to do after she kicked his office door shut. She reached behind them and locked it.

"You're okay with my plans?" he asked. "Even if it means me sharing a bed with you until I get a place of my own?"

She pulled back, licking the taste of him off her lips. "Yes, I'm okay with that. But you breezed right over the part about you being in love with me," she pointed out.

"Good point. I. Love. You," he repeated. "Not a trace in a breeze in that."

Her smile was just like the next kiss he had planned for her. Hot and naughty. And fast.

She moved him to his desk and had him on his back before he could even blink. Callen didn't mind the no time to blink, but there was something else he wanted to do. While Shelby kissed the living daylights out of him, he fished around in his center desk drawer and came up with the rectangular box.

"One more gift," he said, working it between them so she could see it.

Shelby saw it, all right, but she didn't seem nearly as interested in it as she was in unzipping him. Still, she took it when he practically shoved it into her hands. On a huff, she opened it, looked inside.

Her expression went through two stages. Surprise, followed by confusion. She lifted out some of the contents. A piece of yellow yarn, followed by some purple ribbon. Then some twine.

"Uh, it's a box of…" Then Shelby smiled. Really smiled. "…strings."

"Yes, I know." Callen smiled, too. "Use them."

* * * * *

Coldwater's deputy Judd Laramie has had a hard time putting his past to rest. And things don't get any easier when his childhood friend—and the first girl he ever loved—Cleo Delaney—asks him to become a foster father to three orphaned boys. That's when life really gets interesting…

Don't miss Hot Texas Sunrise, *A Coldwater Texas Novel, by* USA TODAY *bestselling author Delores Fossen, on sale in March 2019!*

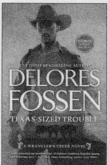

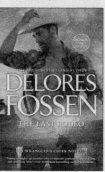

INTRIGUE

EDGE-OF-YOUR-SEAT INTRIGUE, FEARLESS ROMANCE.

Save **$1.00**
off *Rogue Gunslinger*
by B.J. Daniels.

Available wherever books are sold,
including most bookstores, supermarkets,
drugstores and discount stores.

✂ -

Save **$1.00**

off *Rogue Gunslinger* by B.J. Daniels.

Coupon valid until December 31, 2018.
Redeemable at participating outlets in the U.S. and Canada only.
Limit one coupon per customer.

52616091

5 65373 00076 2   (8100)0 12396

HIBJDCOUP1018

Get 4 FREE REWARDS!

We'll send you 2 FREE Books plus 2 FREE Mystery Gifts.

FREE Value Over **$20**

Both the **Romance** and **Suspense** collections feature compelling novels written by many of today's best-selling authors.

YES! Please send me 2 FREE novels from the Essential Romance or Essential Suspense Collection and my 2 FREE gifts (gifts are worth about $10 retail). After receiving them, if I don't wish to receive any more books, I can return the shipping statement marked "cancel." If I don't cancel, I will receive 4 brand-new novels every month and be billed just $6.74 each in the U.S. or $7.24 each in Canada. That's a savings of at least 16% off the cover price. It's quite a bargain! Shipping and handling is just 50¢ per book in the U.S. and 75¢ per book in Canada*. I understand that accepting the 2 free books and gifts places me under no obligation to buy anything. I can always return a shipment and cancel at any time. The free books and gifts are mine to keep no matter what I decide.

Choose one: ☐ **Essential Romance**   ☐ **Essential Suspense**
                    (194/394 MDN GMY7)   (191/391 MDN GMY7)

Name (please print)

Address   Apt. #

City   State/Province   Zip/Postal Code

> Mail to the **Reader Service:**
> **IN U.S.A.:** P.O. Box 1341, Buffalo, NY 14240-8531
> **IN CANADA:** P.O. Box 603, Fort Erie, Ontario L2A 5X3

Want to try two free books from another series? Call 1-800-873-8635 or visit www.ReaderService.com.

---

*Terms and prices subject to change without notice. Prices do not include applicable taxes. Sales tax applicable in NY. Canadian residents will be charged applicable taxes. Offer not valid in Quebec. This offer is limited to one order per household. Books received may not be as shown. Not valid for current subscribers to the Essential Romance or Essential Suspense Collection. All orders subject to approval. Credit or debit balances in a customer's account(s) may be offset by any other outstanding balance owed by or to the customer. Please allow 4 to 6 weeks for delivery. Offer available while quantities last.

Your Privacy—The Reader Service is committed to protecting your privacy. Our Privacy Policy is available online at www.ReaderService.com or upon request from the Reader Service. We make a portion of our mailing list available to reputable third parties that offer products we believe may interest you. If you prefer that we not exchange your name with third parties, or if you wish to clarify or modify your communication preferences, please visit us at www.ReaderService.com/consumerschoice or write to us at Reader Service Preference Service, P.O. Box 9062, Buffalo, NY 14240-9062. Include your complete name and address.

STRS18